A STATE OF CORRUPTION

A STATE OF CORRUPTION

PAUL GEDDES

HOLT, RINEHART AND WINSTON
New York

First published in the United States in 1986 by
Holt, Rinehart and Winston, 383 Madison Avenue,
New York, New York 10017.
Published simultaneously in Canada by Holt, Rinehart
and Winston of Canada, Limited.
Originally published in Great Britain.

Library of Congress Cataloging-in-Publication Data
Geddes, Paul.
A state of corruption.
I. Title.
PR6057.E24S8   1986   823'.914   85-24830
ISBN: 0-03-008164-5

First American Edition

Printed in the United States of America
1 3 5 7 9 10 8 6 4 2

ISBN 0-03-008164-5

For R.B.C.

. . . at times, it seems as if the Mystical Body of Christ were a corpse in decomposition . . .

Monsignor Escriva de Balaguer

When the existence of the Church is threatened, she is released from the commandments of morality. With unity as the end, the use of every means is sanctified, even cunning, treachery, violence, simony, prison, death.

Dietrich Von Nieheim, BISHOP OF VERDEN

A STATE OF CORRUPTION

1

The Swiss handed the scotch to Barralozzi and with a curiously abrupt gesture raised his own glass. His eyes seemed to darken, as though with an intensity of emotion: he was reacting to some sort of stress.

Glancing at the hand holding the glass, Barralozzi saw it was not quite steady. It puzzled him. He had supposed that criminals operating at Steiner's level, even those who were no more than acolytes, like this man, had stronger nerves. But perhaps the Swiss was overawed by him.

'Your good health, sir,' the Swiss said. 'And also that of the Bank.' His English was slow and stilted. He apparently knew no Italian and, since Barralozzi preferred not to speak German, they had settled on English.

Barralozzi nodded, looking elsewhere as he drank. He was not disposed to be patronized by a mere messenger. His original agreement having been with Steiner himself, he had expected all dealings to be with him alone. However, on this occasion, perhaps it did not matter: at least it seemed the Swiss had brought good news.

They were the sole customers at the bar. The restaurant in which it was situated had opened its doors only as they were mounting the stairs from the lakeside where the Swiss had asked they should meet. With mild satisfaction Barralozzi observed that the girl at the cash desk was watching him. She was pale and excessively English in manner but the eyes were interesting. Allowing her his profile as he reached to take a tariff card from the bar top, he read aloud:

'The Cut Above — that is the name of this restaurant?' He raised his eyebrows. 'Cut Above? Above what?' He glanced up to catch the girl's eye.

The Swiss frowned, preparing to grapple with the problem.

7

'The Bar-bi-can.' Barralozzi pronounced each syllable slowly, as though faced with unravelling an encoded message. The sounds were as ridiculous as the spectacle outside this alleged cultural centre. He had stepped from his taxi to be confronted with apartment blocks, their grey balconies curtained with grime, and then a succession of empty, windswept terraces, their interminable red brick leading to the final bathos of dwarf fountains expiring into a dingy lake. 'Bar-bi-cannot, I think.' He said it for his own satisfaction, having no hope the other would be capable of appreciating his facility in English humour.

'In fifty years,' the Swiss said cautiously, 'perhaps it will be better.'

'Or abandoned. Another Fatehpur Sikri.'

Barralozzi watched clouds begin to fatten through the windows of the restaurant. 'Unfortunately there will be no shortage of water to hurry the decision.'

The Swiss smiled with careful politeness. He sensed that Barralozzi was amusing himself with the assumption that he had not heard of Fatehpur Sikri or of the reasons it was abandoned, but he was indifferent. Nor was he concerned at the ridicule of the rendezvous he had chosen. He had specified it when speaking to Barralozzi on the telephone the previous evening because he had seen a poster advertising the Barbican when travelling on the Underground from Heathrow airport and had guessed it would be less crowded than restaurants in the West End. For a little while longer, it was necessary to humour this Roman peacock, preening on his elevated heels as each fresh woman entered the room. He was glad to find himself so immediately repelled: his task was made that much easier. He found it beyond belief that such a person could be allowed to rise to high office in the Institute for Religious Works, charged with handling funds held in sacred trust for the Church. It could only be viewed calmly if seen as part of a wider landscape of Evil. But Evil could yet be destroyed.

The first course of their meal had been placed on a table next to the window overlooking the lake and terrace.

They sat, Barralozzi with his back to the window so that he could see those entering the room. A diamond in his cuff-link

8

glistened as he shook out his napkin: a Vatican banker was not to be mistaken for a poor priest. 'You are Mr Steiner's private secretary in Geneva?'

'Yes.' Now that they were seated, the Swiss seemed more at ease. 'I make all arrangements for him when he stays there.'

'But he is still in New York at present — ?'

'Until tomorrow. Since I had to come to London for other business he asked me to tell you of progress over the merchandise.'

'You spoke to my sister when you telephoned her house the first time. Who did you say you were?'

'I gave no name. Only that I was speaking on behalf of an American friend of yours.'

'Nothing else?'

'Nothing.'

Barralozzi's spoon hovered above soft avocado flesh. 'Her husband is a minister in the British Government. I naturally do not discuss my business, or the affairs of the Institute, with them.'

The Swiss kept his gaze down so that Barralozzi would have no chance of reading his thoughts, of sensing his anger and contempt.

'The bonds — ' Barralozzi began and then paused while the first of the wine was poured for approval by the Swiss. He watched him pretending to taste it, trying to appear cultivated. He had no wish to play the host but to have this factotum doing so, who would normally not be in his company except to take notes or open doors, was irritating. 'The bonds, you say, are ready.'

'The work was completed yesterday. Mr Steiner spoke to me before I left Geneva.'

'And they will be indistinguishable from the originals?'

'They could only be detected as duplicates if they were sent to America for technical examination. Mr Steiner hopes you will come to Geneva to take possession as soon as he is back in Switzerland.'

'Geneva?' Barralozzi was frowning. 'Milan was the agreement between us. Why does he now say Geneva?'

The Swiss felt himself go hot. He stared at the tablecloth,

trying to recover composure. Rome's information had been wrong; there had been no mention of Milan in his instructions. Someone had assumed that because Steiner had his European office in Geneva, the deal would be completed there. He swallowed. 'Mr Steiner now feels it would be safer to receive the money there.'

He watched Barralozzi turning his roast beef with his knife to examine both sides. He was still frowning. But when he looked up, it seemed that all was going to be well. 'It is less convenient to me of course. But if he wishes — I take it you will provide a container for the bonds — a suitcase perhaps?'

'Of course.'

'And Mr Steiner's associates have accepted that the dollar element of the payment will be restricted to fifty per cent — the remainder to be in lire?'

'Yes.'

Barralozzi nodded to mask relief. Steiner had almost refused to take the offer back to New York, saying that the people providing the forgeries would take only dollars or Swiss francs. Someone, somewhere, had discovered a use for lire.

'However,' the Swiss said slowly, 'there is one fresh requirement. The name of the person to whom you have passed the original bonds — this is to be disclosed.'

'What is the relevance to our transaction?'

'Mr Steiner's associates say they must have the information before they will release the merchandise.'

'But why?'

'It is a rule.'

'Whose rule?'

'The rule of Mr Steiner's associates,' the Swiss said doggedly. He was sweating a little. 'The transaction cannot be completed unless I telex these details to New York.'

Barralozzi sat back, holding his wine glass. He was trying to understand, to imagine the circumstances in which the information could be used to his disadvantage.

He shrugged. 'I do not follow. But if they insist — I cannot say who actually *holds* the bonds at present. They were supplied for the purpose of being deposited with another bank as security for a loan. The bank is unknown to me. But the person to whom I supplied the bonds is Signor Rossano, the chairman of Laportex, the construction company.'

The Swiss was writing it down in his diary. 'And the address of the company —?'

'Turin.' Barralozzi shook his head impatiently. 'You should know this — it operates in Switzerland also.'

The Swiss put his diary away.

'So there will be no problem now?'

'No problem, sir.'

A knot of the anxiety he had almost refused to acknowledge to himself began to loosen in Barralozzi's stomach. He picked up his glass again and turned towards the window. Cloud had extinguished the thin April sunshine that had fitfully softened the buildings earlier. But the ugliness out there now seemed more touching than anything else. How like the British to have produced this place! He could almost find it amusing that in such a setting he should learn that escape from catastrophe was finally assured.

The waiter was beside him, offering to serve cheese and biscuits. 'So what day will Mr Steiner be ready to complete the transaction?'

'By tomorrow evening or the following morning he will arrive in Geneva with the merchandise. I will then contact you.'

'Telephone my house, not the Institute, and if I am not there, leave a number for me to call back. Leave no other message.'

'Of course.'

A party of four, a woman and three men, had arrived at a nearby table. Barralozzi knew before he heard her voice that the woman was Italian; the clothes and the way she held herself were unmistakable. She was past the age he was willing to consider for any form of relationship, but the animation of her movements, the glittering torrent of words from her lips were like a tonic in this drab English world. The woman was castigating one of the men, who was also Italian, about the display of a sculpture. It became apparent that he was the sculptor and in the woman's view had accepted too readily the way his work was being shown. The others at the table waited with uneasy smiles for the storm to abate; more insipid in appearance, presumably they were English, perhaps the organizers of the display. Barralozzi spoke to the waiter pouring his coffee. 'You have sculpture in the Bar-bi-can?'

'On Level Eight, sir.'

He glanced back at the sculptor, irritated at not being able to recognize him.

'You are interested in sculpture?' The Swiss had leaned forward and was resting on his elbows, the hands clasped over the middle of the table.

Barralozzi did not trouble to turn his head. 'I have a small collection in Rome.'

'What was your opinion of the bronze runner on the terrace outside?'

'I don't remember noticing it.'

'The legs are very thin. And the — the *genitalia* — are engorged.' His eyes were alight as though the excitement of his words was almost too much for him. The thought crossed Barralozzi's mind that he was not completely stable.

'*Engorged*?'

'Yes.' The Swiss laughed.

Barralozzi turned to the window and tried to glimpse the sculpture below. The Swiss stood, reaching forward as though to do the same; his right hand, moving over Barralozzi's coffee cup, paused for no more than a second, then came to rest on the edge of the table.

'I think you have the wrong English word.' Barralozzi turned back, mildly amused. 'You mean "large" perhaps?'

The Swiss laughed again, this time with an access of relief. 'Perhaps. I read underneath it that it was sculpted by a woman.'

'One should not question a woman's perception of such things.' He said it for his own amusement, not to excite further this boring Swiss. Draining his cup, he consulted his wristwatch. 'You will forgive me — '

'Of course.' The Swiss rose and waited while Barralozzi extricated himself from the window seat. 'If my taxi to Knightsbridge would be convenient — '

'No, I may look at the sculpture exhibition.' Barralozzi

signalled for his coat. 'You will accompany Mr Steiner at the meeting in Geneva?'

The Swiss was smiling. He shook his head. 'I think I shall not meet you again, sir.' There seemed a hint almost of impertinence in his tone. Barralozzi was conscious of his eyes on his back as he left the restaurant.

He followed the signs to Level Eight and paused to look for further directions. A crowd of people was surging into a room in front of him. They wore lapel badges. Inside the room, display boards had been erected; girls with folders in their arms were handing sheets of paper to those entering.

A young woman crossed Barralozzi's path in the wake of the crowd, stared briefly into the room, and began to climb a nearby staircase, above which a sign said, 'The Conservatory Terrace'. He had no opportunity to study her features, but the perfume, the ash blonde hair caught in a knot at her neck, the perfection of the legs as they climbed, first held, then magnetized him. He followed her.

At the top of the stairs he had the feeling of being in a factory of civilized pretensions with many white-painted iron supports and girders rising to a glass roof. The atmosphere was one of enlightenment awaiting a purpose. Advancing to look for the woman, he found he was standing on a broad balcony and that from a level below him, beyond the balcony ledge, tropical trees and shrubs, laced with vines, were thrusting upwards towards the glass sky.

She was in a corner, staring into the plantation below. He approached until he could see her face. The features were good. She seemed of an age that offered the possibility of both sexual appetite and accomplishment. 'Forgive me,' he said.

The woman turned, still leaning over the balcony. Her expression was not hostile, merely neutral in what he had learnt to recognize as the depressing Anglo-Saxon way.

'Can you tell me what you call that flower in England?' He pointed towards a strelitzia in a flower bed along the edge of the balcony.

She bent down with brisk efficiency to examine a small plant sign. 'Bird of Paradise — that's what it says here.'

13

He gave her his most charming smile. 'It's very beautiful, don't you think?'

'I suppose it is.' There was not the slightest hint of sexual vibration or of any other interest in her voice. He sighed inwardly. Briskness in women, even as physically desirable as this one, he found tiresome.

The woman had straightened and he realized that she was at least fifteen centimetres taller than himself, an unacceptable imbalance. On one of her breasts, a lapel badge read, 'Current Trends in Pain Management'. Seeing his eyes on the badge appeared to act as a reminder to her. 'I think I must get back to my seminar.'

He bowed, then stood to watch the movement of her hips as she receded from him. He still felt desire but it was no longer focused on the woman. It was stupid to have wasted time on someone encountered casually in this bizarre culture factory. After all, a telephone call away, women could be found, wearing no badges but capable of the management of pleasure as well as pain and, if he so required it, both together.

Abandoning the idea of the sculpture exhibition, he walked downstairs to a large foyer and asked to be directed to a telephone. Anticipation, now that his mind was made up, gave him a feeling of well-being. Yet, as he consulted his diary for the number, he became conscious of a sensation somewhere above his stomach that he could not identify. There was no pain; he felt only that fingers had reached within him and touched the innermost core of his being. It was over almost at once. Before he had finished dialling, he had forgotten it.

Only later, embarked on the management of pleasure, did the memory come back. Then he began to fear what the fingers sought.

2

From his desk, by turning his head slightly, Antrim could see that the buds of the chestnut trees lining the gardens of Somerset Square were almost open. In general indifferent to the signs of seasons changing, recently he had found himself looking with each succeeding week, at the way the sun's angle widened on the bookcase in the corner of the room. For the first time he had noticed that spring showers brought a lustre, unseen in other months, to the slate roofs of the bed and breakfast hotels on the far side of the square.

Once, before a wartime administration had commandeered it for its bureaucrats, the building in which he sat had itself been a hotel and this the drawing-room of the best suite. In its proportions, it retained a dignity which the government's Property Services Agency and its forebears had never quite been able to erase. Now it was his domain. Solid Edwardian walls and double doors, combined with the vigilant Baxter at the Private Secretary's desk in the outer office, guaranteed a calm in which to enjoy the triumph of possession.

Two months had gone by since Antrim's appointment as Director of the Central Crimes Bureau had been announced. Outwardly calm, he listened at times to a great exultant shout from his heart. Who could reasonably have foreseen that when Harkness had died on the operating table at Sister Agnes, Antrim, the junior Assistant Director in years and everything else — carrying the several handicaps of a major political row from one of his cases, of the messy divorce from Juliet, and of the antipathy of his more senior colleagues *and* the Yard — would come out the winner?

The great stroke of luck had been the briefing he had given the Prime Minister on the Mancini investigation that autumn day when both Lorimount and Harkness were sick and Fender was away in Ottawa. He knew at the time he had made an impression. But, after that, he had seen the PM only twice and in the company of others who did most of the talking. There was no reason, he had supposed, for him to be remembered; moreover, no likelihood either that the PM would take an active interest in a post outside the magic mandarin circle.

But events had gone his way. Harkness's death, so soon after his taking over, had upset the succession planning. And although Temple and Madge had had the seniority and virtually equal claims, Madge had been blackballed by the Permanent Under Secretary in the Home Office so the recommendation that went forward was for Temple. The Home Secretary, who had taken on ministerial responsibility for the Bureau following the Stradbrook affair, had bought his officials' choice without a murmur. To those few in the know, it seemed settled.

Then all was changed when the PM returned the Home Secretary's minute with a scrawl across the top in the characteristic violet ink, 'I would like Mr Antrim's claims to be considered also. He has youth and drive on his side and that may outweigh the supposed advantages of Mr Temple's longer experience.'

From that moment on, not without some grinding of gears and curses, the machine had gone into reverse. Soundings were taken in this department and that, a new biographical note was prepared and Antrim found himself despatched to the Home Secretary for a briefing session on his latest and hardly sensational case, the underlying purpose of which he only grasped from such straws as the half-amused manner of the Private Secretary who had ushered him into the Home Secretary's presence and the sour punctiliousness of Temple's conduct towards him.

So Temple had gone, without even a farewell party to mark his humiliation, to a directorship of one of the security companies — at twice the salary, Antrim had noted bitterly — while Madge had bitten on the bullet and settled for the senior Assistant Director post. Hostile though they remained, there had been no one in the rest of the Bureau's management who had proved too difficult to whip into line. Fender might have been, had he still been hanging on in the Consultant role given him after his heart attacks. But Fender, thank god, had taken himself off to a retirement cottage in Mayfield. With the occasional kick in the crotch, the rest had buckled down.

Antrim lit a Panatella and tossed the match into the ashtray made out of artillery shell-casing that had somehow been overlooked in his sweeping away of the traces of Harkness. Most of the changes which he had ordered to the room were complete, although the picture situation was not yet satisfactory. The nineteenth-century watercolours imported by Harkness were still there. His own choices, conscientiously modern without being dangerous, were still stored under a table in the outer office, while the man with hammer and hooks and sole prescriptive rights to hanging anything in the Bureau was hunted down by Baxter in the Property Service Agency's many mansions.

But the new coffee table had arrived. On it stood the miniature bronze of the steeplechaser Juliet had given him when they married. The steeplechaser itself had gone with the break-up of the marriage, together with the house in Wiltshire and the rest of the pleasures Juliet's money had created so painlessly. The bronze remained, a talking-point for visitors, if nothing else.

His most radical change had been the installation of a panelled cabinet, with sliding doors, which he could view without rising from his desk. A different display or device was revealed by pressing a button beside his chair: a television screen, an illuminated map of the Metropolitan area with colour-headed pins for operational planning, a separate map of the United Kingdom, a chart of the personnel of the Bureau above the clerical grade, showing age, rank and post held.

Two empty spaces within the cabinet awaited other acts of creation. Antrim had ordered, hesitated, then drawn back, when almost committed to it, a VDU screen, linked to the Bureau's central records. There was a danger, he thought, that it would be seen to reflect a preoccupation with those details which should be left to others. But he hankered for it still.

He pressed his buzzer for his shorthand writer and picked up a file. As the girl was about to enter the room, he saw her being

17

eased aside by Baxter, displaying the proprietorial air he was beginning to find oppressive.

'The Cabinet Office are on,' Baxter said, indicating the telephone. 'Could you speak to Sir Norman before you start dictation?'

Picking up the receiver, Antrim listened until Pagett's voice spoke, then pressed the button for secure speech.

'The PM has a small problem which I suggested you might handle.' Pagett did not use Antrim's Christian name: there remained a period of probation before that intimacy would be granted. Antrim was not cast down. Whether they liked it or not, he was One of Them now. Moreover he was the PM's personal choice. Already he had begun to remind them that he knew it. Harkness, conscious that the Central Crimes Bureau was still a fledgling among government agencies — the controversial offspring of a Commission of Inquiry when corruption scandals had been erupting almost monthly and the police were found to have their feet in the trough in all too many — had believed in avoiding the giving of offence whenever possible. He had averted his eyes when odd financial transactions by the intelligence people came to light; conciliated officials in the Foreign Office and the Department of Trade when over-zealous burrowing had exposed those *douceurs* without which a healthy flow of exports to the Third World would falter; pandered to police vanity whenever the Bureau's investigation of corruption overlapped their province. Colouring Harkness's attitude, Antrim had concluded, was an anxiety that if the Bureau became too conscientious, too efficient, it might stumble across a political horror story like that of Stradbrook, which had finally broken Lorimount's nerve.

Antrim had decided there would be no more of that. He did not see himself shambling through Whitehall with a toothless bulldog at his heels. He had set about staking out the Bureau's territory more precisely than ever before, establishing his right to withold information about criminal activity from the police if disclosure might prejudice the Bureau in its work of uncovering serious corruption. Noses had been bloodied. In Baxter's words, Antrim had begun by cutting a dash.

He was taking notes as Pagett talked, injecting brief affirmations of understanding and the lightest of cynicisms whenever Pagett led a card in those suits. At the end, he flashed Baxter and told him to get Priestley, the head of Investigation.

His tray with coffee and digestive biscuits came through the door at the same time as — not Priestley, but Antonia Strachan. She waited until the messenger had put the tray down and departed before she spoke. 'I understand you wanted James Priestley. He's ill. His doctor says he won't be in for at least a week.'

Antrim pressed the button to slide away the panel covering the Personnel chart. 'What about Francis Cope — isn't he his deputy?'

'In Hull until Monday. I came in case there was something to be done in the meantime.'

She stood just inside the door and waited. She looked very cool. Once upon a time, alone in a room with him, it would have been different. But that was over; just as well, perhaps. He pointed to a chair. When she crossed her legs it was an agreeable reminder, like a book once enjoyed. 'Nice to see you, Antonia.'

She said nothing in reply but widened the corners of her mouth in faint politeness. The black hair was longer, framing her face in a way that emphasized those deeply-set eyes. She was still lovely, he thought reluctantly.

'There's something that can't wait. I hope you're reasonably free?'

'I can be.'

'The Secretary to the Cabinet's been on. There's a delicate inquiry for the PM that's got to be done at once. It concerns the Chancellor of the Exchequer, Charles Ropner. But more especially his wife. Her brother came over from Italy a few weeks ago and stayed with them. Apparently he had a heart attack in their house and snuffed it.

'The brother, whose name was Barralozzi, was a Departmental Head in the Institute for Religious Works — which you may or may not know is the Vatican's own bank. He was a very senior chap although, according to Pagett, he didn't enjoy the highest of reputations in Threadneedle Street.

'It seems that when the PM was at Covent Garden last night

19

some old peer on the Government side, who attends the House only once in a blue moon, thrust a letter into his hand with a lot of mumbling about "your eyes only". The letter, which was marked "Most Secret and Personal" and festooned with sealing wax, said that he, the peer, wished to warn the PM that a major financial scandal implicating the Ropners was likely to break. He also recommended the PM to look into the circumstances that surrounded Barralozzi's death.'

She looked up from writing notes. 'Implying it wasn't a heart attack — '

'Presumably.' Antrim poured himself some coffee. 'This unlikely story unfortunately rang a bell for the PM. A year or so back the Governor of the Bank of England gave Pagett a report picked up by one of his senior people when he was passing through Rome. It said that Ropner's wife had made an enormous killing in the currency markets at the time of the last sterling crisis. With money she'd been able to borrow through her brother she bought sterling when it was at the bottom and just a few hours before the Government's rescue package was announced. The implication was that she had foreknowledge of the package and used it.

'Pagett chose not to tell Harkness about the Bank of England report.' Antrim grimaced. 'God knows how many other things we weren't told when Harkness sat in this room. Instead, Pagett simply discussed the report with the PM. His explanation to me a few minutes ago was that he had had to tell the PM first and the PM had replied it was just malicious gossip and should be dismissed as such — he'd known Ropner for twenty years and was quite sure he was not the man to tell his wife beforehand what was going to be done about sterling and when. Of course it was a difficult time for the Government in other areas — to have had to drop Ropner just then would have been very inconvenient. So we weren't told. Now this new story comes in from the aged peer and the PM starts to get uneasy.'

'Was the speculation arranged through the Vatican Bank?'

'That wasn't in the Bank of England story. But it seems likely — if there's anything in this at all.'

'Do we know anything about Mrs Ropner?'

'Very charming and elegant according to Pagett. He had heard of only one weakness.'

'For what?'

'Money.' Antrim smiled, trying to make her respond. 'She's very partial to it.'

Her expression remained unchanged. 'And now the peer is suggesting Barralozzi was murdered at the Ropners'.'

'Sounds like it.'

'They would hardly have had a reason for that if he'd been helpful over the speculation.'

'Unless he was becoming difficult. Suppose he was threatening that the story of it would leak out unless Ropner helped him in some way. More advance information perhaps.'

'But killing him could have made things worse. Whoever took over from Barralozzi at the Vatican Bank might have discovered what had happened and let the cat out.'

'True,' Antrim said. He put his head back to brood.

Now that he was no longer watching her, she could study his appearance. He still dressed well. But perhaps too well: the chalk-striped suit with the double-breasted waistcoat, the Swiss cotton shirt in a shade not found outside Jermyn Street, the Windsor-knotted tie between the cutaway collar's wings — they had all taken on a faintly theatrical appearance as Antrim moved into middle age.

He sat forward and stubbed out the Panatella. Reflection, as Fender had once observed, never seemed to require more than a ten seconds' burst. 'I think we can be almost sure *that* part of the story is balls. The old chap's probably fantasizing — he's read too much about the Calvi business. All the same it sounds as though there may be *something* in the letter since it ties in with what the Bank of England heard. I want you to go and see him. He's the Earl of Wadebury — Matthew Bacton to his chums — and he's tucked away in Cowden Hall in a Somerset village called West Gurney. Definitely eccentric, Pagett says, may even be gaga. Catholic family from way, way back, had their own priest on the premises to keep them holy until the Second World War. Go down there this afternoon if you can discover he's available. Otherwise not later than tomorrow — I want to have something to say to Norman Pagett by Friday.'

'If I'm to get him to talk about the contents of a personal letter to the PM I'll need some introduction.'

'I'll have Pagett's office warn him that a Mrs Antonia Strachan is empowered to hear his confession and will be in touch. Incidentally, a copy of the letter is being sent round. It may have got to Baxter by now. Ask him for it on your way out.'

She stood up, glancing through the notes she had made, and turned towards the door without looking at him again. He wondered if anyone was making time with her now. Since his own affair with her had folded, no rumour had reached him; but people told him less these days. It seemed a waste, if there *was* no one. Fascinating to get back — just once. But it was madness to think of, he couldn't take the risk of gossip seeping out into Whitehall that he was bedding staff only three months after being made Director.

Holding the door handle, Antonia paused. 'One thing — oughtn't we to be finding the whereabouts of Barralozzi?'

'What do you mean? He's dead.'

'His body — whether it's buried here or was sent back to Italy. There may have to be a post-mortem some time.'

He felt irritation that her mind had moved ahead of his own. 'Let's see what we think of the Earl's story first.' He sat back, swinging in his chair from side to side. 'And by the way, tell nobody else about this except your secretary — no, don't tell her either, use mine for typing reports and so on — Baxter will fix that if you ask him. He can also be finding out what happened to Barralozzi's body.'

'You'll want me to brief Francis Cope presumably,' she said.

'No. On this, you'll report to me alone.'

She raised an eyebrow but remained silent. He could guess she had hoped to interpose Cope between them as soon as possible, but he wasn't going to let her. He smiled. 'Nice to have you around again, Antonia. See me as soon as you get back, won't you?'

He noticed moisture on his lips as she went out of the door. He wiped them with his handkerchief. The flavour of the Panatella lingered on his tongue but he was tasting something more satisfying: submission.

22

3

Soft West Country rain began to mist the windshield as Antonia drove into the outskirts of Wells. She glanced at the clock in the office Rover: after all, there would be time enough for a drink and something to eat and still reach West Gurney by two-thirty.

Getting the Earl on the telephone had proved an uphill struggle consuming most of the previous afternoon. A female voice had three times announced in defeated tones that he was not to be found. Various possibilities were offered — that he was in the village, down the orchard or at the local garage where a car repair had apparently been performed to his dissatisfaction. Antonia eventually made contact with him as she was about to leave the Bureau for the day. It was plain from his first words that he had no liking for telecommunications. She tried and failed to make out whether Pagett's office had managed to forewarn him of her existence and purpose. His voice came over a crackling line in clipped and querulous shouts. He sounded as though he imagined himself on a field telephone in a First World War dug-out and regretted they'd ever given up flags. But he was surely not as old as that.

Slowly it registered with him what she was talking about. As he hemmed over fitting her visit in during the morning, she wondered if he would get round to asking her to lunch but he didn't. Two-thirty had been his unornamented choice. Perhaps he was put out that the Prime Minister had thought it fitting for a woman to talk about the contents of that Most Secret and Personal letter. As she was checking the turn-off from the main Yeovil road, he interrupted, 'Is it Mrs or Miss Strachan?' When she laid claim to her former married state, he was somewhat mollified — perhaps he felt less threatened, she thought sourly. She had got the route straight and was about to hang up when he shouted, 'Now when you get to the front door, don't use the bell, it's not working. There's a stave behind the footscraper—knock hard with that.'

She stopped at the first pub with a car park and ran through the rain to the lounge bar. Armed with a gin and tonic and a plate of cold lamb she found a seat in a corner of the room and took out her papers.

She had brought with her the copy of the Earl's letter that Pagett's office had sent over and the family's Debrett entry. Debrett was depressingly uninformative about what he actually did. The Earl was the eighteenth in line. He was just seventy-four, so his experience of the telephone could hardly have been blighted during the First World War. From Downside and Magdalen College, Oxford, he had gone (with nothing acknowledged in the way of activity in the years between) to the Guards for the duration of the Second World War. He had married in 1945. Subsequent activity seemed again unworthy of note apart from procreation and membership of a body for the preservation of English fruit trees. There had been four children, two daughters who appeared to have been married off into northern county families, an elder son named Thomas More Bacton — now farming in Australia — and finally a Francis Dominic Bacton, who at twenty-seven years of age was not recorded as occupied in any way. The rest of the space was taken up by the Earl's arms, in which griffins stared stonily at a mad-eyed owl.

The letter to the Prime Minister had a rather endearing quality. It was written in a large hand that had required three sheets of Cowden Hall writing paper.

Dear Prime Minister,

We do not seem to have met in recent years. I find I cannot get up to the House as much as I would like and I am sure you must be very busy. But you will remember Tanfield and I raising with you the intolerable tactics of the French over their dumping of Golden Delicious. Since then I am sure you will have been glad to see English growers fighting back. Not that some additional official support would be amiss. A close eye needs to be kept on what they are doing across the Channel.

I am coming to London for a couple of days tomorrow and shall telephone your office for an appointment in the hope you can fit me in. However in case it turns out that there is no chance of speaking to you *quite privately* (away from Private Secretaries and so forth) I am putting something down in writing that you need to know about.

I have it on very good authority — someone who has been in touch with people in Rome who are *at the heart* of the thing — that you are going to be faced with a serious scandal in the near future. It will seriously compromise Ropner and his Italian wife. I cannot go into the details but it involves speculation affecting the pound with the help of her brother. In addition, as you probably know, the brother died in their house a few weeks ago on a visit from Rome. It was said to be a heart attack. I recommend you to go carefully into the circumstances in which he met his death. My advice is that you put the security people or an honest policeman — if they are to be found in London these days — on to it straight away.

I am sorry I cannot say more about the facts. But you would be taking a *great risk* if you did not move to head off trouble now.

Yours sincerely,
Wadebury

She pushed aside her plate. There was no evidence of Italian connections in the Debrett entry. But as a member of an old recusant family it would not be surprising if the Earl had contacts in Rome, and more particularly in the Vatican. Perhaps even inside the Institute for Religious Works. Still, the phraseology of the letter didn't inspire great confidence in his judgement. Someone who wrote about people 'at the heart' (and underlined the words too) would probably listen to any tall story that happened to fit in with his prejudices. Even so, there was the earlier report from the Bank of England of a coup in the currency markets. Presumably the Bank was not so gullible. But its story might still have originated from the same source.

She sat back, trying to decide whether to stay for coffee and a cigarette. The room had thinned out since her arrival. At one end of the bar three men formed a group over a liquid lunch: local businessmen, estate agents perhaps. One of them was eyeing her discreetly. She wrote off his companions as provincial Hooray Henrys but he was quieter, with a graceful manner. When their gaze met, he appeared faintly embarrassed to have been caught appraising her, then smiled to indicate it wasn't anything of which to be ashamed. She looked away; even at the most optimistic calculation he was nine years her junior.

She had not foreseen until recent times that she would fall into this depressing arithmetic so easily. Passing the mid-point of the thirties had still to produce notable pluses. No more wisdom, no access of philosophical calm, no greater readiness to find advantage in the other half of the bed being empty. Only cellulite creeping down the thighs, a downcast air to breasts when looked at bravely in the morning mirror, those grim laughter lines at the corners of the mouth. And attractive men, not just the police, looking younger every day.

She stood up, deciding she would arrive early at Cowden Hall, even if it deprived the Earl of his nap or whatever was the post-prandial tradition in West Gurney. As she went out of the bar, she noticed grimly that the man had also decided it wasn't on.

There were no gates, only decaying stone columns where these had once hung at the entrance to Cowden Hall. It was evident too, from the fencing just inside the grounds, that the lodge had been sold off. Antonia's expectation of ancient grandiloquence, slumbering in immaculate, bosky grounds, diminished sharply as she steered the Rover round pot-holes in the quarter-of-a-mile drive to the house. Yet Cowden Hall, when it came finally into view, had a charm that grew with acquaintance. A low-built house, its façade was faced in stone of milky grey. Where the sun that had now crept through the clouds caught it, a patina on the stone glowed a delicate pink. She guessed it to be Tudor or a little before. The windows were mullioned, the gables decorated with stone carvings. Signs of disrepair were evident. But it was a perfect small manor house.

A drive, which broke off to the left from the one by which she had approached, presumably led to the outbuildings; perhaps also to the chapel where once the resident priest had conducted his services. Almost hidden by a hedge on the south side she could see the top of a conservatory, its wooden framework bleached where paint had peeled. It was the house of a family that, perhaps, had never had great wealth and placed no store on outward show. The existence of the front-door shoe scraper for which the Earl had told her to look, no longer seemed incongruous.

She parked the Rover and stepped out into stillness broken only by the gravel's crunch as she walked to the door. Beside it, a wall-trained wisteria was in flower, saturating the air about her with its scent. The stave waiting behind the scraper turned out to be the broken shaft of a spade or garden fork. She lifted it, feeling a shade ridiculous, and struck the door two blows.

The stillness remained unbroken. Looking round for signs of life in the grounds, she glimpsed a flash of movement amongst topiary shaped like candle flames along the margin of a low wall. But it was only a fat pigeon prospecting in newly-mown grass.

She struck the door again, harder. This time footsteps approached and the door was opened by a gangling, untidy man of about twenty-five. He stood mute, a faint blush rising from his neck as he looked at Antonia. Above the round-necked pullover he wore beneath his dark suit, a prominent Adam's apple was visible. He was carrying a basket of eggs. If this was a minion of the Earl's, uniform was clearly not a part of the remuneration package.

She told him of her appointment. 'I see,' he said. 'Yes.' He seemed at first confounded by the situation but finally looked back into the interior of the house, as though reminded it was there. 'Would you — come in?' He deposited the egg basket on the floor and stood aside.

They crossed a hall unevenly flagged with black and white tiles. A wide oak staircase ascended on their right; beside it, next to a high-backed chair, a suitcase and a shoulder bag had been placed. A few rays of the sun had crept in but it felt much colder than outside. Leading into a small sitting-room, the young man crossed to an ancient electric fire standing by a hearth and switched on a single bar before inviting Antonia to sit beside it.

She smiled up at him as he stood, curling his fingers in indecision against the seams of his trousers. He had a pleasant face but it was very pale and the eyes had retreated into dark hollows. 'Are you the Earl's son?'

'Younger son, in fact.' He gave an odd, irrelevant laugh, hardly more than a deprecatory expelling of air through his nostrils.

'If your father's had to go out — ' she began.

He sat down abruptly on the edge of a chair facing Antonia. 'No, it's my mother's kiln, it's overheating. She's a potter.' He smiled and she was struck by the sweetness of his expression, as if a shadow had lifted from his mind for the moment. 'The kiln's in the old stables. My father's gone to see what he can do. I'm sure he'll be back soon if he made an appointment with you. He doesn't forget things like that.'

The speech was lucidly delivered, but it seemed to have cost him a considerable effort. He clasped his hands in his lap and the knuckles grew white. She would have liked to comfort him if only there had been an obvious way. As his eyes moved away from her, she said, 'I'm sure you've got things you want to do. I can look for your father if you don't mind pointing me in the direction of the stables.'

He stood up at once, grateful. 'I do have to — to go, if you'll forgive me. I'll show you the way.'

He led her along a corridor and past what she could see was a large, empty kitchen. There was no sign or sound of life anywhere. She wondered who the defeated female had been to whom she had spoken on the telephone. If the Earl employed servants, they either had the afternoon off or were keeping their heads well down. By a side door of the house he pointed across a courtyard to a path through shrubbery. 'It's at the end, I expect you'll hear him.' He extended a hand, blushing again. 'Goodbye then.' He was very anxious to get away.

She had found the stables and was searching for the way in, when a figure appeared round a corner of the building. It was clearly the Earl. He was shorter than his younger son but there was a familiar shape to the forehead. He was walking very briskly for a man of seventy-four; also, she was depressed to note, with an air of irascibility which suggested that electric kilns affected him in the same way as telephones. His tweed suit, worn with a stiff white collar and an aged striped tie, had patches of dust down one side. Looking up from the path and seeing Antonia, he stopped in surprise. She held out her hand. 'I'm Antonia Strachan. Forgive me for coming to find you. Your son said I might.'

Dust, she now noticed, also clung to the Earl's spectacle lenses which were enclosed in round steel frames. He blinked and took her hand. Ancient instincts of courtesy struggled upwards through his irritation. He patted her knuckles with the free hand. 'Yes, of course, Mrs Strachan, I apologize for not being at the house. A crisis in my wife's kiln called me away. You're not a potter yourself, are you?'

'No.'

'Very sensible.'

With fussily polite movements, he conducted her back through the courtyard and into the house again. 'Did you say you had met my son, Francis?'

'For a few moments.'

They were crossing the hall. The Earl turned to look towards the high-backed chair beside which the luggage had stood earlier. The luggage had gone; so had the basket of eggs Francis had been carrying. The Earl opened a door and stood aside for Antonia to pass through. 'Might as well use my study — drawing-room's not very private.'

Her nose wrinkled at a smell of decay as she seated herself in the chair he had indicated beside his desk. No sun had reached the room; it felt like an ice box. This must, she thought, folding her arms tightly against the chill, be what the rest of the household would call his 'den'. The books in shelves on the walls were stacked in a reasonably tidy fashion but elsewhere, covering all available flat surfaces, was debris, or so it seemed — tattered files, copies of *The Field* in piles of varying height, newspapers, a broken water sprinkler, boxes of cartridges, smoke bombs for mole warfare — there was no end to it. In here the electric fire was of a bowl shape she dimly remembered from childhood. But either it didn't work or the Earl was impervious to cold since he made no attempt to reach for the switch.

Seating himself on the other side of the desk, he pushed papers aside in an effort to clear a line of sight between them. 'So Francis let you in?'

'Yes.'

'Talk at all?'

'No, he said he had to go out.'

The Earl nodded. 'Francis is not at all well at the moment. You may have noticed. I'm glad you weren't troubled.'

He reached suddenly under the desk, brought out a bowl and thrust it in front of her. 'Like apples?'

She sensed that the interview stood more chance of success if she answered with enthusiasm. Facing each other, they sank teeth into golden skin with grave expressions.

'Wonderful keepers,' said the Earl. 'Cross between a Cox and a very much older apple. The commercial growers won't have it, of course. Nobody wants to pay for quality, they say. I don't believe it. But there you are.' He restored the bowl to the floor by his feet. 'The PM looked well the other night, I thought. You must find it very satisfying, working for him. Fine brain.'

She temporized with a smile. If she admitted that she had never ever seen the inside of No. 10, he might decide she was not a fit person for further confidences. On the other hand, if she allowed him to go on believing that was where she had come from, there could be problems ahead. But he was speaking again before she could decide how to play it. 'I suppose he will have given you the gist of my private letter to him.'

'I was allowed to have a copy.'

'Ah.' A bit surprising, was what his expression seemed to say, but presumably she's all right. 'Well, as you can see, it's a bad business. It's been deeply shocking to me. Deeply.' He stared out of the window. 'Once evil gets a foothold —' He shook his head.

Opening her bag, Antonia took out the copy of his letter, a notebook and pen. There seemed no obvious place to dispose

30

of the apple core. The Earl had somehow managed to get rid of his unseen, unless enthusiasm had led him to swallow it. 'I wonder — ' she said, and held it up. Reaching once more under the desk, he brought up a waste bin containing the cores of earlier apple sessions; it was the source of the smell of decay she had noticed on entering the room.

'When we read your letter,' she said, 'it seemed to us there were two separate matters — although I appreciate you may be going to tell me of something that connects them. The first is the involvement of Mr Ropner and his wife in a financial scandal and the second is the death of her brother, Signor Barralozzi, in their house?'

He looked at her a trifle impatiently. 'Well?'

'Taking the first — could you be a little more specific about what they did? Was it speculation based on access to official information — ?'

'Yes.'

'Assisted by Signor Barralozzi?'

'Yes.'

'Using what channels?'

'I can only tell you that the brother was a crook. He held this very senior post in the Institute for Religious Works — ' he paused and glanced at Antonia suspiciously — 'I take it you know what that is?'

'Yes.'

'Well, there you are. The sister with his help was able to do things in the money markets that were most improper.'

'Using information supplied by her husband about Government intentions?'

'Of course.'

'Do you know what the information was?'

'No idea.'

'Or how much money was made as a result of the speculation?'

'A lot. The brother did very nicely too. For himself of course. Not the Church. Oh, no.'

'Do you know where the money is now?'

'I can make a guess. One of these offshore places. Or a Swiss bank. Not in the Institute, you can depend on that. I'd say some account in Geneva — I imagine half the politicians now-adays have fixed themselves with something of the sort, it seems to be the way of the world.' The Earl paused, a man trying to be fair. 'Although I would never include your master in that category. The PM has always had my deep respect.'

She began again, carefully. 'That's very helpful. I see you said the information came from Rome. If you could tell me who we might go to in Italy in order — '

'No.'

'We would be very discreet. Your own name need not — '

'Mrs Strachan, I cannot help over that. I hoped my letter had made it clear. You must have ways of getting at these things through the banks. What about your security people? Put them on to it — they seem to get up to all sorts of things. The information will be there if they look.'

'Your own source would not be willing to talk to us in confidence?'

'No, no, no.' It was his fiercest response yet. 'Not available to you.'

'You mean — it's somebody inside the Vatican — in the Institute?'

'I can't say any more about that.'

She was making absolutely no progress.

The Earl had begun to polish his spectacle lenses after blowing hard on the dust that clung to them. She could sense he was embarrassed to be so unyielding. But he was the sort of person who could find an escape hatch from embarrassment into irritation and she knew it was only a matter of time before he looked for it.

She tried to appear sympathetic, understanding. 'But it *was* the same source, was it, who suggested to you that Signor Barralozzi's death might not have been just a heart attack?'

'Yes.'

'. . . that he was murdered . . .'

'I'm afraid so.'

'How?'

'That I don't know.'

'And Mr Ropner and his wife were in some way responsible — ?'

32

He seized on the remark as his excuse for the irritation she had foreseen. 'Now I carefully did *not* say that in my letter to the Prime Minister. But I have grounds for believing this story of a heart attack is cover-up. *And they must surely have known it!* That seems to me no way for a minister of the Crown to go on. I daresay the reasons had to do with the other business. But I'm only guessing there.'

'Their doctor would have had to connive at any cover-up.'

'It wouldn't be the first time doctors have agreed to say whatever was most convenient.' He spoke feelingly. So doctors belonged in the same black bag as telephones and potters' kilns.

'You can give me no more details about this — how, why and when?'

Rather more considerately, he went on, 'I wish I could.' He looked away from her. 'It's a dreadful business. Unbelievable. In all my days I never thought — ' he trailed off, still looking into space. Then he said, 'I suppose you're not a Catholic, Mrs Strachan?'

'No.'

'I could almost say you are fortunate. Certainly you would have to be a Catholic to understand my feelings.'

There was nothing much she could make of that. Her spirits drooped: it was going to prove a disastrous visit. Despairingly, she began, 'If you could just explain — ' But he shook his head more vigorously than ever, as though she really had gone too far this time.

'You'll have to make your own inquiries. I've put you on the track — follow it. I'm sure the Prime Minister has all the resources from which to draw for whatever inquiry is necessary. Please tell him how sorry I am to have to leave it at that. I only wish I had been spared the duty of reporting this much.'

For a little while she persisted, offering hypotheses for him to pick up, speaking of the Prime Minister's great anxiety, displaying what she hoped would prove a touching apprehension about returning to London with not a single extra fact to offer. He was not to be moved. She might as well accept defeat. She stood up.

33

Now that it was almost over, guilt pecked at him. 'Look, you must take a few apples back.' From a drawer of his desk he extracted a well-used Army and Navy Stores plastic bag and placed half a dozen apples from his bowl inside it. 'You won't find any of *those* in your London markets.'

He waited beside the Rover as Antonia fastened her seat belt, his scalp shining in the pale sun. 'You remember the way?' She gave him a smile, more of resignation than anything else and let in the clutch. 'Give the Prime Minister my warmest regards,' he shouted. In her mirror she could see he had turned before she had gone twenty yards and was hurrying down the narrower drive she had noticed earlier. Presumably the Countess's kiln required further attention.

Swinging the Rover out into the main Yeovil road, after negotiating the mile of lanes that protected Cowden Hall from passing traffic, Antonia saw a solitary figure standing by a bus stop. It was Francis Bacton. At his feet was the suitcase she had seen in the house. She drew up beside him. 'Hullo, again!'

He looked startled, at first unable to recognize her. He wore a long gaberdine raincoat; the strap of the shoulder bag was across his chest.

'Can I give you a lift?'

'It's all right, there'll be a bus soon, I think.' When she persisted, he admitted being on his way to catch a London train.

'But that's where I'm going.' She opened the passenger door.

When he was seated beside her, he held his head stiffly, the eyes looking straight ahead. At first she supposed it was another sign of his shyness until she noticed his hands were working, one thumb incessantly describing a circle on the palm of the other hand. She cast around for something to break the spell.

'Your house is in beautiful country.'

'Yes.' He gave the quick nasal laugh. It was like a wry comment, relating not to the words but to thoughts unspoken. He turned a little more towards Antonia. 'You found the stable all right?'

'Your father was just coming away.'

34

'He's very active, isn't he? Very clear-headed.'

She smiled.

'Unfortunately we haven't been seeing eye to eye.'

'Living with parents can be very difficult at times.'

He shook his head. 'I don't live there, you know.'

Surprised she said, 'I'm sorry, somehow — seeing you with the basket of eggs — '

'I'd just been staying for a few days. My mother asked me to drop the eggs in at the lodge.'

Again came that small irrelevant laugh and suddenly an echo from the past came back to Antonia: Leppard, the Bureau's Registry Head, poor Leppard, everyone's Aunt Sally because of the bugs in the computer at Somerset Square, bullied in the office by day, lashed at night by an ambitious wife who scented the blood on him and saw her dreams vanishing. Leppard, she recalled, had developed that same laugh, kept going with it until the day when, at a presentation of his umpteenth re-jigging of the system, his words began to slow and ebb. Finally they had stopped altogether and Leppard had sat, quietly sweating, until somebody had taken him by the arm and led him away to the first-aid room.

Francis Bacton's voice broke into her thoughts. 'Had you met my father before?'

'No.'

'He's a very upright person. I wish I had his goodness. And his judgement.' He seemed unable to stop talking about his father.

She would have given a more astringent verdict on the Earl and his qualities but, clearly, it would not comfort his son if she embarked on that now. Gently she said, 'Have you a place in London?'

'No, a friend has lent me her flat in Tunbridge Wells for a few weeks — I'm going there. She's gone to join the peace camp outside the nuclear arms base at Chawton Wood. They hope it's going to become as big as the Greenham Common affair.'

He was smiling at the windshield, his mind lifted, eased by this new thought pattern. 'Jennifer's giving up her holiday for the camp. She's very serious about it. In some ways I wish I

35

were joining her. But they're restricting it to women, I think.'

'So you'll be by yourself in Tunbridge Wells?'

'Yes. I want some time on my own. To sort myself out.' He looked away again.

Thereafter his burst of animation seemed spent. She had hoped to question him gently about his father's contacts with Italy, whether the Earl had paid a recent visit to Rome or had received a visitor from there. But her efforts to revive the conversation were met with vague half responses which wandered into irrelevancy. He had returned to a private world where black dogs roamed and his own worth was less than the dust beneath their paws. Finally, putting his head back, he closed his eyes. After a while his breath became rhythmic and he slept.

In the Cromwell Road she woke him. 'If you're getting a train to Tunbridge Wells, you'll need Charing Cross Station. I'll drop you there — it's hardly out of my way.'

He was apologetic for falling asleep. 'I must have been a very dull companion.' In the forecourt of the station she watched him struggling clumsily to extract his suitcase from the rear of the car. Even at his best, his co-ordination would always be laboured. The suitcase became stuck for a while; a handle tag fluttered away to disappear under the seat beside her. Thrusting fingers through his hair to make himself more presentable for formal leave-taking, he eventually said, 'Mrs Strachan, that was very kind.' He produced his rare, sweet smile. 'May God go with you.' She felt warmed by the words.

She had already turned into St James's Street, preparatory to threading through Mayfair to reach the Bureau's office in Somerset Square, when the obvious, the appallingly obvious, struck her. She stopped almost dead and, oblivious to the curses of the taxi driver hard behind, maneuvered into the curb to reach under the seat for the tag. She read it, filled with self-contempt. Stupid, slow-witted, *blind*! Not once, in the past two and a half hours, had the possibility crossed her mind that the bearer of the Earl's intelligence from Rome, the source so peremptorily described as unavailable, could be within touching distance. But here in her hand was a Leonardo da Vinci airport tag, unambiguous and accusing.

She imagined Antrim's face as he listened to her story, and winced. There was just one chance she could be spared that. Ignoring the horns of assorted buses, limousines and taxis, she reversed into the north-flowing traffic to the front of St James's Palace and swung down into the Mall. Jumping one set of lights in Trafalgar Square she arrived unscathed in the forecourt of Charing Cross Station in less than three minutes, abandoned the Rover and raced to the concourse. The platform she identified with a single glance at the departures board. But as she ran towards it, the ominous bell was sounding above the ticket collector's head. He had the gate closed in the instant she got to it.

The train was already picking up speed from a deserted platform, bearing Francis Bacton to an unknown address in Royal Tunbridge Wells, the flat of the admirable Jennifer. She didn't even have her surname. For a few moments, she thought of trying to race the train in the Rover so that she would be there to meet it. But at this time, home-going traffic south of the Thames would make it impossible. There was no way of avoiding the truth: she had made a prize mess, a complete, imperial balls-up.

4

For Baxter — that blandly enigmatic concierge on watch in Antrim's outer office, the one whose nod was mandatory for entry to the lair beyond — adjustment to his new powers in many ways resembled Antrim's. In Baxter's case, however, the change had held no element of surprise. He had long been marked out as a front runner to take over as Private Secretary when Jane Farnes moved on. Of this he was well aware. It was his habit to pursue the conduct of his career, the plans for its unfolding in the years ahead, with the Bureau's Establishments branch; as Baxter saw it, his employers must be monitored no less closely than they monitored him, to ensure that his talents were not allowed to waste. Seeing that determined face at his door, more than one in Establishments had sighed and ground his teeth. But the ability could not be denied. It had been agreed that, failing the Director's blackball, here should be the next stage in Baxter's upwards progression, this vantage point at the heart of the Bureau.

It was true that when Harkness died, Jane Farnes of the Pre-Raphaelite look, had still done only two years at the desk and might reasonably have been left to bed the new Director in. No one could deny the success with which she had accomplished Harkness's purposes in terms of timely briefs, urgent meetings with elusive ministers, Glyndebourne tickets, the better served tables at the Athenaeum — even to the matching of the faded curtains in the south window of his office. Knowing all this, Antrim would not have refused to have her, his senses in any case having been quickened by that steely charm in the Burne-Jones wrapper.

But Jane Farnes herself, once she knew that Antrim was to be the new Director, not Temple or Madge, had made it plain she wanted out, had no appetite for servicing Antrim after six and fending him off in the hours before.

So Baxter had come in, on almost the same day that Antrim passed through the double doors; and the latter, after a twinge of regret, concluded that Baxter's ambition, strident though it could be at times, would serve him well for as long as their interests coincided.

He had proved a paragon in these early months of their joint reign, arriving three-quarters of an hour before Antrim in the morning to put the final touches to his programme and staying late at night, smoothing out the craters caused by unforeseen explosions, getting Antrim's runway serviceable again.

When Antonia entered the room, he was consulting the Army List to identify a brigadier in Weapons Procurement who might have approved the over-generous contract which was the Bureau's newest concern. He gave her his tentative smile which, combined with country-air complexion and diminutive size, led many to underestimate him. 'Back from the sticks then — '

His feelings about Antonia were neutral. She presented no threat in any professional sense and was too undevious to maneuver against him. Though he had sometimes reflected that she was attractive, even desirable in the way that reaching their thirties made some women, his libido was a docile thing, subordinated to other purposes. Moreover Antrim had had an interest there which might revive.

Antonia nodded towards the double doors. 'Free?'

Baxter shook his head. 'Gone. There's a dinner for the Head of the Philippines Anti-Corruption Office so he's round at his flat changing.' He began to turn over papers on his desk, searching for something. 'He said he wanted you to telephone him there before a quarter to eight — assuming you got back in time.'

She seated herself on a corner of the desk, relieved that the afternoon's events were now to be reported over a telephone and not face to face.

'How was the aged peer?' Baxter asked.

'Very uncommunicative. He refused outright to say more. Simply gave me a bag of apples.'

'Apples?'

'Yes. Would you like them?'

He shook his head, amused. 'Tiresome for you — all that way. Still you saw him in his habitat. Bridesheadish?'

'Nearer to Cold Comfort Farm.'

Baxter had discovered what he had been searching for. 'Here's something that may interest you, Signor Barralozzi's earthly remains are still with us. He's buried in the Italian cemetery at Hackney — I managed to find that out this morning.'

'Might come in useful.'

'Himself was rather less hypothetical.' It was his own term for Antrim, chosen to distance his style from Jane Farnes's habit of always dignifying Harkness with his name or rank. 'He may tell you more.' He gave her the enigmatic look which said, But of course, he may not.

'Anything else?' she asked.

39

'Another call from Pagett — he'll certainly want to discuss that with you. There's a news item in the *Standard* you ought to look at.'

One of Baxter's telephones rang and she took the opportunity to leave him. He lifted his arm in farewell while speaking into the receiver, a man contented with his lot; there he would stay for some time yet, she guessed, digesting morsels that had entered his web, savouring the thought of others to come.

She had told Transport that she needed the Rover for another day and drove it back to her flat in Little Venice. By the time she had found a parking space in Blomfield Road and squeezed herself past the bed of the new upstairs' tenants, jammed against the newel post of the first-floor landing, it was five minutes past seven. She opened her door, snapped on a light. The familiar scent of her own stored silence greeted her. The corners of her mouth were pulling down. Not as terrifying as Francis Bacton's, but threatening enough, her own black dogs were there, waiting to take over if she didn't look out.

She began the routines of evasion, poured a whisky and drank it, poured another, then replaced the bottle at the very back of the cupboard behind the water jugs, to hamper temptation. Then to the kitchen: switch on radio, remove entrecôte from fridge, peel potatoes, ignite cooker, sit, kick off shoes, light cigarette, avoid all thoughts of tomorrow; drink second whisky.

The immediate hurdle was the call to Antrim. Impossible not be be reminded that once he might have been here, sharing the whisky, the entrecôte steak and later her bed. Back in those days, she had begun to believe that, as his marriage to Juliet drifted more irreversibly on to the rocks, he was going to need her as she needed him. When she had finally seen the light, realized that Antrim needed no one except himself, she had at first thought it would be intolerable working with him in the same building. But his trip to Australia had removed the immediate embarrassment and when he returned it was to a different Division. She had thought his promotion would remove him further from her. But now, having long stopped caring about him, amazed that she could have blinded herself to his ruthlessness, his arrogance, his lack of charity towards older colleagues on the slide, like Madge — even Fender who more than anyone had helped him prosper — she was face to face with him once more, working for him, taking his orders; letting him see her get things wrong.

The telephone rang. She swore, looking at her watch; it was still only twenty-five minutes past seven. As in the past, but for different reasons, Antrim had become impatient and decided to ring himself.

But it was her mother's voice, not Antrim's: another glove flung down to morale; but, for this ritual however practice had equipped her. In the successful daughter's voice, she spoke of the drive down to West Gurney, the first glimpse of the façade of Cowden Hall, the stave for beating on the front door, the Earl and his bloody apples. She received in return observations that were more localized, the meaning of which lay often in the pauses, or even in words with little meaning in themselves but which deciphered subsequently would be found reassuring or warning. And that was that, for another day or so; a web quite unlike Baxter's, with nobody in particular playing the spider but where one stayed alert to sense the strands varying their pattern.

Deciphering would have to be left until after she had dealt with Antrim. She picked up the receiver once more and dialled his number. He answered at once. 'I'd begun to wonder if you were staying the night with him.' He was being hearty with a slightly malicious undertone. 'So what did you get?'

'It was a frost I'm afraid.' She told him without varnish the details of the conversation with the Earl.

'You mean he added *nothing*?'

'Not as far as hard facts are concerned. Just reiteration of how shocked he was, etc., etc. And this curious comment about how shocked *I* would feel if I were a Catholic.'

He laughed shortly. 'Because Barralozzi worked in the Vatican's Bank?'

'No, there was more to it than that.'

'But what?'

'There's some underlying connection that's very troubling to him.'

41

She heard him sigh. 'So you got absolutely no further.'

She was approaching the big jump. 'Not quite. I'm fairly sure that the younger son, Francis, whom I met briefly, is really the Earl's source, the bearer of the news from the people "at the heart" of the thing. He's recently been in Rome. From tonight he's staying at an address in Tunbridge Wells — I'll know exactly where by midday tomorrow, I hope.'

She held her breath waiting for Antrim to explore the holes in her account. But all he said was, 'What is he? Some sort of merchant banker?'

'Not from his appearance. He looks rather unbusinesslike. Also I think he's heading for a nervous breakdown — if he isn't already in the middle of one.'

'What about the Earl's mental condition?'

'I wouldn't say either of them are actually deranged. Just a bit odd.'

'God,' he said. 'What a pair! And that's all you have, is it?' Before she could reply, he went on, 'I can see my car's arrived outside — I'll have to go. Now listen, have you seen the *Standard*? The midday edition carried a story that's got the PM worried. It mentions a report from Italy that the Bank of Rome have been asked by the Vatican to look into possible irregularities in the Vatican Bank's investment activities. It also says that there are rumours of some mystery surrounding the circumstances of Barralozzi's death.'

'So it's coming out already.'

'Whatever "it" amounts to. Anyway the PM has asked that I talk to the Ropners. I've an appointment to see them both tomorrow morning. He's not agreeable to any mention being made of the Earl's letter or of the Bank of England report. I shall have to make as much as I can out of the press story.'

'If it can wait until I've tackled Francis Bacton there might be more ammunition to use.'

'No, the PM wants a report by twelve o'clock. I'll see you afterwards in case there's any follow-up action needed. Come to my office at twelve-fifteen.'

If he said goodbye, she didn't hear it. She went out to the kitchen again and placed the saucepan of potatoes on a boiling-ring. Thoughts of a third whisky tapped at the casement but she managed to divert her attention to preparing a salad. From upstairs the sounds of the new tenants getting their bed into place could be heard. The confident prediction to Antrim of knowing Francis Bacton's address by midday tomorrow was going to come home to roost all too soon. Between now and a quarter past twelve tomorrow, she had to get some sleep, drive to the Atomic Weapons base at Chawton Wood — which must be at least eighty miles away — locate the right Jennifer amongst the assorted woollen hats camped outside, persuade her to reveal her home address, drive back to London and face Antrim once more.

Placing the steak under the grill, she said finally, 'What you need is a drink,' and went to the cupboard.

5

In the end, it turned out simpler than she had feared. By breakfast time, driving through the light mist that had succeeded a night of showers, she found herself confronted by the perimeter fence of Chawton Wood nuclear base. The peace camp had occupied a strip of the grass edge of the road, away from the base entrance, about two hundred yards along the fence. She parked the car against a field gateway some distance beyond the camp. A police van was the only other vehicle in sight. A few policemen stood about, chatting; one began to do small jumps in the middle of the road, shaking off the chill of early morning.

She walked slowly back towards the camp. There were fewer women visible than she had expected from her recollection of TV news shots, perhaps thirty in all; but there might be more, she supposed, still abed in the small brown tents. Food and drink were being heated on stoves and a radio was tuned to a news bulletin. In front of a tent larger than the rest and pitched so as to constitute a sort of reception point, a tall woman stood with two companions. Unlike the others she wore no hat; her black hair, cut short above the ears and at the neck, glistened damply in the mist. The woman's eyes had fastened on Antonia while she continued to talk to the other two, then moved to appraise the Rover. She had the look of a leader.

As Antonia drew level, she could hear the woman talking about the need for additional tents to be pitched. Apparently six more women and a child aged two were expected. At ease but attentive, the two lieutenants nodded. They only turned to examine Antonia when the woman said, 'That's all.'

Antonia smiled a greeting. 'Could you help me? I'm looking for someone named Jennifer. She comes from Tunbridge Wells. I think she joined the camp a day or two ago.'

The woman kicked at a hummock with a wellington boot. 'Who are you? — a friend?'

'No, we haven't met.'

'Local Tunbridge Wells press?'

'Actually I'm the friend of a friend of hers. She's let her flat to him while she's here. I need to find him. But I haven't got the exact address.'

Antonia could see, now that she was near, that the black hair was streaked with grey, but not at random: nature was being helped. The woman looked Antonia full in the eyes for rather longer than the occasion seemed to demand. 'I'm Claire Wylie. Where are you from?'

'London.'

'You *must* have made an early start.'

'Five o'clock.'

The woman made a complimentary inclination of the head. She was handsome with a strong nose and chin. 'Care to join us — ?' She made the sort of noise that asks for a name.

'Antonia Strachan.'

'Care to join us, Antonia?'

'I'm rather tied up at the moment.'

'Married? Or what?' She delivered questions in a voice that had no time for circumlocutions.

'No, I meant I have a full-time job.'

'Well, spend your holiday here — *if* you think Peace is

important. This is going to be bigger than Greenham Common before we've finished. We learnt a lot there. What about it?'

Relief came in the form of a blue Mini which drew up on the grass beside them. The girl driving it looked out at Claire and grinned. 'BBC no, but ITN *yes*! They think the crew should be here at two o'clock.'

'This is definite?'

'Definite.'

Claire threw back her head and yodelled. Other women, gathering round the Mini to hear the news, broke into a ragged cheer. They made off to the tents behind to spread the tidings. One of the policemen further up the road looked round and began to walk slowly towards the Mini.

The tall woman had turned to call to somebody, then remembered Antonia. 'You want Jennifer. Right — she's the one in the red anorak over there.' She pointed. Lowering the hand she placed it on Antonia's forearm and squeezed, moving the fingers gently as she did so. 'Don't forget what I said. It would be lovely if you'd join us.'

Breaking away, Antonia saw that the policeman was abreast of them and had observed the gesture. There was the faintest flicker of amusement in his eyes. She looked at him stonily and went after Jennifer.

About Jennifer's rear view as she bent over a camp stove there was a comfortable shapelessness that was somehow reassuring after Claire. Hearing her name she straightened, revealing a flushed but smiling face; she had the eyes of someone who assumed the motives of others were as unmean as her own. Once, in the days when merely plump, she must have been pretty. Then at some point, she had presumably bartered appearance for the consolations of gluttony, embracing it as the jolly vice.

Holding a mug of tea while she poured sugar into it from a packet, she listened to Antonia in delighted amazement that anybody should be seeking her out. That it should only be for the purpose of locating some one else didn't seem to matter. 'So you're a friend of Francis's too!' she said.

Lying to some one so guileless seemed especially

45

contemptible. 'Not exactly. I was visiting his father yesterday and gave Francis a lift to London in my car. I'd just like to contact him again.'

Even that came out wrong. She could see from Jennifer's expression that she scented a budding romance which it was now in her power to advance. Yet to disillusion her could only make for difficulties. She waited.

Jennifer took a pull at the mug after offering the other side to Antonia. 'He's so nice, isn't he? He helped me a lot at University. A really good person.' She sighed. 'Pity in a way that he gave it all up. Yet I'm glad as well.'

'Sorry, I've lost you.'

'I mean I'm glad he gave the Church up. He's the sort who worries over everybody. It would have been a burden. He feels too responsible, wants to give himself one hundred and ten per cent to things. You know?' She brightened. 'Anyway, the address is 45c Jefferson Street. It's off Grosvenor Road, if you know Tunbridge Wells.'

'I don't but I'll find it. Is there a telephone number?'

'I'm afraid not. If somebody has to get me in an emergency I rely on a friend who's got a phone and lives in a house nearby. That's where I left the key for Francis.'

'You haven't seen him since he came back from Italy?'

'No, he wrote in the middle of April from some hostel he'd gone to when he gave everything up. I think he was at the English College first but he moved from there. He asked if I knew of a place he could rent for a week or two. Since I'd already decided to spend my holiday here — ' Jennifer threw a hand sideways with a cheerfully resigned expression to mark the distinction from the Algarve or even Southend on Sea — 'I wrote back he could have my place for a bit.'

Behind Jennifer, one or two children were now visible, playing among the tents. A woman emerged to shake out a blanket. Someone went up to her, perhaps to convey the news brought by the girl in the blue Mini. She was nodding her head in grim satisfaction.

Jennifer's eyes had turned towards the woman with the blanket. 'We're hoping to be on the box again tonight. It's quite a breakthrough. I must do something about my appearance in case my mother's looking in.' She gave the derisive laugh of one who knows that cause is lost already. 'How was Francis when you saw him?'

'He didn't seem very well. Is he highly strung?'

'He's too sensitive. I think it was his father who wanted him to become a priest.'

'You've no idea what he went to do when he left the English College?'

'Not a clue — something else for the Church I suppose.'

'And he didn't give you a hint why he finally gave it up?'

'No. He said in his letter that he'd made a mistake and the responsibilities were heavier than he felt able to accept. Very unlike him, that.'

Claire's voice could be heard, raised in command. She wanted everybody to gather round her. Women shouted to the more distant tents, passing the message on.

Antonia said, 'I think you're wanted.'

Jennifer put down her mug and began fastening her anorak for Claire's parade. 'Give Francis my love. I hope he's going to be all right.' She looked at Antonia with a trace of archness. 'He really needs someone to look after him.'

Laggards were still making their way to Claire's conference as Antonia reached the Rover. One girl had stopped to do a jig round the policeman who had come to learn the news brought by the Mini. 'Will you dance with me on telly?' Her boots splashed the contents of a puddle against his trousers. He looked at them in a resigned way and made his way back to his colleagues.

She sat for a few minutes in the car, making notes of the conversation with Jennifer. By the time she had turned and was driving past the camp again, the women were dispersing from the parade.

The absence of men, a certain domestic untidiness with laundry drying and children running to and fro, the air of drabness and discomfort, had an echo in something not seen, but imagined: the camp followers of an army, patiently waiting out of sight of the battle, could once have presented this sort of scene. Presumably there were occasions when just such a group had rebelled against the men's *affaire* with death. Did

47

they sing, do little dances, call to passers-by to join them? Did they ever succeed in turning the army back?

By twelve-thirty Antrim had still not returned to his office. Flicking over the pages of *Punch* (the only reading matter provided for visitors to his ante-room, now that he had withdrawn *Private Eye* for his exclusive attention), Antonia began to wonder if, under his inquisition, the Ropners had embarked on some startling confession. But no politician, surely, had ever been known to confess anything. He couldn't be at No. 10, since, according to Baxter, the PM had postponed the twelve o'clock deadline for a report. He might have looked in on Pagett at the Cabinet Office if he had a particularly succulent bone to lay on the carpet or if fresh direction was needed. But she knew he would have to leave for lunch with an FBI man before one o'clock. There seemed little point in waiting. She was almost out of the door when Baxter's telephone rang with the news that Antrim was on his way up.

Antrim appeared, walking at speed, the man of affairs driven by the clock yet relishing its pressure. Tossing to Antonia the practised smile that once had not seemed empty at all, he beckoned her to follow him into his room. 'Sorry to keep you.'

As Antonia settled into the chair in front of his desk he glanced through messages that had been placed on his diary by Baxter, grunted, went to the lower half of the bookcase, poured himself a gin, held up a second glass inquiringly to Antonia. When she shook her head he said, 'Prudent as ever.'

He came back to sit in the high leather chair behind the desk and stretched his legs out in front of him luxuriously. He was pleased with himself.

Baxter's head appeared round the door. 'Would you like me to sit in on your discussion?'

'I — ' Antrim let the syllable linger on the air before finishing his sentence with a bang — 'don't think so, Graeme.' He smiled fixedly until Baxter shut the door again. And that, she thought, was Baxter's taste of the whip for the day.

Antrim lit himself a Panatella. 'Well — the Ropners are now

prepared to admit that Barralozzi's death wasn't quite as it appeared.'

'That it wasn't from a heart attack?'

'Oh, he had that all right. But there's rather more to it than they'd previously let on. The truth turns out to be farcical rather than high drama. The heart attack didn't happen — didn't begin to happen, at any rate — in their house. Barralozzi became ill in the bedroom of the Royal Landau Hotel to which he'd gone with a girl. He'd apparently ordered her to be sent over in the middle of the afternoon from the usual sort of agency. This one calls itself Company International.

'He didn't lose consciousness when he had the attack because he told the girl to telephone his sister and explain his predicament. Mrs Ropner, instead of saying, Get a doctor, went round to the Royal Landau and, using a wheel chair provided by the hotel, got him into her car, back to her own house and into bed there before she summoned her local medico. While the doctor was on his way he had another attack. He lived for only a few minutes after the doctor got there.'

'Whyever did she move him from the hotel room?'

'If her brother was going to die — and he'd apparently had one heart attack in Rome a year ago — she wasn't going to let it take place in a hotel room in the regrettable circumstances described. That also seems to have been the brother's main concern, oddly enough. Perhaps working for the Vatican makes one like that. Mrs Ropner also said that the girl hadn't really conveyed to her on the telephone quite how ill her brother was but I don't think that made much difference. Anyway the Barralozzi escutcheon was not to be sullied. A ropy financial reputation can be laughed off apparently, but not, according to Alida Ropner's lights, death in the arms of a hotel tart.'

'And Ropner knew all about this?'

'After the event, apparently. I suppose he decided the best thing to do was — nothing. After all, what *could* he do?' He drained his glass and fetched himself another gin.

'Did they tell you this quite willingly?'

'They weren't eager to. But when I produced the news item

and pointed to the reference to mysterious circumstances and added the PM had asked me to inquire into it, Ropner turned to her and said, "Alida, you'd better come clean." After a bit of eye-snapping, that's what she did.'

Antonia said reflectively, 'It could be a put-up story — to conceal something else about the death.'

'Oh, no.' He was irritated by her reaction. 'Too many possibilities for cross-checking. They couldn't risk it. She's a compulsive talker once she starts — I'd be there now if it weren't for the fact that she's off to Italy for the funeral of some family friend. She gave me the name of the whore, the number of the hotel room, the agency — everything. Which leads me to what I want you to do. Get hold of the girl, so that when I see the PM he can be told we've got corroboration. At the same time you can find out if Barralozzi said anything about his other interests while she was — satisfying his requirements.'

Antrim let his eyes rest on her face, willing a reaction, a flicker of unbidden memory to undo her calm. She looked back blankly. 'I was planning to see Francis Bacton this afternoon — I've got his address in Tunbridge Wells. There's no telephone but I could drive down in an hour or so. I've also discovered he was a priest. He was at the English College in Rome. Then he suddenly threw it all up. This must tie in with the Earl's talk about how shameful to a Catholic what he knew was.'

Antrim was scarcely listening. 'I daresay. But leave the business of seeing Francis Bacton for the moment. I want you to talk to the tart and dispose of that angle.' He tossed back the remains of his gin. 'Get hold of Sellars at the Yard — he's got lines to all these call-girl agencies and can make sure the girl's told to come clean.'

There was no point in arguing with him. 'Did the Ropners admit anything else — on the other part of the Earl's story?'

'Not really. Since the PM had forbidden me to put it to them directly, I had to make do with the report of the Bank of Rome inquiry and asking Alida Ropner if this was likely to get into any business her brother had conducted for her. She played an absolutely dead bat. Just once remarked that *of course* he'd occasionally tipped her off about good investment opportunities he saw coming up. I thought Ropner himself was sweating a bit at that point, but not seriously. In other words, if she *did* bet on sterling at the right time, he may have his suspicions but I don't think he put her up to it. More likely she got some lead out of him — or read it in one of his official papers he brought home to work on — and then told her brother so that they could make a killing between them.'

'So your provisional view is that the Bank of England report may or may not turn out to have been correct, but that there's probably nothing in the Earl's belief that Barralozzi was bumped off.'

Once more, Baxter's head appeared round the door. When Antrim glanced at him, he said, 'I think you should be leaving for your lunch.' Antrim rose briskly to his feet. As he walked over to the side table on which he had placed his top coat on coming in, he rested his hand briefly on Antonia's shoulder and pressed, a reminder of other moments when flesh had met flesh. Once more he was testing her reaction.

'By tonight,' he said, 'I expect to have confirmation that that part of the Earl's story is moonshine.'

She raised her eyebrows.

'I've arranged for Barralozzi's body to be exhumed. Informally.'

'Informally?'

'Yes. I decided it would save a lot of worry if we took a private look at the corpse.'

Even knowing him, she was shaken. 'Have we done that before?'

'I don't think so. Harkness would probably have wet his pants at the mere thought. *And* Lorimount. But I've no doubt on this occasion it will prove to have been justified. It's the only way of quickly putting the PM in the position of knowing how big a smell there is. My guess is that I'm going to be able to reassure him on the death angle.'

'When will you know the result of the examination?'

'We got the body up last night — a rather useful exercise for Wontner's section. It was taken straight to Jamieson, the pathologist I managed to persuade to help us over this. He telephoned me just before I left to see the Ropners. He'll need the rest of the day to complete his tests — we're putting the coffin back tonight — but his first look points strongly to straightforward coronary failure. Which is what I expected.' He stood, buttoning the coat and smiling.

Well, she thought, in Baxter's favourite phrase, Himself was certainly cutting a dash. She gathered her papers together and stood up. 'Did Mrs Ropner have anything to say about where her brother might have been in the earlier part of the day? In case we need to pursue that after all —'

He was not to be discomfited. 'I did slip in a question about it. She didn't know. But he took a telephone call from a man — a foreigner, by which I established she meant, not English and not Italian — soon after breakfast. There was a reference to some American business. Barralozzi went out at about eleven o'clock, obviously to meet the caller. She didn't expect him back to lunch — in fact not before the early evening. The Ropners were giving a dinner party to which they'd invited a few bankers for him to meet.'

Antrim paused with his hand on the door. 'Just in case Jamieson does start back-pedalling on the cause of death, find out from the girl if he talked about the person he'd seen. Pick up anything you can. You'll probably find her interesting anyway.' He grinned; but she knew that, after all, she had dropped a sliver of worry in his mind.

He was waiting for a response. 'All clear?'

'Yes.'

'Good girl,' he said. 'See Baxter when you get back.'

6

It was a handsome house, set back in a little courtyard, pilast-
ered and white-painted and altogether delectable. A stone's
throw from Harrods, the house agents would have said, and,
given a sling and a strong right arm, they might even have
proved it. Urns of geraniums and trailing ivy stood sentinel
along the York stone path to the front door; behind a magnolia
tree that overhung the path, the windows glowed in the early
evening sun.

No name plate, Sellars had said, they're much too classy for
that. No parking space either, Antonia noted with increasing
frustration, nosing the Rover past for the second time. She
drove into and round the neighbouring streets, hoping in vain
to see the car of some home-going shopper pulling away from
the curb. She was already ten minutes behind the time Sellars
had fixed for her with Company International when she gave
up the struggle and left the Rover with a prayer on a double
yellow.

The woman who answered the door looked Spanish, a
housekeeper-type in a black dress. When Antonia gave her
name, she nodded silently, obviously forewarned of the visit.
She led the way across pale marble to a door with a heavily-
flowered fingerplate and a handle to match. Knocking, she
stood back for Antonia to enter.

Sunlight, softly filtered by gauze curtains, slanted across a
polished oak floor and velvet upholstered chairs to dwindle in
the nap of flock wallpaper the colour of apricots. Beyond the
sun's reach, flanked by pieces of Chippendale, some more-
than-respectable china was visible in a wall cabinet. A gas log
fire flared in a stripped pine fireplace. All was handsome
bourgeois comfort, or what some interiorist felt would pass
for that.

53

There were two persons in the room. Seated beside the fire, a girl of perhaps twenty-three or -four was leafing through a *Tatler*, a honey-blonde, lightly tanned, with full lips and remarkably long legs; a silk jersey dress, cut high in the neck but low beneath the armpits, added appropriate zest. She looked like a valuable capital asset, as delectable as the house.

The other, who stood beside the half-open door to another room, was a smaller woman in her fifties. She was as carefully dressed as the girl, but for a grander role. On her tightly waved hair she wore a tiny hat of sapphire blue; her dress was pleated silk with, nestling in the front, a two-string necklace of pearls. She might have been a society columnist on her way to the Dorchester to cover a charity auction.

'Mrs Strachan,' the small woman said, without preliminaries. 'You're later than I expected. Six o'clock was the time I agreed with Mr Sellars.' She had something of the headmistress about her.

'I'm sorry, I had trouble parking.'

The woman shook her head at such foolishness. 'Driving yourself round here is hopeless. I never do. If you've no driver, you must take taxis.' She was very crisp. Pointing to one of the velvet chairs, she seated herself on a *chaise-longue*. 'I suggest we get down to business since Michelle may not be free much longer. Before we start, I'd like to make something clear. It's well known to Mr Sellars, but perhaps not to you. The policy of the company in general is not to talk to anyone about its clients. We have a world-wide business and a reputation for absolute discretion which we intend to keep. At our end of the market, clients expect and get complete privacy.'

The woman extended the fingers of a hand and looked at her rings. She was wearing so many, it was no doubt prudent to check them from time to time. 'However, in this instance, since the client is unfortunately dead and I always try to be helpful to Mr Sellars, we are prepared to make an exception. On an informal basis though — no affidavits, no evidence in court, nothing like that. I hope that is clearly understood?'

'I understand.'

'So what questions do you want to put?'

'Well, perhaps we could begin with how Michelle first met Signor Barralozzi.'

'It was a normal booking through my office here — he would have had my number as a Rome member of our club. In fact I spoke to him myself. After he explained his requirements I reserved the room at the Royal Landau and arranged for Michelle to meet him there.'

Antonia looked at Michelle. She had put down the *Tatler* and was in the process of lighting a cigarette. 'Was he quite well when you first met him?'

Michelle seemed to take a while to get her thoughts together. Then she shrugged her shoulders. 'Yes. Just complained a bit about his lunch, said it had given him indigestion. I rang down to Reception and got them to send some stomach tablets up. But he didn't take them.' She had a south London accent, fast disappearing under something more anonymous. 'By the time they arrived it wasn't bothering him. He'd got quite lively.'

A telephone rang in the adjoining room. The small woman rose and went to deal with it, closing the connecting door behind her. Her voice could be heard, rather less crisp than before but still very businesslike.

'So when did he have his attack?'

Michelle drew deeply on her cigarette. 'When he was — finishing. He hadn't had any trouble until then. But suddenly I saw he was having difficulty getting his breath. His colour changed, went almost grey. I pushed him on to his back, got a pillow under his head and wondered what the hell to do.' She lifted her eyes to Antonia. 'Would you have known what to do?'

'Send for a doctor.'

'The rule is that if there's any sort of trouble — *any* sort — you telephone here first. I was just dialling the number when I noticed he was beginning to breath properly again, so I stopped. He opened his eyes after a while and stared at me in a helpless way. I sat on the bed looking down at him and just sort of hoped. It was — eerie. Eventually he managed to get a few words out, asked me to telephone his sister. I offered to get a doctor then but he said, no, just tell my sister I've been taken ill and where I am, she'll know what to do, I don't want a doctor here. So I did what he asked. When I phoned her, she said she'd be right round and I was to do nothing else. Actually I rang through to Mrs Rivers here then and it was agreed everything should be left as arranged with the sister.

'While we were waiting for the sister he got a bit better and tried to stand up but he couldn't manage that. Then the sister came — very bossy woman — she had a wheelchair sent up and between us we got him out of the hotel and into her car. She checked where I was from, took my name, pushed a tenner into my hand and said she hoped I'd forget about it. Since I knew Mrs Rivers had his card number and the bill would have gone through the club anyway I wasn't worried about that side. And that was the last I saw of him.' She looked into the fire. 'Poor bastard, I was sorry when I read the papers. But, God, he gave me a fright.'

'Did he tell you anything about what he'd been doing that day before he met you at the hotel?'

'Not much. Just about this lunch that hadn't agreed with him.'

'Where was that, do you know?'

'In a restaurant at the Barbican Centre, he said. It had a funny name — the something-or-other above — he asked me what it meant — I've forgotten now. He said the Barbican was a mess in his opinion. He didn't think much of the man he'd had lunch with either although he said he'd brought good news.' Michelle lit another cigarette from the stub of the old one. 'He told a story about him he thought was funny.'

'Any idea what he meant when he talked about good news?'

'No.'

'And the man —?'

'He was another foreigner — but not Italian.'

'American?'

'No — he couldn't speak English properly according to Signor What's-his-name. That was the point of the story.'

'In what way?'

'He apparently said something about a statue outside the restaurant having a hard on.' She raised her eyebrows. 'Understand?'

'Yes.'

'Well, apparently it hadn't.' Michelle sighed. 'Mind you, with the GLC nothing would surprise me. They run the Barbican, don't they?'

'I'm not sure.'

'I bet they do,' Michelle said. She seemed to be on the threshold of a political outburst, her lips no longer provocative but rancorous; she was beginning to look like a voter.

'Did Barralozzi say anything about what he'd been doing before he met this man?'

'No.'

'Or talk about his work?'

'Just said he was a banker, that's all.' Michelle stretched and turned away from the fire. She was getting bored. Beneath the silk jersey dress, her body moved as though in some curious way it had been freed from contact with the fabric. Without conscious effort, she conveyed the idea of nakedness moving behind a screen.

There didn't seem much else to ask. 'While he was with you, he didn't eat or drink anything?'

'No. Mind you, he might have taken a pill when he went to the bathroom at the beginning. Some of them do. But if so, I didn't see.'

The small woman had reappeared through the connecting door. She stood waiting impatiently. When Michelle failed to notice her, she called, 'Michelle, you're on your way, dear.'

Michelle looked unenthusiastically at her cigarette. 'Where?'

'Lake Side Towers, Room 84, seven o'clock. Straight.'

'Anyone I know?'

'Mr Reiner.'

'Oh, no!'

The woman had clearly foreseen that some spine-stiffening might be necessary. 'You know you can handle him.'

'Jesus.'

'He said he had something for you,' the woman said encouragingly.

'I'll bet.'

It seemed a good moment to leave. Antonia stood up. 'Thank you.' Michelle gave her the slightest of nods. She was

57

staring bitterly into the fire, arms crossed, hands gripping the shoulders as though she had become cold.

The woman led the way out of the room. As they crossed the hall, Antonia asked, 'Do you live here?'

'I have a flat on the top floor. It's a company house — the president of the company uses it when he visits from New York. He's flying in tonight.'

'And Michelle?'

The woman opened the front door. 'Michelle has a house in Canonbury. Her husband's an actor — very nice man.' She was being friendly now that Antonia was leaving. Sunlight made brilliant the small sapphire-blue hat on her head. It had a look of permanency. Perhaps she wore it all the time. 'Remember me to Mr Sellars,' she said. She bent to flick a dead leaf from amongst the geraniums in one of the urns.

As Antonia crossed the street, she could see that the Spanish housekeeper had appeared with a trowel; there was a discussion going on about the condition of the flowers. Standing beneath the magnolia, they made a pleasant picture, two women getting the house perfect for when the master flew in.

The security guards had lowered the shutter at the entrance to the Bureau's garage by the time Antonia got back and she had to ring to be admitted. Apart from the office runabouts, the parking area was empty. With luck even Baxter by now would have returned to the suffering software programmer who shared his bed in Beckenham. In which case, she was spared delivering a report to him as Antrim had asked. Baxter she had once taught as a new arrival to the Bureau when his fingernails were seldom clean and he had commuted by Vespa from lodgings in a less leafy part of Kent. During the Mancini investigation he had been under her control. She had required him to ask her whenever he proposed to leave the office for the night. Baxter would not have forgotten that.

She visited his room, hoping that silence would greet her. But it was not to be. Baxter still sat at his desk, his jacket hung on the back of his chair, his tie loosened, dictating into a recorder. He was trying out Antrim's mantle for size and finding it an agreeable fit. His eyes wandered across the wall opposite him while he lovingly fashioned the periods of a draft minute. He looked as though he was intent on making a night of it, would be only too ready to extract every morsel from any story she could tell, and to glaze it with his own wisdom for presentation to Antrim the next morning.

He waved her to a seat and ran on for a few moments more, to let her hear the concision of his instruction to the duty typist privileged to collect the cassette at seven-thirty the following day. Then, letting his arms fall with a sigh down the sides of his chair, he said with relish, 'What a day!'

She made an attempt at ducking out. 'Look, you're busy, why don't I save you the trouble of making notes of the little I've got? I'll be in first thing tomorrow and can tell him myself.'

He shook his head. 'He especially wanted me to let him know your news when I call at his flat on my way home tonight. I'm taking the pathologist's report on the corpse of Signor B — it's just come in.'

She sat back, resigned. She might as well bring herself up to date anyway. 'What was his final verdict?'

Baxter looked amused; something had given him a lot of pleasure. 'Complete turn around.'

'A turn around?'

'Absolute. Himself was quite shaken when Jamieson telephoned this afternoon.'

'It wasn't just a heart attack?'

'He had that all right. But Jamieson found traces of a substance which he believes was the trigger, the true cause of death. It's primarily a derivative of Digitalis in a new compound developed in Germany. Can produce symptoms indistinguishable from a normal heart attack in someone who had a dicky heart to begin with. As the Signor had.'

'Could Barralozzi not have been taking it as medication without realizing the danger?'

'Jamieson says it's inconceivable anyone would have prescribed it for him — it would have been seen as potentially lethal.'

'Does the report say how it's normally administered?'

'Best in liquid. Has a bitter taste which may be disguised in

59

coffee and some alcoholic drinks.'

'And the time-lapse before it takes effect . . .?'

Reluctantly Baxter sorted a memorandum from the papers on his desk and studied it. He was irritated to find himself answering questions instead of asking them. 'Varies — usually up to six hours.'

Antonia closed her eyes to think aloud. 'So if Mrs Ropner had told her doctor of Barralozzi's heart attack a year ago, in the absence of any suspicious circumstances he would have thought he was faced with a simple recurrence. Whereas, unless we think against all likelihood that the sister did it, he was murdered by someone who slipped the poison into his drink before or during his lunch.'

'What's your reason for thinking it happened at lunch?'

'The time factor plus what I learnt at Company International.' She told him Michelle's account of her pillow talk. Baxter's eyes glistened. 'It fits with the sister's mention of the telephone call — the one he took from somebody who was neither English nor Italian.'

She had to give Baxter his due: although excluded from her earlier conversation with Antrim, he had somehow winkled out the salient facts during the afternoon. 'That doesn't take us far towards identifying him.'

He was working up a head of enthusiasm. 'Perhaps there was a table reservation at the restaurant. The other man could have made a booking. In which case he would have given a name — they might still have a note of that in the head waiter's book.'

'How would they distinguish one name from another?'

'Apart from the fact that the name ought to be foreign, the booking will probably have been for two people. And since we can provide a physical description of Barralozzi as one of the two, the waiter who served them might enable us to relate the table to the booking.'

It was a long shot but worth a try. As she began to say as much, Baxter cut in. 'I'll drop in at the Barbican tonight after I've called on Himself and see what can be got. Leave it to me.'

Damn him, she thought, if I don't watch out, he'll simply take over. But I can't very well order him *not* to go. Why has this happened? Am I wet, so obviously not in control of the inquiry that anyone can feel like horning in? Perhaps, in Antrim's phrase for those whose energies and motivation he finds deficient, I'm Over the Hill.

Busy now with the task of sorting the files and papers on his desk, preparatory to locking them away, Baxter said casually, 'By the way, you won't of course have heard — ' He jerked his head towards Antrim's office. 'He's decided to bring an old boss of yours in on this. Fender.'

Astonishment replaced self-analysis. 'Ludo Fender!'

He nodded. 'He was more than a bit put out by Jamieson's news, which went against his reading of the case. He seems convinced now that as your not-so-batty old peer implied, it may have some very odd angle to it. He wants a fully paid-up Papist to talk Francis Bacton into spilling the beans about whatever it was he picked up in Rome and there isn't one on the premises he thinks is experienced enough. So he telephoned Fender in his country fastness and asked him if he would come back for a small investigation.'

She knew Baxter was watching her as he piled papers into his trays, he wanted to see how she took it. She shrugged. 'I'm sure he'd do it very well — if he's really willing.'

'Apparently he demurred until he heard the background. Then curiosity got the better of him. So he said, "Yes." I've arranged for a car to pick him up early tomorrow — he lives in a Sussex village called Mayfield. It's about fifty miles out so we should have him here by eleven. After he's been chatted up by Himself you're apparently required to brief him in detail. I'll give you a call.'

She rose. 'Well, I shall enjoy seeing Ludo again.'

'You went to Ottawa with him on some hush-hush case, didn't you?'

'Yes.'

With difficulty Baxter fitted his files and bulging trays into the security cupboard against the wall, shut the door and spun the tumblers. 'I never knew him properly. What was he like? All I remember is a very fat man who walked slightly sideways and expected one to get out of his way in the corridor. Somebody said he was incredibly devious.'

61

'About right,' she said. 'But somehow one didn't mind in the end.' She walked to the door, conscious that he was expecting her to explain that. But on Baxter it would have been a waste of breath. She wasn't sure she could, anyway.

Back in her own room to collect her coat, gingerly she fingered her self-esteem. She decided that, although the news had not been agreeable, she didn't need to lick any wounds. Also there would be compensations. She would be spared any more direct dealings with Antrim. She could get on with her own work again. And, if the case had to be handed over to anyone, she preferred Fender to all the others she could think of.

Surprise that Antrim had brought himself to ask for his help remained. Fender, after all, in Antrim's eyes, had been one of the old gang who'd condoned the pussy-footing of Lorimount and Harkness. Moreover Antrim had been Fender's subordinate, a role he had never enjoyed. Only grudgingly had he ever admitted respect for Fender's foresight, his cunning, his skill in handling those the Bureau had to question and who believed their status or power should exempt them from scrutiny. She knew from the time of the Mancini investigation how much Antrim had resented Fender's unwillingness to reveal his mind until the very last moment, how much he had grumbled about that exasperating ambiguity, which, while shyness played some part, was really the mask behind which he chose to conceal motive and opinion.

She had suffered enough from those aspects of Fender's character herself. And yet, deep inside that lumbering hippopotamus figure, was something for which she felt fondness. There was a dimension, unconnected with his size, that she seldom sensed in others. Maddening in his secretiveness, he would yet, at times, reveal his thoughts with an engaging humility, to give a glimpse of that dark reservoir in which emotion had been dammed up since his wife's death. Then one knew that the eyes peering out of that wall of monstrous flesh saw things differently from Antrim and the rest. If he loved secrecy for its own sake, there was an imagination there which fed on it and glowed and gave off warmth.

She would be glad to see him again. But, closing the door

behind her and making for the Underground, she also knew she wished he had turned Antrim's invitation down.

7

Antrim lifted his chin above the telephone mouthpiece, smiling bland apology in Fender's direction. 'Forgive me, Ludo — must put this chap back in his box.' He pressed a button and turned away.

Easing himself forward in the armchair that Baxter had produced when the one in front of Antrim's desk had proved too snug, Fender let his gaze wander round the room. It must be eighteen months since he had visited it, called up by Harkness to elucidate a more than usually cryptic file note. Now that poor Harkness was gone, the main change seemed to be a contraption which virtually covered one wall and consisted of a series of sliding panels. It was vaguely reminiscent of something seen in a television panel game. One of the panels was open, revealing a Central London map with coloured pins in it. Hard to believe that so many joint swoops with the police were now being undertaken as to necessitate that sort of thing. The inter-communication system at the side of the desk was also new — no doubt a great deal more sophisticated than in his own day. Surprisingly, there was no VDU screen, but it would almost certainly come; Antrim had always had a weakness for gadgetry. That perhaps would be his memorial, his special imprint on this graceful room; and then they would all be gone, the ghosts of provincial ladies, up for the shopping and taking tea on an Edwardian afternoon.

The curiosity that had impelled him to accept Antrim's invitation was ebbing away, to be replaced with the faint repulsion he should have foreseen. Now that he had heard Antrim's account of the Barralozzi-Ropner affair, he could guess only too well how it would turn out, for all Antrim's suspicion of some special Catholic dimension. Barralozzi would be found to have been playing games with criminals who had then decided to rub him out. They would never be identified. Nor would anyone get to the bottom of the jiggery-pokery, in which Alida Ropner, and perhaps Ropner himself, had been engaged with Barralozzi. It probably meant that, one way or another, the Vatican Bank had made an expensive fool of itself. And what was new in that?

True, he had always wanted to see what Antrim looked like, wearing the Director's hat. The news of his elevation had certainly come as a surprise. He had not supposed that Antrim would be amongst the runners for at least five more years and, even then, that his defects would be sufficiently apparent to disqualify him. Did some blame for what had happened attach to himself? He couldn't deny that long ago, when Antrim was posted into his own Division at the Bureau, it was he who had marked him out for early advancement, having observed and admired his restless energy, his professionalism, even that glinting ambition which others found obtrusive. Only later, seeing the womanizing, the impulsive and brutal streak that could jeopardize an investigation, the steady drift towards sleight of hand with facts when briefing the powerful, did misgivings form. But by then it was too late. His own influence in the Bureau was on the wane. Harkness had said, Don't worry, Temple will be in my chair and he knows the form with Antrim. Then suddenly Harkness was dead and Temple was nowhere — nowhere with influence, anyway.

So here Antrim was — arrived. In appearance much the same — a little more jowly perhaps, a few more flecks of grey in that immaculately groomed auburn head. The suits were as well-cut as ever — not quite flashy but running things fine. The manner had changed, however. Never lacking in confidence, it now had the briskness of somebody who no longer considered the possibility of contradiction. And there was something absolutely new. In contrast to the controlled politeness of greetings in the past, there had been a positively ornate welcome as Fender had been shown into the room by Baxter. Antrim had jumped up, advanced from his desk and fussed

round extravagantly while Baxter went through the panto-
mime with the chairs, as though Fender was at once inordinately geriatric and infinitely precious.

'Ludo,' he had said. 'How terribly good of you! It really was
convenient, was it? London is probably the last place you want
to come to these days. I really am most grateful.'

Repellent, Fender had thought. But then, memory had
pinched his arm: was that meaningless cordiality so very different from the way he himself had greeted people in not
dissimilar circumstances, while the brain mapped out the
handling of the interview and the eyes searched for signs in the
face which would offer guidance as to tactics?

The telephone conversation — with the Ministry of Defence, he had been able to deduce — was still going on. Putting
that department back in its box, an interesting challenge by
any standards, was after all proving less than easy. Colour was
pricking the centre of Antrim's cheeks. He raised his voice,
twice expressed himself in unambiguous negatives. The noise
from the receiver at his ear was equally uncompromising.
Finally he put the telephone down. Pressing a button he spoke
again, this time to Baxter presumably.

'You heard all that? I shall want to send a note to the Home
Secretary in case the bastards try to go round the back. Remind
me.'

Antrim poured more coffee into Fender's cup and his own.
The pot was silver. Fender did not recall that from Harkness's
time; it was the first change to which he felt well disposed.

'Well,' Antrim said. 'You've heard the facts as I know them
but I daresay there's more detail you ought to have.' He lit a
Panatella, visibly needing to calm himself down after the
telephone conversation. 'Antonia Strachan is going to brief
you — she's been working to me on the inquiry so far and can
fill in the gaps. You remember her, of course.'

Fender reached for his cup. 'Of course. How is she?'

'All right — not that I see much of her. She works under
James Priestley normally.'

'So she didn't marry the Canadian —Muir?'

'Was that on the cards?' Antrim frowned, hardly able to
believe it: that aggressive, touchy RCMP officer with the

ice-blue eyes! 'Well, it obviously came to nothing.'

Fender shook his head. 'She ought to marry again.'

Antrim glanced at a paper on his desk, either indifferent or irritated. 'Anyway — she knows you're taking over and will be conducting the interview with Francis Bacton. There's no need for you to have her along.'

'On the contrary I should like her to come with me. I value her judgement.'

Antrim shrugged. 'As you wish. What matters is having you in charge. I feel sure you'll be able to get on to a wavelength with Bacton in a way that wouldn't be open to a non-Catholic.'

Fender sighed inwardly. Horses for courses were clearly the order of the day now. He thought of the complications that must be cropping up under that doctrine — a black for a black presumably, and a Jew for a Jew. Lesbians for Lesbians? Establishments must be having quite a headache. They were all in for a rocky ride under Antrim. Slyly he murmured, 'I was interested that you decided to take a look at Barralozzi's body.'

'It was a quite straightforward operation.'

'What happens if it has to be dug up and post-mortemed again — formally? The fact that your tame pathologist has had a go will be apparent.'

'I'll meet that problem if it arises.'

'You're not telling the police you've discovered a murder — '

'No. The evidence is not absolutely conclusive anyway.'

The spots of colour had returned to Antrim's cheeks. Fender smiled. 'So you don't think the Home Office are likely to find out and kick up dust — '

'If they did, I think the PM would step in on my side. He made it plain when I last saw him that he expects the Bureau to be a good deal more active and venturesome than was the case under Harkness — or Lorimount for that matter. After all we've been given a certain flexibility the police lack. I took the view that over Barralozzi we'd have to exercise it, otherwise there'd be no progress.' He wasn't giving the smallest hint that the pathologist's discoveries had come as a rude shock. But they must have done.

Fender smiled again. 'You feel you can live with the risk — '

66

'It's what I'm paid for, Ludo.' Antrim held the Panatella pointing skywards between thumb and forefinger, the model of a public servant accepting responsibility. He glanced at his wrist-watch. 'Do you mind if I hand you over now? I'm due at a meeting in a quarter of an hour.'

'Of course.'

Antrim spoke on the telephone, then reached for his brief-case and placed a file inside it. 'We could perhaps have a chat when you're back from seeing Bacton.'

'I may get nothing.'

Antrim shook his head to convey unbounded confidence. 'You taught me all there is to know about interrogation — remember? He'll be putty in your hands.' He snapped the briefcase shut. 'Of course, whatever happens, we'll pay you a consultancy fee for the hours you spend on the case. I'll get Baxter to find out the Treasury scale. That all right with you?'

'Thank you.'

Antrim stood beside his desk, casting round for small talk as they waited for Antonia to appear. 'How do you spend the days down in Mayfield? Gardening? Parish Council? Retirement not weighing too heavily?'

'You'd be surprised how busy one becomes away from the world of telegrams and letters.'

'I suppose so.' But it was evident he couldn't imagine it.

The door opened and Antonia appeared. She was paler than when Fender had last seen her. The smooth planes of the forehead and cheeks were the same, and the mouth, with that hint of an ironical comment at the corners. But there was too much shadow under the eyes and the pupils seemed darker, even duller. Struggling to his feet, he thought, Not unhappiness necessarily, but perhaps some loss of hope, of optimism. Or it could be worry. He wondered what the situation was with her parents.

He took her hand in both of his, squeezed it but said nothing. She was, for all the change he had observed, very beautiful. In this instance he could acknowledge something previously avoided in thought. If he had met her a quarter of a century ago, after Catherine had died in that Calcutta nursing home, he would have wanted to marry her. But he hadn't met her.

Instead he had grown fat and ugly.

'You look marvellous,' she said. 'So much younger.'

'I feel younger,' he said.

Antrim had his arm round Fender's shoulder, ushering them both towards the door. 'Why not use the conference room — it'll be more comfortable than Antonia's office.'

In the ante-room, Baxter was hovering with some message. Antrim took it and flashed them his practised farewell smile. 'Lovely to see you again, Ludo.'

Seated at the table in the conference room, Fender took out pipe and tobacco pouch. Alone with Antonia, he was aware that his appearance was not as spruce as he would have wished. A fifteen-year-old suit, the pockets overloaded with bills, receipts, clippings about butterfly sightings, even seed packets, as well as the ordinary things; suede shoes in need of heeling; a bow tie he now recalled was becoming greasy round the knot. She would suppose he was letting himself go. Perhaps she would suppose right. He looked covertly at his shirt cuffs. There was the beginning of a fray but at least they were clean. A little more confidently he began to fill the pipe.

Antonia sat at right angles to him. She was turning the contents of her file, checking the position and annotation of the cardboard flags she had inserted among the serials. She had kept her hair long he was glad to see. He could remember with absolute clarity the moment in the foyer of the hotel in Ottawa when, thinking he was asleep, she had bent over to awaken him and her hair had moved across his face. He had smelt the hair and then the scent of her skin. And then he had opened his eyes and thought what a grim joke desire had become for him, imprisoned in this revolting carcass, a man who had to look at chairs twice before sinking into them, who panted on the smallest flight of stairs. Briefly he had been tempted to touch her, to feel the texture of the skin from which the scent had spoken to him. Of course, she might draw back with tightening muscles and a forced smile masking repulsion. But if, for some inconceivable reason, she did not — if she responded — Then he had shaken his head and smiled at her, putting the ridiculousness of it behind him. But he had remembered the scent and the touch of the hair.

She placed the file in front of him. 'I've pinned flags in. They cross-refer the serials to bring out the main points.'

'Admirable,' he said. 'That will be very useful.'

She leaned back in her chair, smiling.

'How are you?' he asked.

'Fine.'

'You're in James Priestley's Division I hear.'

'Yes.'

'A nice man.' He folded up the tobacco pouch. 'But in this case I gather you've been working directly to Antrim.'

'I was the only person available the day it started. So he was stuck with me.' She smiled again.

He could not resist probing a little. 'How are things — now that he's Director?'

'He knows what he wants, which I suppose is good. But I hardly see him, of course.' She wasn't giving anything away. He had never directly acknowledged that he had known about her *affaire* with Antrim. He believed she was aware he had guessed. But she had given no hint.

'And you,' he went on, 'still in that flat in Little Venice?'

'Just. If the rates go on rising I'll have to move.'

'You don't share?'

'No. For reasons I don't care to analyse, I'd find another woman depressing. And the men are getting either too old or too young. Those I meet anyway.'

He digested it, considering the nuances while asking her if she would mind if he lit the pipe. 'And your parents — how are they?'

'My father's virtually an invalid now. If my mother fell ill I don't know what I'd do about them. Give this up and go there for good perhaps. I quite like Shropshire. As it is I have to drive there most weekends to give her a break from nursing.'

She wasn't enjoying the conversation and he could scarcely blame her. He struck his match. 'Well, I'd better start reading. How long will this take me?'

'Thirty minutes.'

'Then perhaps we could talk about it. Over lunch.'

'Just as you like.'

69

'And shall we go to Tunbridge Wells in search of Master Bacton this afternoon?'

She raised her eyebrows. 'You want me to come?'

'Of course.'

'I don't want you to feel obliged — '

'I'm not concerned with obligation. I would like you to be present at the interview. And to have your professional judgement afterwards.'

She shook her head but he could see she was pleasantly surprised. 'Really?'

'Yes.'

'In that case I suggest we drive down in an office car. I can drop you at your house afterwards. Mayfield's only about half an hour on from Tunbridge Wells, isn't it?'

'Less. You must stay to tea.'

She rose to her feet. 'I'll book the car and come back in twenty minutes.' Her eyes, he persuaded himself, were brighter.

When she came back, the cardboard flags it had taken her half the morning to annotate and pin inside the file had all been removed and were scattered about the table like autumn leaves.

She laughed. Fender looked up, smiling a question. She shook her head. 'Don't mind me.'

8

A car journey of any distance with Fender, she was now reminded, was *audibly* ruminative.

The humming began before they had negotiated an exit from London's south-eastern entrails, a meditative drone while his eyes wandered over the passing scene. When she had first experienced it, in Ottawa that autumn investigating the Stradbrook allegation, she had wondered if nervousness prompted by her driving had started him off. But slowing down had seemed, if anything, to encourage imagination and add to the volume.

At that time it had been continuous Elgar. Today the choice was more free-ranging. Fender moved without a pause from Mozart to Rossini and back to Mozart, the phrasing broken up to match the development of thought. It was an irregularly pulsing stream of consciousness from which she had no escape.

They were now on the Sevenoaks bypass. She swung the Rover into the fast lane and pressed the accelerator hard, willing the engine's sound to penetrate that mental auditorium. For a while he carried on, then sighed, as though satiated, and was silent. She switched on the radio to consolidate success.

A news bulletin was in progress. The women at Chawton Wood had collared the media again, this time by climbing the fence into the base with the help of commando-style equipment smuggled into their camp the previous night. One of them was going to be charged with obstructing the police in the performance of their duty. She wondered if Claire, that handsome predator, had bagged the honour.

Fender was shaking his head from side to side. 'You don't approve of the peace women?' she asked.

He grunted unintelligibly. She felt the case should not go by default. But as she was on the point of telling him about Jennifer, surrendering her holiday for principle, he pre-empted her. 'I am of course deeply reactionary and chauvinistic.'

They had entered the slip road for Tunbridge Wells. He stared gloomily through his side window. 'I hope this doesn't prove a profitless exercise. I fear it may.'

'Why?'

'Even if we succeed in finding Francis Bacton, from your description of his condition, I doubt if we are likely to get a coherent or reliable story out of him.'

'In that event you can still try the Earl yourself. He obviously knows much more than he would tell me. I imagine he doesn't take women seriously enough to feel they can be trusted with all his confidences. You'd probably get on well with him.'

It didn't come out as lightly as she intended; but he showed no sign of having registered the nuance. 'I fear his memory of me may not be favourable.'

'You've met him before?'

'A year ago — we had an argument of the usual Catholic sort. I seem to remember telling him he had forsaken the honest gold of tradition for the tinsel of trendiness. He was not pleased.'

She laughed aloud. 'Trendy isn't the description that occurred to me. How did he deserve that?'

He shook his head as though to indicate she would, or should, not be interested. 'I had not expected the representative of a distinguished recusant family to say he supported the abolition of the Tridentine Mass.'

'You prefer the Mass to be said in a language ninety-nine per cent of the people don't understand — '

Resisting provocation, he said mildly, 'I believe in a ritual that makes no compromise with the ordinary.'

'But does it have to be a mystery?'

'I believe in mystery. Without mystery one has a sky without stars. Rome should always remember that even if the Earl doesn't understand.'

'Isn't Rome in your good books?'

'I have a fair store of bones to pick with the Pope, should he happen my way.'

Fender lifted his eyes to the far distance, relishing the imagined encounter, an almighty dressing-down for His Holiness. Once the focus for his irritation had been Lorimount, the Bureau's first Director; Lorimount seated at his desk, endlessly toying with that symbol of his vacillation, a very small silver pencil, while, from the chair opposite, Fender sought in vain to instil him with firm resolve, any sort of resolve. Afterwards Fender would return to his own office and sit with his fingers drumming the sides of his chair, while his cheeks darkened and his neck swelled until it seemed to overwhelm the collar of the Oxford shirt. In those days had come the first of his heart attacks.

Now, with Lorimount long retired to his Derbyshire farm, it seemed there was a new whipping-boy, this one more majestic, infinitely less temporal. 'Have you been to Rome?' she asked.

'Many years ago. Unfortunately I hadn't then formulated my indictment. Nor did I have an entrée to the Vatican, which doesn't exactly throw open its gates to the critic.' He lifted a cautionary hand and pointed. 'Grosvenor Road. Slow down. There is Corunna Street, turn left. Now we have to look for Jefferson Street. What was the number of the house?' With a disconcerting swiftness, he had resumed his old identity as the one who gave the orders.

The house containing Jennifer's flat was part of a Victorian terrace. On the corner where they turned out of Corunna Street, the approach to it was a row of shops, including a supermarket, its windows raucous with luminous paint signs; beyond the terrace, houses stretched in an unbroken line of bourgeois detachment, unviolated by commerce. The terrace itself had become a bridge of transition, largely occupied by accountants, insurance agents and solicitors. Only No. 45C seemed to have stood its ground, a last domestic bastion in a lapping tide of change, signalling survival by the variety of its curtains and the occasional glimpse of a paper pendant shade.

On the bell plate by the front door were nine buttons, with a Dymo-ed name beside each. Confronted by the plate while Fender was still completing the process of disembarkation from the Rover, Antonia became aware of a disagreeable fact: lulled by the ease with which she had located Jennifer amongst the woolly hats at Chawton Wood, she had forgotten to ask her surname.

She stared at the plate, willing some intuitive miracle that would spare her having to make such a humiliating admission to Fender. The names stared back. Only Farouk seemed to offer itself for tentative elimination.

She was saved, in the exact moment that Fender reached her side, by the door opening. Behind a shopping trolley to which a Jack Russell terrier was attached, stood a middle-aged woman in a donkey brown coat and maroon trousers. She had the bright-eyed look of an inquisitive bird. It was the next best thing to a miracle. If, between them, the woman and the Jack Russell did not have a comprehensive coverage of everything

73

that moved in the house, appearances counted for nothing.

Offering a placatory hand for inspection by the dog, she said, 'I'm looking for Mr Bacton. I think he moved into a flat here the other day. It's been lent to him by Jennifer.'

The woman smiled. 'That's right, dear, he had to ask me where the electric meter was. You'll find 9E at the back on the third floor.'

'Do you know if he's in?'

'I think he must be. Have you tried the bell?'

'Not yet.'

'It sometimes doesn't work. But I'd have heard him go past my door if he'd gone out.' She looked up at Fender, a trifle overcome by his bulk. 'Are you relatives?'

He gave the woman what Antonia recalled as one of his benedictory smiles. 'Just friends.'

The Jack Russell, impatient to be off, had begun to drag the trolley between them, drawing the woman, her fingers still clutching the handle, after it. Notwithstanding the maroon slacks, it was clear he wore the trousers. Moving jerkily past them, the woman said, 'Mind the stairs on the upper landing — the carpet's very worn just there.' They disappeared towards Corunna Street and the shops, the dog intent on the exacting business of reconnaissance, the discharge of carefully measured markers at vital corners.

Fender pressed the bell for 9E. When there was no response, he looked reluctantly through the open door at the staircase. 'Perhaps he's out after all.'

'She said the bell didn't always work. I think we should go up.'

He sighed. 'I'll follow you.'

As they climbed they could see that, on the upper floors of the house certainly, the division had been, not into flats but into flatlets, single room accommodation with shared bathroom and lavatory on each floor. Cooking odours mingled with the smell of dust from shrunken skirtings beside the stair treads. Through landing windows a metal fire escape was visible on which had been erected a contraption for drying laundry. A radio was playing somewhere.

Antonia reached 9E while Fender was still toiling up to the

second-floor landing. She looked over the banisters to satisfy herself that he was going to make it, then knocked.

There was no voice or movement from inside the room. She turned the handle of the door, calling as she pushed it back a few inches. The wallpaper beside the door was bright with sunlight. Reaching her side, Fender said through laboured breath, 'Don't say after all that — ' then stopped, sensing in the same instant as Antonia that it was not sun illuminating the wall but lamplight and that it would be shining on something else.

Francis Bacton lay on a divan bed behind the door. He was fully clothed except for his shoes which had been removed and placed beneath the bed. His face was turned towards a small side table on which stood the lamp. Beside the lamp were a tumbler and an empty water jug.

It was a scene of exceptional neatness. The bedclothes were uncrumpled, the pillow barely creased. Even the empty aspirin bottle had been placed in the wastebin beneath the tiny sink opposite the bed. Francis had wished to make it a tidy end. The only thing he couldn't control was the white froth that had spurted from his mouth and was now a dried coating for the lower part of his face.

Fender moved to do what she shrank from, placing fingers against the cheek. When she lifted her gaze to his eyes, he said, 'I should think at least twelve hours.'

She nodded silently, sick with a mixture of horror and melancholy. If Antrim had not stopped her driving down the previous afternoon as she had planned — Turning away from the bed, she said, 'I suppose we may find a note.' Her voice sounded unfamiliar to her.

The note was in an envelope, propped at one corner of the mantelshelf and addressed to Miss Jennifer Caswell. It had been left unsealed for the police to take a look. Francis had thought of everything.

She unfolded the note. It was brief and written in italic writing that showed surprisingly few signs of stress.

Jennifer dear,
I was so grateful to you for giving me refuge. Can you now

forgive me for repaying you in this way? Please try to. I hoped things would seem different here and at first they did. But things have got bad again, very bad.

Take care of yourself, Jennifer, I pray for your happiness,

Love,
Francis

Antonia handed the letter to Fender and watched him read it. As he refolded it, she saw him wince slightly and felt comforted. 'I suppose I'd better go and call the police,' she said.

He replaced the envelope on the mantel shelf and turned to face the room. 'Perhaps we should first make sure there's nothing else of interest.' Moving to the bed he reached down to feel inside the pockets of Francis's jacket, then proceeded to lay the contents on the side of the bed: cheque book, diary, comb, pen, shop receipts, a handwritten plan of the relationship of Jefferson Street to the centre of Tunbridge Wells, perhaps the bequest of the thoughtful Jennifer. Replacing them all in the pockets except for the diary, he moved to the suitcase which stood beside a hanging cupboard and groped amongst the still unpacked clothing for papers or notebooks. Finally satisfied, he picked up the diary again and lowered himself into the only armchair in the room to study the contents. He appeared to have forgotten Antonia's existence.

She looked about her for other signs of Francis's brief existence in the room. But away from the bed there seemed hardly an imprint. On a small table used for meals was a clean plate with a knife across it; beside the plate were a Bible and a folded newspaper, as neatly placed as everything else. She could feel tension mounting inside her. Eventually she said, 'Anything interesting?'

Fender closed the diary and held it towards her with a sudden gesture. 'I'm not sure. There are some addresses and telephone numbers in Rome we should make a note of in case they turn out to be useful. And I find one or two of the entries in the early months of this year — curious.' As she began to turn the pages, he said briskly, 'Look, since we can't very well pocket it, I think we must photocopy all the pages on which

76

there's writing. There must be a library or a post office nearby where there's a machine on which you could do that. I suggest you slip out while I hold the fort. Leave the door on the latch. If somebody comes in while you're out and locks it, ring and I'll come down.'

He was once more ordering her about. She compressed her lips; but it seemed sensible. She put the diary in her bag. 'Difficult if I meet the woman with the dog. She's got to know sometime what we found when we came up.'

He brushed the problem aside. 'I'm sure you'll think of something. Just remember she mustn't come here until we're ready to call the police.'

When she had gone, he went to the suitcase he had opened earlier and began to search amongst the shirts and underclothing. Eventually his fingers located a velvet bag secured at its mouth by drawstrings. He loosened the strings. Inside the bag were a small whip, a chain with pointed links and a pair of leather gloves; sown into the palms and fingers of the gloves were brass nails.

Replacing the bag in the suitcase he crossed once more to the bed and unfastened Bacton's clothing until he could examine the upper part of each thigh. Lacerations caused by the pointed links of the chain could be seen on both legs; in one place they had gone septic.

A faint nausea rose in Fender's throat. In this drab room that Francis Bacton had chosen for his last refuge, the contents of the velvet bag seemed grotesque. He was struggling with revulsion. But who was he to judge the rightness of those acts, that pain?

He turned away from the bed. He would have liked to pull back the curtains at the window and let in the daylight. But the police had better see the room as they had found it. Sitting down again in the armchair to await Antonia's return he closed his eyes; but the thoughts that came were both violent and melancholy. He opened them and reached for the newspaper on the table beside the Bible. He had read almost to the end of the item where the newspaper had been folded before its meaning began to stir in his consciousness.

ITALIAN COMPANY CHIEF IN DEATH CRASH

Firenzuola, Thursday — After two unsuccessful attempts, Italian police using special hoisting gear today raised from a ravine near here the car containing the body of the head of the giant construction company, LAPORTEX, Enrico Rossano. Signor Rossano, who had left the house of a friend nearby, twenty-four hours before, to drive to Milan was only discovered after an extensive search. There had been fears that he had been kidnapped. The road is not especially difficult at the point where the car plunged into the ravine and the preliminary view of the police is that a mechanical defect developed. Signor Rossano's death comes at a time when the LAPORTEX group after several years of crippling losses is showing clear signs of having turned the corner under his energetic leadership. The LAPORTEX group have been responsible for many prestige building projects in Italy, including the controversial Luciani Hostel for Pilgrims which was built near the entrance to the Vatican.

9

The garden of Fender's cottage faced south and overlooked a valley. Entering from the High Street and passing through a short dark hall to the room beyond, presented the stranger with a *coup de théâtre*, so dramatic was the change from the clutter of village life to the empty aspect of the valley; from the noise of traffic to a stillness broken only by a clock's even tick. If not quite two-faced, the cottage was a world of sleight of hand, a fitting home for Fender.

The window at which Antonia stood gave on to a terrace, with the garden running away below. She could hear Fender in the kitchen next door, opening and closing cupboards in search of cheese biscuits to have with their whisky. The ten-

78

sion in her stomach was at last beginning to slacken. From the time they had finally called in the police until now had been all of three hours. The sergeant, stepping self-importantly from the patrol car in front of 45c Jefferson Street and examining her Bureau identity card, had shown disbelief that such things were issued to women unchained from typewriters and filing cabinets. Later he had taken a dislike to Fender, declining her assurance that, while no longer in possession of such a card, he could be regarded as bona fide. Only after he had been persuaded to speak on the telephone to Baxter did he grudgingly decide to accept their account.

Evening sun, slanting across the tiny lawn, enveloped a bed of antirrhinums. Along the wall at the bottom of the garden, another bed held rose bushes and shrubs and was edged with white alyssum. She tried without success to imagine Fender bent over the beds to minister to all this: there must be someone who did it for him.

He appeared, pinkly discomposed and grunting apologies. In his hand was a plate on which biscuits had been spread in an unsuccessful attempt at artistry. She took one to please him. 'I was wondering if you looked after the garden yourself.'

'I am death to all plants. The woman who takes care of my other needs has a husband who comes in once a week.'

'Your London housekeeper didn't come with you then?'

'She felt she would miss the great city, her daily intake of diesel fumes. That may have been her excuse for getting rid of me of course.'

'At least you have butterflies here — I saw three a moment ago. I remember you complaining that you never saw them in London.' She stared from the window, suddenly snared by another memory.

He snapped a biscuit, watching her. 'What else do you see?'

She smiled, shaking her head. 'I was thinking of something else. The very first present my husband gave me was a brooch in the shape of a butterfly. The wings were a pale blue enamel. I had a burglary recently and it was stolen. It was the thing I hated losing most.' She handed him her glass to be refilled. 'And you're not lonely here?'

79

'Certainly not.'

'No dog? No cat?'

'Other people's are quite enough. In a village, cats are conscientious visitors.' When she remained silent, he went on, 'Being alone has many compensations. Perhaps you've discovered for yourself.'

She laughed and adopted what she hoped was a look of robustness. 'Having it all one's own way becomes a vice in time.'

'Such a small vice,' he said. 'But perhaps not so agreeable at your age.'

In a moment he would embark on a roundabout inquiry to discover why she was not living in a log cabin in Alberta or wherever Muir now was and she had no satisfactory answer ready. To ward off the inquisition she glanced at her watch. 'I suppose I ought — '

'You can't leave now.' He appeared taken aback. 'I insist on your staying to dinner. There's a small restaurant across the street where I often go.'

She hesitated. He went on, 'It's too late to return to the office. And we ought to talk about the next steps.'

Certainly there were plenty of questions she wanted to put to him. He still hadn't explained what he had found interesting in the diary. 'I was going to drive down to my parents' house later tonight.'

'Why not tomorrow?' he said. He was as close as he would ever get to pleading.

He disappeared upstairs while she telephoned her mother with the change of plan. The voice at the other end sounded relaxed enough; no hint of crisis, it seemed, save for the blackfly on the roses. She had returned to the window over the garden by the time Fender reappeared. He was wearing a fresh shirt and a smarter suit than she had supposed him to possess; his hair had been brushed more or less flat. It was clear he had decided their dinner together warranted exceptional measures. She felt mildly flattered.

They were finishing off their drinks when the telephone bell sounded from the hall. Fender levered himself up and went to answer it. She could hear his voice without being able to distinguish the words. Whoever was at the other end was having to listen a good deal. When he returned he looked pleased with himself.

'That was Antrim. He'd telephoned your flat for news and getting no reply decided to ring through here. I offered to put you on but he thought it unnecessary.'

'What was his reaction to Bacton's death?'

'That it was — inconvenient.' He savoured his choice of word. 'Of course, I understand his feelings. He has an appointment with the PM fixed for Monday afternoon and hoped for something further about the Ropner business with which to beguile him. However he's now asked if I would try tackling the Earl myself to get more.'

'Did you agree?'

'I said that provided a car and driver could be made available, I would do my best.' He offered Antonia the last Bath Oliver and, when she declined, bit into it with relish. Crumbs settled on the ledge of his stomach. He was inordinately satisfied with the turn of events. 'How long would you say the journey to West Gurney might take from here?'

'Possibly three hours.'

'I might try telephoning tomorrow morning.'

'It's going to be very soon after he has the news of Francis's suicide.'

'Yes, I wish that could be avoided.' He sighed but was not noticeably abashed. 'Perhaps by Sunday he'll feel able to talk.'

'Coming down from London you said that he wouldn't be disposed to talk to you — because of the argument you had over the Mass.'

'Did I say that?' He frowned in an exaggerated way. 'No, no.' He was dismissing the idea as though she had invented it herself. 'It was just a friendly discussion. We agreed to disagree.'

She watched him screwing the cap back on the whisky bottle, his thoughts already down in West Gurney. Gemini, she had once worked out his birth sign to be, after another occasion such as this. She remembered him moving, without shame or even apparent awareness from morose attachment to one point of view to embrace the opposite, when something occurred to change his humour. It had wasted a whole day's work for her. Some in the Bureau, at the receiving end of these sudden changes, had looked for the answer in deviousness. They were not amused by her charitable references to the Heavenly Twins. Something about the telephone conversation with Antrim, allied to what he had seen that afternoon, had fired him — had renewed his sense that power was within him to exercise. Everything was possible once more. Before long he would be giving her orders again.

Fender consulted his watch. 'Dinner, I think.'

The restaurant was the lower half of a timbered and tile-hung house and very small. For Fender, entering was akin to the maneuver of docking a liner. Chairs were eased back, tables adjusted, coats cleared from the hanging rack, in the interest of lowering him into the far corner of the room where he would have the remaining diners under his gaze. Seated, he exchanged with the proprietor items of obscure intelligence on village matters, bowed to another familiar face, then settled down to authoritarian pronouncements on the dishes offered by the menu.

She waited until he had given approval to his soup before opening her questions.

'You were going to tell me why you thought the story of the car accident in the newspaper could be significant.'

'I might be wrong,' he said, 'quite wrong.'

She sat watching him. He was at his least convincing when portraying modesty. Eventually he went on, 'Could you look out the copy pages of the diary? They will help to explain what I mean.'

She took them from her handbag. There had been no chance even to glance at them since she had returned to Jennifer's flat from her session of photography, narrowly escaping a head-on encounter with the woman and the Jack Russell terrier.

'Look for an entry around January 10th, beginning "Left . . .",' Fender said.

She read, ' "January 11th — Left E.C." Presumably "E.C." stands for "English College" since that's where Jennifer said he had been studying.'

He nodded. 'She didn't know where he went from there.

82

But you'll find a similar entry almost exactly three months later.'

She turned over the pages. 'Yes, April 10th — "Left V.d.L." '

'If we knew what those initials stood for, it could be useful. "Via" something perhaps, or "Villa". Anyway that seems to be where he spent the intervening months. Then, shortly before April 10th, something happened which caused him great distress. Having left "V.d.L." he wrote to your peace woman, Jennifer, and asked her to help him find a flat in England. She writes back and says he can borrow hers. Later that month he returns to West Gurney and tells his father what it was that so disturbed him. What was it?'

She waited, knowing better than to upstage him when he was in this mood.

'It was the death of Barralozzi. That had happened in London on April the 8th. We can assume, I think, that the news would have been in the Italian papers by the following day. He knew, as soon as he heard, that there was something wrong about the death. His knowledge led him to leave "V.d.L." and into what, you saw, was a nervous breakdown. He gets to No. 45C Jefferson Street and, as he tells Jennifer in his note, things seem different — better — at first. So why did they get so bad again that he committed suicide?'

Fender broke off to try the wine he had chosen. When their glasses had been filled he raised his eyebrows at her and she guessed she was now being cued.

'You believe it was the news item about Rossano's death —'

'I would gamble any money that Rossano's car did not go off the road by pure accident. As with Barralozzi, he was murdered in such a way that with ordinary luck it would be thought to have been a chance happening — in Barralozzi's case a heart attack, in Rossano's the momentary lapse of attention by a tired driver. And Francis Bacton realized that.'

'But what was the connection between the two deaths?'

'We can only speculate at this stage. But we know Barralozzi's reputation in financial circles was poor. And while we don't know anything about Rossano's honesty it seems his company did construction work for the Vatican. Perhaps badly. Perhaps they were involved in a fraud against the Vatican.'

She just managed not to laugh. 'You're not saying the *Vatican* was behind their deaths!'

'No. But I *am* saying that Francis Bacton *may have been persuaded of that* from knowledge he acquired in the three months after he left the English College. Wouldn't that be the obvious explanation for his father's attitude when he saw you — that Francis had told him as much and had even convinced him of it?'

The arrival of poached salmon steaks halted the flow. Fender sat back and stared contentedly at wine bottles stacked in bins inside an old fireplace. She knew what he was doing, from past experience: building a pyramid of extravagant assumptions for the pleasure of challenging others to prove the foundations were unsound.

She began cautiously. 'Accepting that Rossano's accident *was* murder — and presumably it may never be possible to say with certainty one way or another — isn't there a more likely explanation for the two killings?'

'And that is —?'

'That Barralozzi and Rossano were both involved with a criminal group; the Mafia, say. They could have been concerned in a fraud against the Vatican, just as you suggest. The Mafia decide they know too much and must be eliminated — but quietly so that there won't be a fuss followed by inquiries. Francis Bacton learns of what is in store for them as a result of — of hearing the confession of one of the criminals. He finds the knowledge intolerable.' She paused, conscious that her extemporization was running into the sand.

Fender was smiling. 'And the Earl's shame as a Catholic — ?'

'Francis sought guidance from a very high level in the Church and was told he could not breach the confessional in order to save their lives.'

Fender went on smiling. 'I think not.' But she detected signs that she had sobered him a little. 'We must certainly remain open to all possibilities, however.' For a moment she thought he might be considering a change of horses but all he said was,

' "V.d.L." — we must hang on to that. That's where we shall find the key.'

She picked up the diary pages again. 'Apart from the addresses and telephone numbers he'd listed, weren't there other entries that interested you?'

'Do you see that from the beginning of February onwards until the middle of April when he left "V.d.L." the word "Discipline" appears regularly, sometimes with another word after it, *"cilis"* for example?'

'Yes.'

'It's a reference to self-mortification — punishment inflicted on himself. The entries start only after Francis Bacton left the English College. That seems to me significant. While you were having the diary pages copied I decided to take another look in his luggage. In the bottom of the suitcase I found the instruments he had used for his Discipline — a whip with five thongs, a *cilis* and leather gloves with brass tacks fixed to them.'

'What is a *cilis*?'

'A *cilis* looks like one of those chain collars made for dogs, except that the links have points which are very sharp and penetrate the flesh. It's worn round the top of the thigh. The gloves, well, I don't understand how or when they are used.'

'Isn't that all rather primitive in these days?'

'It is to me. But I must accept it is not so to some other Catholics.'

'You believe that wherever it was he went after he left the English College, it was an environment where self-mortification of a very extreme kind was enforced.'

'And secrecy.' He was looking into her eyes. 'I don't really think it involved taking confessions from the Mafia.' He was not trying to provoke a response from her now, his expression was serious, even solemn.

Half an hour later she stood in the High Street, beginning to wonder if after all he had been so very extravagant in his assumptions. 'It's bizarre, however one views it,' she said.

'So is most of life, if only one looks closely enough.'

'I admit I'm curious to know what you get out of the Earl.'

'Come to Antrim's office at eleven on Monday and you'll hear.'

'Did he say I was to be present?'

'I told him it was my wish. This is a joint investigation — you and I together.'

It was a half-truth and diminishing too, she thought; but she was glad he had said it. She moved towards the Rover. Fatigue was starting to grow behind her eyes. The village was quiet now with only the occasional car to disturb the night. From the churchyard, a few yards further up the street, the smell of mown grass was being carried on the lightest of breezes. It would be pleasant to go to sleep with that scent in her nostrils. She glanced at Fender's cottage across the street and wondered if the breeze would carry it through the upper windows. Supposing she said to him, 'I wonder if I might stay the night,' how would he take it? Probably better not to find out. 'Thank you, that was lovely,' she said. 'Good luck with the Earl. I hope you like apples.'

She reached down to unlock the car. She was conscious he had opened his mouth to say something in reply and had then decided against it. Holding the car door open for her, feet trimly together, head slightly on one side, Fender assumed a protective stance. At the top of his head spikes of short black hair moved in the breeze.

When she was seated he put his hand through to press her shoulder. 'Take care.' The fingers lingered, not conveying the sort of message Claire Wylie had signalled but not impersonal either. He was reluctant to let her go. For all the appearance to the contrary he had been at pains to convey earlier, he was lonely.

On the road north to Mark Cross, she decided she could guess what he had thought better of saying as she got into the car. He had wanted her to stay. She lowered the side window and shook her head, smiling at the perfume from hidden fields.

10

One thing had become clear to Fender, even before he entered the drawing-room at Cowden Hall: if he was to succeed where Antonia had failed, the Countess and not the Earl would have to be his target.

Not that the Earl's welcome had been unfriendly in its mildly irascible way. His only reference to their past argument about the Mass, as he conducted Fender across an icy hall to the Countess, was bland enough. But his son's death had obviously not persuaded him that he should be more forthcoming. This had been apparent in the stilted conversation they had had on the previous evening, after the Earl had returned from his grim mission to Tunbridge Wells to view the body. Only reluctantly had he accepted the idea of Fender making the journey to Somerset. He was a man who, once a position had been taken up, saw its defence as a matter of principle, even when circumstances had removed the original cause for making a stand. On the drive down, sitting in the back of the Bureau Daimler, Fender had told himself that he would erode the Earl's obduracy by a mixture of reasoned argument and reminders of public duty. Here it no longer seemed realistic.

The Countess, presiding over a Crown Derby tea service at one end of a *chaise-longue*, had not at first sight seemed the stronger, either in character or physically. With her unsteady walk, her wild white hair and gaunt features to which face powder had been half-heartedly applied, she had a general appearance of disorder; and now grief had added its own ferment. Yet, when she had finished distributing the cups of tea and sandwiches, he saw that her hands went into disciplined repose, only loosely clasped in her lap, and she listened with an intentness that signalled authority. Her pottery, he thought, might well display disturbing shapes and patterns;

but it would be robust, made to last.

In the minutes before the tea tray had been brought in, by a silent woman addressed as Alice, there had been little time for serious conversation. The Countess had used the opportunity to put to him what were presumably her key questions for strangers, her litmus testers: the whereabouts of his present address and place of worship, the nature of his forebears — was he one of the Yorkshire Fenders? — his marital status, finally, his view of Papal globe-trotting. When he mentioned Antonia's visit to the Hall, she showed almost total ignorance. Communication between her and the Earl was obviously an uncertain thing.

It was the Countess who made plain when they could move to business, sitting back against the faded velvet of the *chaise-longue* and saying, 'Well, now, Mr Fender — ' in a tone that was almost brisk.

He began carefully. 'Forgive me for pressing you with questions at such a very painful time. I only do so because there is urgency from the Prime Minister's point of view. I know you felt unable to speak frankly to Mrs Strachan. But I thought it possible that your son's death might have released you from — from a confidence which previously bound you.'

As a matter of form, he had turned to look at the Earl while he spoke. The Earl stared obstinately into his tea cup. 'I fear that is not how I see it, Fender. I provided the PM with everything he needed to know for the purposes of government. I felt that was my duty. The other implications were not the government's business, they're the Church's. Because of that I thought it right to talk to the Archbishop when I was in London. It was up to him to do the necessary.'

At least, this was something new. 'The Archbishop — you mean Westminster? You called on him?'

'I did.'

'And gave him the rest of the story?'

'I didn't feel free to go into detail. But I gave him a sufficient outline.'

'Did he take any action?'

The Earl jerked his head in disagreeable recollection. 'At first he was disposed to say it was all balderdash. When I told

88

him I didn't go around peddling balderdash, he promised to make inquiries. I had a letter from him yesterday. In so far as it made any sense at all, it was passing on some assurance he'd apparently got from Rome that there was nothing to worry about. The implication was that I had been led up the garden path, or had misinterpreted something. I found it extremely disappointing.'

It was the moment to grasp the nettle. 'Your informant was Francis — '

Behind steel-rimmed spectacles the Earl's eyes went smaller, blinked. He shot a glance at the Countess. 'Yes, as a matter of fact.'

'Do you think the knowledge he possessed led him to take his life?'

'Of course. It was profoundly shocking.'

'Although it seems Rome doesn't think so — '

The Earl snorted. Palms flat on his knees, he sat stiffly upright, eyes fixed on the Countess. 'Rome!!' A struggle between anger and grief was going on in his mind.

Fender turned to the Countess. A single tear had streaked the already uneven powder on her cheek. When she saw his glance, she shook her head, as though to dismiss the tear as a false witness. In a level voice, she said, 'I think you should tell Mr Fender all we know, Matthew.'

The Earl looked at her fiercely, then allowed an expression of resignation to cross his face. 'Very well.' The fierceness had been an act. This was what he had wanted, a decision taken for him, principle overturned, not by his own hand but by an external force. He took his spectacles off to polish them.

'You know, I suppose, Fender, that our son was in the priesthood — '

'Yes.'

'Last year he went to Rome to attend the English College. At first all seemed well. He was looking forward, once he had completed his studies at the College, to coming back to pastoral work not far from here. Then, about Christmas time, we received a letter from him which we found very odd. He said that he had been told he was needed to serve the Faith in special work and was leaving the College in the early part of

January. He was not free to tell us what he would be doing but it involved undergoing a period of training and some sort of testing.'

'Did he give an address to which he was going?'

'No, he simply said he would not be free to write to us during the training and that it might last up to six months. We were naturally mystified. I wrote to the Vice Rector of the English College, whom I know slightly, to ask where Francis was. He wrote a very kind letter saying he regretted very much that the College had no idea. When leaving Francis had apparently said he was not at liberty to give any explanation at that time. He offered a solemn assurance that it was not connected with any loss of faith and that in fact he would be continuing in the service of the Church on work which had Papal blessing.'

'The College could make no suggestions as to what that meant?'

'None. They seemed as mystified as we were. They had great hopes for Francis's future.' The Earl's voice faltered. He replaced his spectacles with over-elaborate care. 'Towards the end of April he suddenly appeared here, quite unheralded and looking very thin and pale. He told us that he had decided the Church was after all not for him, that he had come home to collect a few of his possessions and was then going to the flat of a friend he had known at University. When we asked what he was going to do there, he said he wanted to be on his own for a while to sort himself out. We were naturally very distressed. He had obviously been through some traumatic experience. But when his mother and I tried to get him to talk about it he would say nothing at all.

'Then, one night, when we were sitting in here after dinner, he suddenly put his head in his hands and said he'd go mad if he kept it to himself any longer. Apparently while he was at the English College he became friendly with a Spanish priest. He'd mentioned this fellow once or twice in his letters. It wasn't clear exactly what he did in Rome except that he'd been engaged on research for the Vatican into Catholic history. One day this priest told Francis he had been appointed to form a special group which was undertaking the investigation of persons who were bringing the Church into disrepute by their conduct. He said the Pope had concluded some body which would function separately from the Church's normal means of inquiry and discipline was needed. This body, which would be his personal instrument, controlled from his own office, would consist of specially selected priests to be known as *Vigiles*. Nothing to do with the Office of Vigilance which looks after security — the group was to be quite new. And, according to the Spaniard, he had been authorized to approach Francis to join these *Vigiles*.'

'This was within the framework of the *Curia* presumably?'

The Earl looked irritably at Fender as though convicting him of inattention. 'No, that was the whole point apparently. It was separate, quite separate. At first Francis was reluctant to leave the College where he was very happy. He was particularly upset when he was told by the Spaniard that he would not be free to tell the College what he would be doing. But he also felt keenly about some of the things that have gone on in recent years. In the end he decided it was an honour that he'd been approached and he would be failing in his duty to the Church if he refused. So he left the College and joined this Spaniard.'

'What exactly were they supposed to do?'

'He was told that the *Vigiles* would consist of sections each with a different task. He was being trained to be a *Quaesitor*, an investigator. On his return to England he would have a secret role in addition to his normal pastoral duties. He would be required to investigate and report on instances of wrongdoing by the priesthood here. To help him in his task he would be entitled to recruit ordinary persons in the Church of whose discretion he felt confident. After he had administered an oath of secrecy they would be regarded as lay members of the *Vigiles* and be known as Co-operators. The reports were to be sent to this Spanish priest — direct, not through any Church authority here. When I said I found it impossible to believe that any of this had the Pope's authority, Francis said *he was quite satisfied that it did*. He also said that a very senior member of the *Curia* had been given a personal responsibility to supervise the work. The Spaniard was visited by him on at least one occasion while Francis was with the *Vigiles*.'

91

Fender sat forward abruptly. 'He said that *from his own knowledge?*'

'Yes.'

'Who was this person?'

'He wouldn't mention any names. He said he felt bound by his own oath of secrecy to that extent. He still believed in the importance of the work.'

A shape entered Fender's vision from his left side, rose and landed lightly on his shoulder. It was an Abyssinian cat, tall-eared and tawny. It reached forward boldly to examine the contents of the plate Fender held in his hand. The Countess called a vague reproof with no effect. With his other hand Fender drew the cat on to his stomach. It looked into his face, appraising him sharply and without pleasure: another *Quaesitor* in the family, it seemed. He turned to the Countess, wanting to test her reaction to the story. 'And it was through this group that your son learned the story of Barralozzi helping the Ropners in currency speculation.'

She nodded.

'He was quite certain about it?'

'Oh, yes, he seemed to know all the financial details. He'd been very shocked at first and was unwilling to believe it could be true of Ropner himself. But the group's inquiries were very thorough, there was no reliance on gossip or rumour. They received information from a number of people in Rome in building up their cases — not just persons in the Church.'

'But then something happened that decided Francis that he couldn't remain with the *Vigiles* — '

'Yes, the news of Barralozzi's death.'

'Why did that make a difference?'

The Earl looked up from studying the carpet by his feet. His expression suggested that he suspected Fender of deliberately seeking to provoke him. 'Because he was convinced they'd killed him! *That's why!*'

'He was told that?'

'No, of course not. But when he heard the news of the death some suspicions that had been growing in his mind suddenly took shape. He realized that during his training he was being led towards accepting the proposition that it might not be enough simply to expose a corrupt individual, that sometimes an act of exposure might damage the Church even more. But, over and above that, one day he had been in the room this Spanish priest used as an office. The fellow was called outside for a moment. Francis saw on his desk what he realized was an organizational chart for the *Vigiles*. He noticed that in addition to the *Quaesitores* and a section called simply Records, there was another section of which he had never been told. They were called *Ultores* Do you know what *Ultor* means, Fender?'

'*Ultor?*'

'Yes.'

Fender's memory was searching the ragbag of schooldays — Latin lessons on hot afternoons, the book open on the desk lid where he had carved his initials like everyone before him, the smell of sun-sweet grass floating through the open windows — he was searching and not quite remembering. 'Something to do with Mars, Mars the Avenger — ' Then he had it. 'One who punishes.'

The Earl said, 'Exactly. A Punisher.'

They sat in silence with their own thoughts. Eventually Fender said, 'It was still a very big jump for Francis to make — to conclude that Barralozzi had been killed. After all — '

The Earl interrupted him. 'When he thought back he re-membered something else. During his training with the *Vigiles* one of the first cases of which he'd been told was that of a priest in the *Curia*, an American who had regularly smuggled drugs from Italy to the United States. He had been paid a lot of money by criminals. One day this priest drowned while swim-ming. He had been alone and it was assumed he had developed cramp. Francis had commented to the Spaniard that it was a pity it had happened before they had been able to have him exposed. This fellow said it was better sometimes for an infection to be cauterized than to go on suppurating. It was only later it occurred to Francis that it was an odd choice of word.'

'*Cauterized?*'

'Yes, cauterized. When Barralozzi's death was reported he went to the Spaniard and challenged him outright — would he give an assurance that the *Vigiles* had had no part in Barralozzi's death? The Spaniard wouldn't give a straight answer — simply said that Francis should remember men like Barralozzi could cause grave harm to the Church's reputation and his death had been for the best. Francis left the group the following day and went to stay at some hostel in Rome where he tried to decide what he ought to do.

'He thought of going back to the English College to seek guidance but was embarrassed at the circumstances in which he'd thrown up his studies. He considered talking to somebody in the *Curia*. He even thought of seeking an audience with the Pope. But he was tortured by his belief, and the signs he had seen to support it, that the *Vigiles* were acting on the highest authority. In the end he did nothing — by this time he was not at all well. And he told nobody about it until he talked that night with us.'

The Earl cleared his throat noisily. 'I fear we subsequently had a strong disagreement over his unwillingness to come with me to the Archbishop or even to let me say anything about his suspicions that Barralozzi and the American had not died naturally. This damned Spaniard retained a very powerful influence over him. He left for the flat in Tunbridge Wells the day your Mrs Strachan came to see me. Of course we didn't realize at the time just how unwell he was. It's obvious now that when he found himself alone again it all became too much.'

There was another silence. The cat was trying to climb on Fender's shoulder again. He put it on the carpet and closed his eyes, trying to get his thoughts into some sort of order. 'If I could return to the Ropners for a moment — when you wrote to the Prime Minister you said that a scandal would break in the near future. But from what Francis told you it was surely unlikely Barralozzi's activities were going to be given publicity. So how would his dealings with the Ropners have come out?'

'Francis said that all that information had been supplied by someone over whom the *Vigiles* had no control. He felt sure it would get to the press before long.'

'This Spanish priest who is head of the *Vigiles* — what is his name?'

'I told you, Francis wouldn't mention any of the names.'

'But had he never talked about him in his letters earlier — before he joined the group?'

'He once referred to him by his Christian name — Felipe.'

'And apart from the fact that he'd been engaged on research into Church history, that's all we have ——'

'Yes.'

Fender shook his head. 'A remarkable story.'

'No,' said the Countess. 'Wicked, Mr Fender. Wicked beyond belief.' She gripped the side of the tea trolley for emphasis, her mouth quivering. 'Someone must speak to the Pope, tell him what this terrible priest is doing in his name.'

The Earl had gone to stare out of the window. He turned round with one of his irascible and accusing looks. 'Damn it, *he knows!*'

The Countess was shaking her head violently. 'Oh no, Matthew, that is too much.'

'Remember what Francis was told.'

She composed her mouth tightly, clearly unwilling to remember anything. Fender glanced at the Earl. 'Could you remind me exactly what he *was* told?'

'That all the activities of the *Vigiles* had the personal approval of the Pope, whose instruments they were. Those were the words of this Spanish priest when Francis agreed to join him.'

'Then he was lying,' the Countess said. 'The whole thing is inconceivable.'

'So what about this damned chap from the *Curia?*' the Earl said.

'The Vatican is a jungle. There are people with wild ideas there. The Pope cannot know everything that goes on or is done in his name.'

She sat back, a woman who had stated her position and was unlikely ever to budge from it. She had the same unreasoning stubbornness as the Earl. Fender felt the cat rubbing against his ankles. They were waiting for him to speak, to offer his own indignation to add to theirs. Playing for time, he reached down to stroke the cat. The story beggared belief. Were it not for just two things, he would have seen himself returning to London to tell Antrim that he was sure Francis Bacton had been off his head and that his parents were the pathetic victims of his delusions. But there *were* those inconvenient facts: the Bank of England report of the Ropners' financial killing, picked up long before Francis Bacton had returned home to tell his story; above all, the drug in Barralozzi's body that could only have been used for the purpose of triggering his heart attack. They weren't to be laughed off as part of a sick man's fantasy.

He steepled his fingers, conscious of something almost forgotten, excitement, growing inside him. Even-handedly, he turned from one to the other. 'Whether the Pope knows or not, there does seem to be a need for enquiry.' He felt a faint surprise that he had managed to put it so calmly.

11

Antrim smoothed his lips with saffron silk. 'Fascinating, of course, Ludo, absolutely fascinating.' He replaced the handkerchief in his breastpocket and pushed his coffee cup away. 'But how much can you really believe?'

Fender lifted his hands from his stomach and spread them. He said nothing.

Antrim was smiling politely. 'Are we to suppose the Pope puts contracts out on people nowadays?' He let his gaze shift to Antonia, seated a little behind Fender, one arm resting on the conference table. She had marked the first really warm day of spring by wearing a summer dress. The point of her shoulder was bare; where the bone shaped the skin, light from the window made it glow. She was turning a pen over and over in her fingers, her eyes on the file in front of her.

'Bacton was obviously going off his head. Isn't the most likely explanation that the atmosphere of this curious group he joined — all that mortification of the flesh — got too much for him and when he heard the news that someone they'd been investigating was dead, he started fantasizing? If so, one rather wonders if there's anything to be gained by your going to Rome, Ludo.'

He spoke with his tongue in his cheek, hoping to bait Fender a little. Fender had virtually announced that the trip should be the next move, without waiting for his own comments. It would be just as well to remind him of the reality of their present relationship; otherwise he would start behaving as though he was in charge again. The memory of those years of taking Fender's orders lingered like the taste of vinegar.

'The fact that Barralozzi died when he did *could* be no more than an odd coincidence. If he was in with criminals they might have been responsible for the killing.'

But of course he didn't believe that now and he knew they didn't either. He saw Fender stirring and cut in before he could speak. 'On the other hand the allegation against the Ropners can't be left where it is. The PM was very frank when I last saw him. Ropner's standing in the party is extremely strong. The Chief Whip has come up with nothing adverse through his channels. To drop Ropner on the basis of a rumour picked up by the Bank of England, fleshed out with a statement at second-hand from an unbalanced and now deceased priest, is clearly not on. There is another factor as well, I learnt it from Pagett only on Friday night. This is very delicate — but it seems that the PM intends to step down next year. His health isn't good and Pagett says his wife has extracted some sort of promise from him to that effect. For complicated reasons the choice of a successor is likely to fall on Ropner. So it's becoming of supreme importance to be sure there is nothing irredeemably nasty in the woodshed.

'Both the PM and Pagett recognize that if the Ropners did make a killing in the currency markets with Barralozzi's help, their profit will by now be in a numbered account in Switzerland to which we'll never gain access. There's apparently no question of the Met. being asked to pursue any of this with the Italian police. So it's up to us. We need a source in the Vatican Bank who can dig out details of the transactions put through by Barralozzi and provide the link — if it exists — to the Ropners.' Antrim sat back in his chair and rested his feet on the desk. 'So it seems we agree, Ludo — you'll have to go to Rome to recruit that source.'

Fender examined the bowl of his pipe for ignitable remains, then put it away in his pocket. He was trying not to look too pleased. 'There *is* someone there I might get help from, a priest named John Hebden whom I knew quite well once. He went to the Vatican a couple or so years back. I believe he has a fairly lowly post in the *Curia* — nothing to do with the Bank, I'm sure — but he may be able to put me in touch with someone who works there and would be co-operative. There are two outstanding things however which should perhaps be cleared at this stage.' He was, Antrim noticed, being almost deferential. 'Do you feel the circumstances now justify your insisting on being told the identity of the Bank of England's source? Presumably it's somebody in Rome.'

Antrim awarded him a nod: as long as he stayed like this, they were going to get on. 'I've already spoken to Pagett about it. He promised to have a word with the Governor today. What's the other thing?'

Fender turned in his chair and reached for the file in front of Antonia on the conference table. Balancing it in his lap he turned the pages, searching for something. Antrim let his gaze rest on Antonia again. The skin of the arm resting on the table was lightly tanned. She must have been sunbathing over the weekend. Or, now he thought about it more, perhaps it was the result of gardening for the geriatric parents in Shropshire. In the past few days she had begun to present against his will the same challenge that had intrigued him at the time his marriage to Juliet was unravelling. He rose from his chair and went to stand behind her while he straightened the angle of one of the Patrick Proktors which had been hung at last, in place of Harkness's watercolours.

Fender looked up from the file. 'Yes.' He had a finger on a paragraph in one of Antonia's notes. 'Baxter's efforts to identify Barralozzi's lunch companion — what progress there?'

'Some. The table at which Barralozzi sat in the restaurant was reserved by one of two people, either a Mr Weber speaking from the President Roosevelt Hotel or a Mr Pick who has, or had, a rented apartment in Park Lane. The waiter who should be able to say for certain which it was comes back from holiday in a day or two. Baxter will see him then.' He turned back from the picture. He could see the nape of Antonia's neck and the hollow of the back where the dress curved away. 'If we can get a firm identification, Antonia will follow it up while you're away.'

Where the hair began in the neck there was a tiny mole. He could remember his hand reaching under the neck at just that point, pushing the hair away while she still struggled to free herself, lifting her head until he had her mouth and began to feel her giving up the fight at last. He crossed to his seat again, irritated that she should disturb him. 'By the way, I'm going to arrange that an old colleague of mine who's now in the Embassy in Rome is told that you're coming, and may need help. I don't want him let in on the actual story, of course, but he should be able to check out those addresses and telephone numbers in Francis Bacton's diary if you decide they really could be relevant.'

'That would be very helpful.'

Only in vague terms did Antrim nowadays speak of his past employment in the shadowy reaches of intelligence. Old colleagues were seldom further particularized. He had come to think this part of his life might be seen as imparting a seediness to his reputation. Now that he moved freely amongst the mandarins, he did not wish them to be diverted by sardonic thoughts of him rifling diplomatic safes. In the Bureau itself, he took care to be similarly reticent, even when talking with those, like Fender, who had known him long ago.

'I think his office should be the channel for passing any messages that are necessary. We can use the diplomatic wireless net then — I don't want conversations over an open line between here and Rome.'

'Of course.' Fender hesitated. 'I have one small request. It's for Antonia's continued assistance to me.'

He was taken aback. 'You mean in Rome?'

'I should find it invaluable. She has the facts at her fingertips in a way I haven't. And there may well be some interviews which she would be able to conduct more effectively than I.'

For a moment Antrim wondered if she had persuaded Fender to get her a trip to see the sights. But when he glanced in her direction, he saw she had looked up and appeared as surprised as he was. Curiosity replaced irritation. Impossible to take Fender's reasons seriously: by now he knew the facts in his usual intolerable detail; and for him to have changed in character so much as to accept the possibility that anyone was better fitted to conduct an interview than himself, was out of the question. There must be more to it. But what? An old man's vanity, wanting the world to see him with an attractive woman at his side, and to wonder? A late candle of desire flickering again in that unlovely carcass, lighting up a hope of conquest in a Rome bedroom, one last grand penetration before the night closed in? He stared at Fender's clasped hands, rising and falling on the ledge of his belly. Some of the fat had disappeared since his retirement but not enough to remove the wrinkling below the waistband of the trousers or the glimpse of dead white flesh where the shirt gaped above. The whole thing was ridiculous, revolting.

And yet — His mind went back to the Stradbrook investigation. On that occasion too, Fender had insisted on taking Antonia with him to Ottawa. Secure in the knowledge that she was sharing his own bed, he had thought nothing of it. But had he read the plot all wrong? Were there moments in Ottawa which Fender hoped to repeat? It was bizarre. But could he rule it out?

He cleared his throat. 'I was relying on getting Antonia back to her normal work. However, there's a young officer named Trent —' he pressed the button that opened the staff chart on the wall and frowned at the names — 'you won't know him but he shows great promise. I wonder — '

Fender interrupted him without raising his head. 'It's tiresome of me, I know, but I do think that if I'm to go at all, it will have to be with Antonia.'

He was digging his toes in. It was impossible to feel sure that he would not withdraw from the whole exercise if he was thwarted. Antrim sat back. 'All right, Ludo, let me think about it.'

Fender said softly, 'That's really very good of you.' Steadying himself against Antrim's desk, he lurched to his feet. 'Now, will you forgive me? I'm lunching with a man who has some news about sightings of Large Blues. He believes there is now a colony near Chipping Campden. If this is true it's very exciting.'

He reached the door a little before Antonia and patted her in what appeared to be a wholly avuncular fashion. 'Would you think about where we might stay in Rome? If there's an old-fashioned *pensione* in Trastevere not taken over by American matrons on cultural safari, that would suit.'

To Antrim he said, 'You'll let me know when Pagett has prised out of the Governor the identity of the Bank of England's source? My guess is some financial journalist with Vatican connections.' He sailed past Baxter, hovering in the open doorway, as though he was mere ectoplasm. He was back to his old insufferable form.

As Antonia was about to follow him, Antrim said, 'I want a few words.' He shut the door and pointed to a chair. 'What was all that about the man he's lunching with, by the way?'

'Butterflies. It's a passion of his.'

He shook his head in contempt and seated himself on the edge of the conference table, watching her. 'If you prefer to avoid the Rome trip — ' He let it hang in the air.

'No,' she said, 'I'll go.' She spoke flatly and he found it impossible to tell whether she was pleased or indifferent.

'You're sure?'

'Quite sure.'

He went back to his own chair, snapping his fingers, telling himself he was wasting his time over her but reluctant to let her leave. 'I want you to bear one thing in mind while you're there. Our interest begins and ends with the Ropner angle. What the group to which Francis Bacton belonged does or doesn't do is not the Bureau's business. Right?'

Her gaze was expressionless. He went on, 'I suspect Ludo is hoping to turn over a few stones in the Vatican in pursuit of purely Catholic interests. I don't want that. Nor, we can assume, does the PM.'

'I might not be in a position to stop it.'

'You'll be in a position to warn me if it's beginning to

happen. I rely on you.'

Her cheeks were beginning to flush. 'Is that all?'

If he tried, he told himself, he could make her come running; he just didn't care to try. 'Yes, that's all.'

12

They stepped from the plane into a velvet evening, into a world still warmed by the day's embers. After the pandemonium of Heathrow, Leonardo da Vinci airport seemed relatively peaceful. Waiting for the baggage carousel to enter labour, Antonia felt a pleasant lethargy descend, a cataleptic calm erasing stress. Even in the taxi to Trastevere, the mood persisted, dulling misgivings that the *pensione*, selected in haste, with minimal help from the travel agent, might prove a disaster.

In the event, it was better than she had hoped, a place of high ceilings and long shutters, of brass beds and bathrooms with giant taps and towels that smelt of sun. When, after a shower, she joined Fender for a meal in the garden on the roof, she felt that she had at least got them off to an auspicious start.

On the aircraft, he had ordered drinks with which to toast a twilit coastline and then dozed, apparently tired. Now, in an aged lightweight suit she guessed to be a legacy of his Indian days, he was restored, livelier even than when they had dined in the restaurant opposite his cottage. At such times, he would share perceptions and feelings in an almost childlike way which was infectious; so that other things, seen but hardly registered at the time — the tendrils of the vine on the pergola above them, reaching into the candle's arc, the waiter's white jacket, now dazzling with light, now a luminous blue shadow as he moved to the darkness by the steps to the kitchen — would return in memory later with a special character. He seemed to have put from his mind their reason for being in

Rome, and talked of his last visit, of opera at the Baths of Caracalla and waffles at Babington's tearooms. But when she thought he was fumbling in his pocket for his door key, preparatory to going to bed, he produced his pipe, clicked it experimentally between his teeth and said, 'So, about to-morrow — '

She reached down for the document case beside her chair and braced herself. 'The Embassy,' he went on. 'We'd better contact Antrim's faceless friend. Did you say it's not the person he thought it would be?'

'It's a woman now, Harriet Ackerley — apparently one of their rising stars. I could go there first thing in the morning to make contact and check out the stuff in the diary.'

He grunted his agreement. 'Ask her for any ideas about what "V.d.L." might stand for. A list of roads beginning with those initials would be helpful. While you're doing that I shall try to see John Hebden — presumably there's an Information Office at the Vatican which will tell me where I can find him.' He was consulting a small notebook of his own which she had not seen him use before. 'That leaves the American journalist, Frank Stolz, who gave the Bank of England their story — have you got a biographical note?'

When she had telephoned Fender at home with the news that the Bank of England had disgorged the details of their source, he had purred his satisfaction at the accuracy of his guess that it would prove to be a journalist and asked her to collect what background on Stolz she could. She took her note from the document case and handed it to Fender.

The facts available from directories and Fleet Street had been thin. Stolz was apparently thirty-five, the son of American missionaries who had both died in China. He had been educated outside America but had gone to New York to take a degree in journalism. Soon afterwards he had moved to Rome and established himself as a free-lance writer. A book about the influence of the Mafia on the economic life of Sicily, with side-swipes at the Church for supine acceptance of the situation, had earned him a lot of enemies in Palermo and probably a few in the Vatican. Most of his writing was financial journalism but he had recently turned out another book, this time on the consequences of Reaganomics, which the US Administration's critics were fond of quoting from. He was unmarried.

Fender handed back the note. 'I think he should be yours.'

'Mine?'

'Yes, I don't see him responding well to me. Try to see him later tomorrow.'

Startled at his willingness to delegate Stolz so readily, she said, 'Shall I tell him exactly who I am — about the Bureau and so on?'

'I see no reason why not. Explain you've been asked to check out the story he told his Bank of England friend.'

'He may not be inclined to disclose his source unless I offer him something in return.'

'We can come to that later, if necessary. Use the first meeting chiefly to size him up.' He was speaking nonchalantly, almost as though he was not particularly interested; but it occurred to her that it was perhaps his way of underlining his confidence in her and bolstering her own.

Later, undressing for bed, she thought of Antrim's instruction to look out for signs of Fender veering away from the pursuit of the Ropners. Perhaps it had begun to happen and that was why he had handed her Stolz on a plate while he went off on his own to his friend in the *Curia*. It seemed quite probable. But she wasn't going to lose any sleep for Antrim's sake.

Harriet Ackerley smelt of expensive scent and was intimidatingly elegant. As she flicked over the copy pages of Francis Bacton's diary, she smoked a thin cheroot and pursed her lips. 'Looks routine enough. Of course you have to realize that in this country even the simplest inquiries can take an intolerable time.' She put the pages in a folder and wrote something on the cover. 'How much time have you got?'

'Not long. There's a fair amount of pressure on.'

She raised an eyebrow at Antonia as though she'd heard that one too often. She looked forty-odd with good features that were a little too hard to be attractive. No work was visible on her desk, apart from the Foreign Office print she had been reading when Antonia arrived and a few embassy circulars;

presumably she kept the real stuff in the steel cabinets which ran along the wall behind her. On a side table were a studio portrait of a large black cat, a bottle of mineral water and a folded silk scarf that exactly matched the blouse she was wearing.

'How's Antrim?' she asked. 'Pleased to get the job, I suppose.'

'I think so. You knew him?'

'Oh yes, I knew him. All too well.' She looked into a corner of the room, cheroot angled gracefully over one shoulder. 'I would say you're *very* welcome to him, my dear.'

There seemed no suitable response. Antonia opened her notebook. 'I gather we're using your ciphers if we need to pass messages. When there's one for us I can come round to pick it up if you'll ring me at the *pensione*.' She wrote. 'This is our address and telephone number.'

'A little ucky these days, Trastevere,' Harriet Ackerley said reflectively. 'Try not to get raped, won't you?' She stood up. 'And you're just following up a corruption lead — ?'

'Yes.'

'Not Italian of course —'

'Not the people we're interested in.'

She nodded. 'Well, any little sidelights you come across, you'll let us know, I hope. We like to keep abreast of things.'

At the door of the Embassy she looked casually up and down, taking everything in. She was cooler than ice. 'I expect we'll be in touch,' she said, waving the cheroot. 'You won't get in our way, will you, darling?'

The room Fender entered was depressingly plain, its gloom barely relieved by the glimpse he caught of cloisters and greenery through the barred window behind the desk. On a separate writing table against the wall were an empty brass candlestick, a blotting pad that had not been changed for a while and a ballpoint pen attached to the table by a chain. The devotional paintings that looked down from the walls had the air of having been rejected from a better place. Only the marble floor and the glimpse through the window suggested that place was very near.

Seating himself on the other side of the desk, Hebden caught Fender's expression and smiled. 'I'm sorry it's a little dismal, Ludo. I would have taken you to my office. But we are asked to use these interview rooms for visitors.'

'Are your pens chained against the Devil?'

'No, there is an economy campaign going on. And one must exercise normal prudence when dealing with the public.'

'You make it sound like the Post Office.'

'Of course. We are in a very similar business — conveying messages.'

Watching Hebden's smile broaden to that point where there was always uncertainty whether it would dissolve into laughter or be replaced by a look of innocence, Fender thought, He is quite unchanged. For a man in his sixties he looked absurdly youthful with the pink and freckled face that had refused to tan under the Roman sun, and the sandy hair in a boxer's bristle. A slight smile was seldom absent from his face. It gave the impression that he was looking behind the words of a conversation, that he was willing to be amused but not deceived.

Fender reached for the travel bag under his chair, placed it on the table and took out the litre bottle of Glenlivet. 'I hope I have correctly recalled your medicine.'

Hebden held up his hands. 'My dear Ludo, how very kind!' He held the palms close together as though about to clap. 'When will you come and share it with me?'

'Whenever you ask me. I expect to be here for a week.'

'I live near the Porta San Patrizio in a small apartment of which I am very fond. Perhaps tomorrow evening?'

'That would be perfect.' Fender drew out his pipe and tobacco pouch. 'And how is life in the Vatican?'

'You see a bureaucrat before you — not what I expected to be when I first set out in the Church. But this place can sometimes be interesting.'

'I have thought of you leading a very privileged existence.'

'Moderately privileged.'

'Solaced by beauty, soothed by ritual, sequestered from reality —'

Hebden laughed.

'And a duty-free shop to boot.'

106

'Ah, yes,' Hebden said. 'The pleasures of the flesh. Those also.'

'The enjoyment of one such pleasure by a colleague of yours was part of the chain of events that brought me here.'

'Which colleague was that?'

'He's dead now. Barralozzi of the Institute for Religious Works.'

'The banker.'

'Yes.'

'Not by my definition a colleague, not in the strict sense. But I saw him about the place. I think perhaps I can guess at the pleasure.'

'He seems to have had a credit card for a call girl agency with world-wide branches.'

Hebden produced a sigh. 'I have not been issued with one. Perhaps all bankers have them now. I cannot answer for anybody else here of course.' He looked mischievous. 'The odd cardinal perhaps?' He went on solemnly in varying tones of voice. ' "Here is my Vatican Gold card." "Thank you, sir, that will do nicely." ' He let the laughter take possession of him and then abruptly subdued it with his handkerchief. 'You see how ill-informed you are about my contact with reality. When I am occasionally unchained from here for a holiday, I go to stay with my niece in Scarborough. She is married to a twenty-one-inch television screen in a walnut veneer case. Why are you so interested in Barralozzi and his habits?'

'His sister is the wife of a Cabinet Minister, Ropner. We have a report that Barralozzi helped them in speculating in sterling on the basis of secret government information of a likely move in the exchange rate. Proof is what I need — evidence of the transactions. Our best chance is that records exist in the Vatican Bank. I need an introduction to somebody there who would be prepared to let me see those records. Unofficially of course.'

'You hoped I could arrange it?' Hebden's eyebrows were raised.

'There is no one else I can ask.'

'Why not an official approach to the Secretary of State?'

Fender lit his pipe and looked round unsuccessfully for an

ashtray. 'That would not be thought appropriate.'

Hebden shook his head. 'I know hardly anyone in the bank — just one or two cashiers I recognize across the counter — certainly nobody to whom I could introduce you.'

'Haven't you a friend in the *Curia* who might be better placed and whom you could get to make an informal inquiry?'

'I doubt it. I will try to think, of course. But in any case it would be difficult to ask for what would be a breach of trust.'

It was too soon to be discouraged. But he had not expected quite such an unpromising response. He sat back and dropped the spent match in the travel bag.

'Perhaps I should return the Glenlivet?' Hebden was smiling again.

'It was not a conditional gift.'

'Thank you. I was not serious.'

'But you'll think about it a little more, won't you? There are in any case aspects which affect the Vatican directly.' He hesitated, uncertain how far to go at this first meeting. 'The investigation of the report in England has uncovered things which, if they are true, I find very disturbing. They would disturb you too.'

'At my age I am not easily disturbed, Ludo. And if you are going to tell me that Barralozzi was corrupt, that would not be news, either to me or the authorities here. I had heard rumours about Barralozzi long before he died — that he had a personal fortune which could not have been obtained honestly.'

'Did you ever hear Barralozzi's name connected with Rossano, the head of Laportex, who died in a car accident last week?'

'No. But perhaps I can guess what you are going to tell me about Rossano also.' Hebden folded his arms, looking pleased with himself. 'I happen to know that a firm of surveyors from Milan were invited recently to examine and submit a report here on the Luciani Hostel for Pilgrims which was built by Laportex. The report states that the foundations are danger-ously unsound because the work was not carried out to the specification in the contract. Rossano is known to have per-sonally ordered the omission of certain materials and steps in the work which could only have that result. Is there something more about Rossano?'

'I have a theory — no, a conviction that his death was not an accident.'

Hebden shook his head. 'I've no idea, but I'm quite ready to believe it. This is a violent country. And Rossano was a crook.' He traced a line with his finger through a dust film on the desk. 'So what else is disturbing you, Ludo?'

Fender paused to collect his thoughts. 'I fear there is something rather sinister going on in Rome.'

'Within the Church?'

'Yes. My information comes from a young English priest who was living here earlier this year. Unfortunately he's now dead. His name was Francis Bacton and until January he was at the English College. Did you ever meet him?'

Hebden rubbed the sandy spikes of hair on his scalp and frowned. 'I think I may have done so once when I visited the College. A very intense young man, but nice. I'm sorry to hear of his death.'

'Bacton was one of the two sources through which we learnt of the dealings between Barralozzi and the Ropners. He told his parents before he died that the facts had been obtained by some mysterious group of priests which he joined when he left the English College. The group seems to be concerned with corruption and other forms of crookedness inside the Church, and more especially the Vatican. I want to get at the facts the group have obtained about the Ropners. It is led by a Spanish priest who is clearly a powerful personality and it practises a degree of Discipline which I would have thought was unusual in these days.' He described the contents of the bag he had found in Bacton's suitcase.

Hebden sat with his hands clasping the Glenlivet bottle. He had dropped his eyes from Fender's face. Eventually he said, 'What are you asking me, Ludo?'

'For help in locating the group. They are apparently known as *Vigiles*.'

'*Vigiles*? I have never heard of them. Why do you fear they are connected with something sinister?'

'They seem to be taking matters rather too much into their

own hands. At least I hope that's the extent of it.'

'You're not being very explicit.'

'Forgive me. There are some things I'm not free to tell you.'

'I see.' Hebden looked at his watch. 'Shall we continue our discussion in the gardens? I expect you'd like to see them. I go there before lunch most days.' He stood with the bottle. 'If I could borrow your travel bag for the time being — ? I should prefer not to be holding this quite so suggestively and then run into the Holy Father.'

They strolled for a while then seated themselves on a bench in the shade of a willow tree. 'So what do you think?' Hebden extended an arm. He smiled as though he had issued a challenge.

Fender let his gaze wander over grottoes and rockeries until it reached a banana plant. 'I would rather not say.'

'You can be frank — these benches are not fitted with microphones.'

'I find it a hideous jumble.'

'Of course. Like the Church. But on the good days I think how much love went into creating even the most vulgar of the things you see.'

'And on the bad days —?'

Hebden paused, staring into the distance. 'On the bad days — I reflect that once, sitting in this place, I would have smelt the pitch burning on the Christians as they were being tortured in Nero's circus. Everything in the world has happened here.'

A gardener in a panama hat passed by, holding a bundle of asparagus. He gave an almost imperceptible nod. On another bench, a lone figure in biretta and soutane was reading a book in the full glare of the sun. The only sound from the city beyond the gardens was a gentle hum. Hebden said, 'You say you're anxious to discover where Francis Bacton went from the English College. Have you considered the Opus Dei people?'

'Should I?'

'Perhaps. I mention them because you spoke of these *Vigiles* being led by a Spanish priest. The Spanish influence is strong in Opus Dei — it was founded by a Spaniard, Escriva. And also because of the contents of the velvet bag. I know that they favour the use of the whip and the *cilis* for mortification.'

'Isn't it primarily a lay organization?'

'There's a section for priests to which Bacton would no doubt have been a welcome addition. As a body, OD has a rather complicated structure. There are the numeraries who take vows and live in Opus Dei residences, and supernumeraries who simply lead ordinary lives in the community at large. There are also people called co-operators whose function I don't really know. Occasionally I meet some one who is in OD headquarters here — we share musical tastes — but I have hesitated to question him — they are reticent about some things.' Hebden shrugged. 'However, I'm bound to tell you, Ludo, that they control their residences strictly and I am sure you will find nothing remotely sinister there.'

'Tell me about their aims.'

'Their aims? My friend would say that they consist in helping people to sanctify their activity in the world.'

'I have always thought that "sanctify" was rather a rubber word.'

Hebden clicked his tongue. 'The Church *invented* rubber words, you know that, Ludo.'

'And what is your view of Opus Dei?'

'They enjoy a fair amount of support here. Some say the Pope is very well disposed — he's rumoured to have been seen praying at the tomb of Escriva, the founder — but that was before he became Pope. Their critics say that OD is a church within a church with unhealthy ambitions.'

'I asked what *your* view was.'

'Mine? Well, they are — how shall I say? — great *goers*. Yes, indeed!' Hebden laughed wickedly, shaking his head until he decided that it would not do and composed his features again. 'No, to be serious, they work hard and have some good people. They do go on rather about the amount of evil in the Church. They see themselves as the only people who can get it back on the right path, of course. *Very* keen. As for their instruments of mortification which one may not like, you'll understand better if you read the history of Spanish Catholicism.'

From the distance came the noise of a single cannon shot. It

III

was followed by the bells of churches ringing out the Angelus, with those of St Peter's, behind where they sat, sounding the bass. Fender rose slowly to his feet. The clamour was oddly exciting, commanding.

Hebden smiled up at him. 'There is a phrase of R.H. Benson's which has stayed with me. It must have been written about a moment rather like this. "Now I am in the *centre* of Papistry." I understand what he felt.' He bent to pick up the travel bag. 'I fear I must leave you now, Ludo. But we can talk again tomorrow evening.'

As they walked from the gardens, Fender said, 'Would you do something for me — introduce me to your friend in Opus Dei? I would like to ask him if Francis Bacton did in fact join them and if so where was his residence.'

'Is that all you want to ask?'

'For the moment, yes.'

Hebden nodded. 'Since he is quite senior, he should certainly know. If he's free, I'll ask him to come to my apartment tomorrow evening. His name is Hernandes, Monsignor Luis Hernandes.'

'That would be very kind.'

'He thinks I am rather unserious, I fear. He is also severe on the weaknesses of the flesh. We may have to keep the Glenlivet out of sight.' Hebden hesitated. 'There are things you have not told me. I don't ask to know. But since he is my friend, I hope — '

'I shall not embarrass you.'

At the exit, Hebden pressed his hand. 'I hope your fears, whatever they relate to, turn out to be false, Ludo. We have no need for bad news here. No need at all.'

Crossing St Peter's Square, Fender was conscious that the exhilaration of a few minutes before, when the Angelus rang out, was being replaced by something else: foreboding. With it came a bleak melancholy.

Sweat trickled down his spine as he emerged into the full glare of the sun. Hebden's farewell had seemed both an appeal and a warning. He looked back at the dome of St Peter's and it no longer appeared beautiful to him. Somewhere about him other events were taking place; he could hear the screams and smell the burning flesh as the Christians were lifted high on the pikes, to give the Emperor a better view.

13

The voice at the other end of the telephone was of someone at ease with the world, whatever surprises might be stacking up out there.

'Antonia Strachan,' Stolz said. He repeated the words, as though enjoying the sound they made. 'That's what I call a very nice name.'

When she told him why she wanted to see him, there was silence and she had a moment's anxiety. But he came back amiably enough. 'Right, let's get together. I'm not sure I recall all I said to Rollo Pawson, it's a while back now. But I'd be happy to have you jog my memory. Do you work at the Bank of England with Rollo?'

She told him she didn't but would explain when they met. He described how to get to his apartment on the Corso and they agreed on seven o'clock.

From the time she had left Harriet Ackerley at the Embassy, it had taken almost the whole day making contact with Stolz. He apparently had no office other than his apartment; from there, during the morning, a maid or cleaning woman speaking no detectable English had answered in negative yelps. In the afternoon there had been no reply at all. It was now after six.

Fender had returned from seeing Hebden while she was having lunch and sat briefly at the table, declining to eat. He appeared depressed. Promising to tell her about the meeting with Hebden when they met for dinner, he disappeared to his room with a bottle of mineral water and some cheese biscuits. She began to wonder if this sudden transition to a Roman summer was proving too much for him. Getting no reply when she knocked on his door as she was leaving to see Stolz, she opened it and was relieved to be greeted by steady breathing. She scribbled a note to say where she had gone and left him in peace.

For no good reason, she had pictured Frank Stolz in some modish eyrie with leather chairs and smoked-glass tables, his word processor winking alongside a bottle of Jack Daniel's. Instead she found herself borne by wheezing lift to the fourth floor of a *palazzo* and entering a world on which modern technology had left little visible mark. The apartment seemed vast: rooms opened into other rooms through double doors and each had its frescoed ceiling and high windows overlooking the Corso. The furniture was seventeenth- and eighteenth-century with the exception of a few settees and table lamps. From the main reception room to which Stolz led her, she was able to look out on to a terrace almost as large as the *pensione*'s roof.

Stolz greeted her with an appraising look, long enough to be complimentary without threatening imminent siege. 'You live up to your name,' he said. He was compactly built and very tanned with eyes that were perhaps a touch melancholy. In a casual encounter she would have placed him as European with a trace of Slav, had it not been for the accent and the laid-back manner. He wore a silk shirt, unbuttoned enough to show he was not a medallion man, cream trousers and moccasins of the same colour.

He had mixed a jug of dry Martini already, producing it from a cold cupboard behind a walnut-inlay panel. On a long coffee table were silver dishes of olives stuffed with nuts and a plate of caviar canapés. Fender, with his six biscuits, she thought uncharitably, could take a lesson here.

When she told him she worked for the Crimes Bureau, Stolz looked uncomprehending; it was plain he had never heard of it. She explained its functions and he listened politely, asking no questions. Finally she said boldly, 'Hence my interest in your story about Mrs Ropner. I came to ask if you could see your way to putting me in touch with your source.'

It was not the way Fender would have played it. But she had a feeling that with Stolz it would be better to put her cards on the table from the start.

He was smiling. 'That's asking quite a lot'.

'I realize that.'

'I wish I could help. I really do. But I can't. My source just wouldn't talk to you.'

'Why not?'

'It's the way things are.'

'His identity would be protected.'

'He'd never be convinced of that.'

'Can you at least tell me what sort of a person he is? Somebody concerned with investigations in the Vatican perhaps?'

He frowned briefly then shook his head. 'Nothing like that.' He picked up her glass to refill it; he seemed to be turning something over in his mind. When he came back with her glass he said, 'You may as well know this much — The reason this guy wouldn't talk to you is quite simple. He happens to be in the US Embassy.'

'A diplomat?'

'You could call him that.'

Through the open doors a telephone rang a room or two away and Stolz went to answer it. Antonia took her drink to the terrace and looked at the flowers along its edge. When he came back, she said, 'I see you like Madame Hardy.'

He looked puzzled. 'What?'

'The white rose with a green eye — it's an early damask called Madame Hardy.'

He examined it with care; clearly it was for the first time. 'Who was Madame Hardy?'

'I've no idea.'

'Beautiful. Very cool.' He lifted his eyes. 'And desirable.' When it seemed he was going to get obvious, he turned away to lean on the ledge of the terrace. 'I'm sorry I can't help you over meeting my source. But I may be able to give you some additional information if you're interested.'

'I'm very interested.'

'The price is dinner with me.'

It occurred to her that might not be all. But, if so, she would meet the problem when it arose. She nodded, smiling.

He went off to the telephone again to ring a restaurant. 'Al Vacario,' he said when he rejoined her. 'We can eat in the garden there and I'll show you the people who tell me the other things I hear.'

She noticed he was received at the restaurant with some ceremony. When he caught her glance he winked.

'They certainly know you,' she said.

'I eat here a lot. It's not so much the food as the fact that the Chamber of Deputies is nearby. There are always people from there dropping in. They like to talk, I'm a good listener, everybody's happy. Particularly if I pick up the tab.'

Over hors-d'oeuvres he asked, 'Supposing I give you some more information, who has to know?'

'My office, the Secretary to the Cabinet, the Prime Minister, one or two Private Secretaries — that's all.'

'It wouldn't be made the basis for criminal proceedings?'
'No.'

'Or passed back to anyone here in Rome?'
'No.'

He still hesitated but eventually seemed satisfied. 'All right, Antonia, I'm relying on what you say. First you have to understand that what I discovered about Mrs Ropner's currency dealing was incidental to the main story that interested me — Barralozzi. A lot of the detail has come from my own sources. But the Ropner angle only appeared in what I was told by my friend in the Embassy. We have a business relationship — I give him the sort of gossip I know his people want, he tells me things in my area. I'm working on a book about the Vatican — not just on the financial side but the whole works.'

'Hasn't that been done rather a lot lately?'

'Not in depth. I'm going to surface a raft of scandals no-body's heard of yet. When I do, from the Pope downwards they're going to take an awful long time to recover.'

Stolz rose to shake the hands of four men in succession as they passed the table, exchanging rapid repartee in Italian. She saw them examine her with flattering care. When he resumed his seat he said, 'They wanted to know you but I said you were a policewoman. Well, about Barralozzi: he wasn't all *that* interesting but he had a nice racket. The Vatican Bank holds — used to hold, rather — in safe custody for a Spanish institution

116

the name of which doesn't matter, twelve million dollars'
worth of US bonds — all issued by big league companies.
Barralozzi knew those bonds were going to be with the bank
for a minimum of three years. Their physical existence in the
bank was audited every twelve months. Otherwise they were
his to play with. What he did was use them to raise money on
short-term loans either for himself or for others to whom he
leased the bonds for a fee.'

'You mean the bonds could be deposited with some other
banks as security for cash loans — '

'Correct. If he lent them out, it was never for longer than
four months and he had to be satisfied that the investment for
which the cash would be used would pay off within that time.
This usually meant something crooked.'

'Is that how he helped Mrs Ropner?'

'Yes. She had the use of five million dollars' worth of the
bonds for her currency dealing. In return Barralozzi was cut in
on the information that made the dealing a sure thing. That
was the story as I knew it when I saw Rollo Pawson here last
year although I couldn't give him the detailed background I've
given you. Since then events have moved on. Barralozzi leased
a very large proportion of the bonds to an Italian businessman
whose name I've never discovered. The term as usual was for
four months. Before it was up, Barralozzi was given the news
that because of other problems the Vatican Bank had been
having and which you must have read about in the press, the
Bank of Rome would do a special audit of all holdings in
advance of the annual audit. When he discovered there was no
chance of getting the genuine bonds back in time, he hit on the
idea of having duplicates made — forgeries in other words. He
made contact with an American named Steiner who is the
biggest operator in bond fraud in the world. Steiner agreed to
have the missing bonds counterfeited. There's a man in
Chicago who does this so well that provided the bonds aren't
returned to the States for authentication nobody knows the
difference. The Bank of Rome were only going to do a
physical audit.'

'And then Barralozzi died — '

'Yes, before the counterfeit bonds could be deposited in the

Vatican Bank. By now the audit will have revealed a nasty gap in the holdings.'

'Is there going to be publicity?'

He shook his head. 'No. You can depend on it the bank will compensate the owner of the bonds and add something on top against an agreement to keep quiet.'

She put down her fork. 'Quite a story. And you say he wasn't all that interesting.'

'Not in comparison with some of the other guys in that place.'

'You sound very cynical.'

When he only shrugged, she said, 'Could we go back to Mrs Ropner? The story seems to concern only her. Is there any good reason to suppose her husband was involved?'

Stolz smiled. 'Let me tell you the sequence of events as far as I can put it together. Eighteen months ago your government was pushed by the movement of world oil prices into approving a big reduction in the rate for North Sea oil. The size of that reduction unsettled the markets. Sterling was already slipping because of industrial trouble and it began to plummet. The Bank of England stood back and watched it go and everybody knew the reason was that only a week or two before your PM had said in a major speech that interest rates should not be used to try to prevent any currency finding its true level. Of course there had to come a moment when he'd eat his words and authorize intervention in the markets. Or did there? Nobody felt absolutely sure what he was going to do, whether or not he had a level at the back of his mind to which he was ready for the pound to go. But Ropner knew. And Ropner was the man with access to the figures which would be the deciding factor. All he needed, at most, was to judge the moment when the PM would accept that the case for lifting interest rates high enough to stop the sellers of sterling in their tracks was unanswerable. That moment, according to the best informed financial writer you've got, came just before a routine Cabinet meeting which wasn't even expected to talk about sterling. The PM authorized Ropner to go into the meeting with an emergency package consisting of a three-point interest rate hike and some other measures designed to reassure foreign investors in sterling. Within an hour of the announcement of the package that afternoon your currency was climbing very fast in all the markets.'

Stolz paused, watching the waiter refill his wine glass, enjoying the moment. 'What that financial writer doesn't know is that while, by my calculations, that Cabinet meeting was still going on, two separate private orders to buy sterling were going out into the markets. You'd need a Geiger counter to trace them back. But one was for Barralozzi. The other was for Mrs Ropner. On those facts would you say Ropner was not involved?'

She shook her head slowly.

'Just one more thing: the block of bonds Mrs Ropner used to raise the cash left the bank vaults three days after the oil price drop was announced; and they came back ten days after sterling began its rise.'

'But you can't persuade the source who's seen the evidence for this to talk to me — '

'Not a chance — it's US Government information and he's not going to give it to a Brit.'

She sighed. 'What I need is proof of the currency dealing and the fact that it was on Mrs Ropner's behalf.'

'You'll never be able to get that.'

'Do you think there are any records in the Vatican Bank which implicate her in what Barralozzi was doing?'

'I doubt it very much. If there had been, he would have had plenty of time to destroy them once she'd returned the bonds.'

'Then the Ropners are safe — even if the PM decided they should be confronted with the story, they could say it was a malicious fabrication.'

Stolz was moving the base of his wine glass to and fro beside his plate. 'If — just *if* — I were able to get you some evidence in documentary form that showed there had been a deal of some sort between Barralozzi and the Ropners during the time of the sterling crisis, could you guarantee that my name would not figure in any of the reports to your politicians?'

She hesitated, knowing that she ought to talk it over with Fender before giving a promise, but knowing too it was a moment which might never recur. 'Yes.'

He was silent for so long she thought he was going to back-track but then he nodded. 'Give me a day or two and I'll know if it's possible.'

'Would you be getting it through your own sources or your friend in the Embassy?'

'You mustn't ask questions — or even expect anything at this stage. I'm simply going to try.'

Over coffee Stolz talked about Italian politics, about the struggle between Left and Right and the Church's role in it. He was very knowledgeable, amusing too, but detached in that chilling way she associated with journalists who'd got beyond seeing any cause as being worth more than a story. Only once did he seem near to caring, when he described the research he had done for his book on the Mafia in Sicily. After asking her which British politicians she knew, he surprised her by acknowledging he had met Ropner at some Italian government reception. 'Quite a guy,' he said. 'Isn't he supposed to be the toughest anti-Soviet in the British Cabinet?'

'I've heard something like that.'

'I don't think the United States Government would be too pleased if they knew I was helping destroy his career. He may be the State Department's great white hope for the UK.'

'On the basis of what one sees elsewhere, you'd probably be saving the State Department from itself.'

He laughed. He liked her, she knew, and he wanted her to like him.

When he suggested going on to a night club, she almost agreed. She was enjoying herself. Moreover she could make out a professional case for it. On the other hand she wanted to end the evening while she still had a clear head. She refused, offering vague concern about Fender's condition as her excuse.

She had surprised him. 'You're here with a man?'

'Yes, he's a colleague.'

'What's his name?'

'Fender, Ludovic Fender.'

Names, it seemed, turned him on: he repeated it as he had done Antonia's, earlier in the evening. 'So what do you call him — Ludo?'

'I don't call him anything to his face. Somehow it wouldn't

120

come out right. But I think of him as Ludo, yes.'

'And he's — just a colleague?' He was pressing hard to get the relationship pinned down.

'If you saw him, you'd know he wasn't "just" anything.'

She declined to enlighten him further. He paid the bill and walked her down the street in search of the taxi for which she'd asked. On the way he saw a woman with roses for sale and went to buy a bunch. They were dark red. 'No Madame Hardy,' he said. 'She hadn't heard of them. But we thought these were you.'

From the taxi window she called, 'You'll telephone the *pensione* as soon as you have news?'

'I promise.' Stolz stood back. He had taken his jacket off and it was slung on one shoulder. It struck Antonia that for all his relaxed manner there was an elusiveness about his personality that had something in common with Fender. What she had identified as the cynicism of his profession had been, after all, a sort of mask, hiding feelings he chose not to reveal. That he had liked her, she was sure. But beyond, all was in shadow.

There was no light under Fender's door as she went past to her own room. She placed the roses in water in the bathroom basin and kicked off her shoes, telling herself it would be pointless to disturb him now, the morning would be early enough for him to hear the score. But, as she began to undress, his knock came.

He was in pyjamas and dressing gown, pink as a schoolboy and smelling of eau de Cologne. He looked totally restored from whatever malaise had attacked him on his way back from seeing Hebden. 'I heard your footsteps,' he said unnecessarily.

She persuaded him to sit down and resigned herself to a postponement of bed. After all she had some progress to report. At the end of her account of the meeting with Stolz, he contrived to look both pleased with her and satisfied with himself. 'I knew I was right to leave Stolz to you. But you did very well.'

His own account of his talk with Hebden was rather thin. She suspected he had omitted a lot of the detail but was reassured when he said he wanted her to accompany him to Hebden's apartment to meet Hernandes, the priest from the

Opus Dei headquarters. 'You will like Hebden,' he said. 'He has a challenging look which reminds me of you.'

When conversation languished, he half rose from his chair. 'A nightcap perhaps? Shall I fetch the whisky from my room?' She shook her head. 'Ah,' he said, still unwilling to leave. She stifled a yawn as he settled back and began speaking of insects in his bath water.

His loneliness, she could see now, was like a sickness that visited him irregularly. It dulled that intuitive sense of what another person was feeling which he could show in his normal moods. Once, looking up suddenly, she became aware he was watching her with a desperate sort of intensity. He perhaps caught her glance, because he levered himself up. 'We must both need our sleep.' He had assumed an unconvincingly casual front. Watching him leave the room, she wondered if she should be calling him back. It was ridiculous. When she eventually got into bed, she became conscious that the moment when she could simply slip away into oblivion had long since past. Picking up a book, she cursed him. Not only had he made her sleepless, he had made her feel guilty too.

14

Murmuring modest invitation, Hebden moved to stand by the tray of bottles and glasses on his desk top. From a window behind him, the evening sun softened the stubble of his scalp, turning it golden. Antonia had expected him to be wearing a cassock but he was dressed in a neat dark suit. 'Mrs Strachan — ?' he said and parted his hands above the tray.

It was a wider choice of drinks than Fender had forecast as they made their way to the apartment. The Glenlivet was visible beside gin and beer and a single bottle of mineral water. Perhaps Monsignor Luis Hernandes, who had arrived before them, had given Hebden no time to purge the display.

Antonia chose the whisky. When Fender followed suit, Hebden said 'Well — ' to his own glass as though events had propelled him along an unforeseen and now inescapable course.

Monsignor Hernandes sat in a shadowed corner, politely impassive, sole fancier of *acqua minerale*. He was a plump, sallow-complexioned man, dressed in a soutane of a thickness that could hardly be comfortable in these days of fast advancing summer. Behind spectacles in ancient black frames the eyes were dark and remote.

Hebden said, 'Your first visit to Rome, Mrs Strachan? You must let me show you something of the Vatican.' He spoke with the half-smile that at first sight had struck her as sardonic but perhaps was merely astringent. Nevertheless, if this was the expression Fender had found to resemble one of her own, she was not flattered.

Hernandes had turned to Fender. 'I understand you are hopeful Opus Dei can help you in an inquiry.' He spoke in clear but strongly accented English.

Fender clasped his hands. He was wearing his guileless look. 'We have been anxious to trace the movements of someone in the early months of this year — a young priest. It seems possible that he went to live in one of your residences here when he left the English College in January. Unfortunately he gave them no information about where he was going.'

Hernandes frowned. 'We should not have been a willing party to a discourtesy of that kind. We value our relations with the venerable English College very highly.' He had something of the manner of a pedagogue; before his sombre eye, the need for a general polishing of conscience could become urgent. 'What is this priest's name?'

'Bacton, Francis Bacton. Did you know him?'

Hernandes shook his head. 'No one of that name has entered one of our residences. You are sure it was in Italy?'

'Yes.'

'Then he did not come to Opus Dei.' He sipped sparingly from his glass. 'Has he written to no one — his parents or relations?'

123

'I should have explained — he returned to England a few weeks ago, and has since died.'

'I am sorry to hear that.' Hernandes took off his spectacles and rubbed his eyes; without the glasses he appeared kinder, a little more vulnerable. 'What gave you reason to think there might be a connection with Opus Dei?'

'In his belongings there were some instruments which I believe you use in your residences — for mortification.'

Hernandes smiled austerely. 'Mortification is not the prerogative of Opus Dei, Mr Fender.'

'I realize that.'

'A great many in the Church share our conviction that it is a necessary part of spiritual life. Are you aware that Pope Paul VI often wore a hair shirt beneath his robes?'

'Yes.'

'Many others who have nothing to do with Opus Dei follow his example.' He seemed almost to be lecturing Fender.

'I was not simply referring to the use of a hair shirt.'

'Nor was I.'

It was not going too well. Antonia could see Hebden had begun to stroke the arm of his chair uneasily.

Hernandes took another sip of his mineral water. 'What were these instruments?'

'A whip.'

'Yes.'

'A *cilis*.'

'Yes.'

'And gloves.'

'Gloves?' He lifted his eyes. 'What sort of gloves?'

'Gloves with metal spikes.'

Hernandes sat forward.

'*You saw gloves of this kind in his possession?*'

'They were with the other instruments in a velvet bag.'

'And you say he was introduced to their use here in Italy?'

'I believe so.'

Hernandes was staring at him. 'By whom?'

'Probably when he joined a group of other priests at the invitation of a Spanish priest whose first name was Felipe. Do you know of the group?'

124

Hernandes said stiffly, 'We have no such group, Mr Fender.'
They sat in a silence that grew awkward.

Eventually Hebden broke it by addressing Hernandes. 'I
hope you are not offended.'

Hernandes shook his head and produced a thin smile. He
was making an effort to recover his composure. 'Forgive me, it
is — very striking suddenly to hear of someone, some group,
turning back to Suso for inspiration.'

'Suso?' Hebden raised his eyebrows.

'Yes.'

Fender leaned towards Hernandes. 'Could you explain —
who or what is Suso?'

'Suso was a religious who lived in the fourteenth century
and wrote an account of his spiritual experiences. He was a
great mystic.' The pedagogue's manner was back. 'It was
Heinrich Suso who had the gloves made.'

'For what purpose?'

'He feared that in his sleep he might involuntarily try to
remove the hair shirt he wore at night.' He glanced at Hebden.
'You remember of course.'

Hebden said carefully, 'A very remarkable man.'

There was another silence. Then Hernandes said, 'But let us
not dwell on Suso. How are you enjoying your visit to Rome,
Mr Fender?'

Hebden began to replenish glasses. Inclining his head, Hernandes tried to read the label on the whisky bottle. 'Tell me
what is special about Glenlivet?' He was being determinedly
genial.

Antonia waited for Hebden to dispose of the difference
between scotch and malt; he had a gift for sly humour. When
he had finished, she said, 'Monsignor Hernandes, could I ask
something that was not clear to me? Were you implying that
unlike the whip and the *cilis*, the gloves are never used in your
residences?'

He looked politely surprised that she should concern herself
with such things. 'If I did not say that, I meant to, certainly.'

'Anywhere in the world?'

'Anywhere.'

'How can you be sure?' Hebden said. 'Wasn't Monsignor

125

Escriva always saying that Opus Dei was an unorganized organisation? I never quite understood that. But if it *is*, you can't be sure.' He had apparently decided a gentle teasing would now be safe.

A touch of colour appeared in Hernandes' cheeks. He didn't smile. 'There is complete understanding in our residences as to the manner of mortification. The gloves are not used.' He dropped his eyes: it had been a near thing. After a few words to Antonia about what she should see in Rome, he looked at his watch. 'I fear you must forgive me, John —' His use of the Christian name came as a small shock, as though a speaker in a formal address had lapsed into slang. He rose to his feet and bowed to Antonia. To Fender he said, 'I am sorry to be unable to help, Mr Fender. What will you do now?'

'We have some more inquiries to make. Bacton left a diary. Some of the entries may prove helpful.' Antonia could see that it had disconcerted him that the meeting was coming to an end so soon. He placed a hand on Hernandes' arm. 'May I ask you one more question, Monsignor, before you leave? Have you ever heard of a group within the Church known as *Vigiles*?'

'*Vigiles*?'

'Yes.'

'I know of no such group.'

'That is the name of the body which Francis Bacton told his parents he had joined when he left the English College. Within the *Vigiles* he was being trained for the role of *Quaesitor* — an investigator of malpractices in the Church.'

Hernandes shook his head. 'These titles are unknown to me. Are you sure you are not pursuing the delusions of a young man who had lost his reason?'

'At the end — yes, he had lost his reason. But in what he told his parents, I fear he was only too sane.' It was the first time Antonia had heard him commit himself so fully to Bacton's story.

'I see.' Hernandes was staring into Fender's face as though there might be more to be read there than Fender had been willing to disclose. Then he nodded politely and turned to go.

While Hebden was seeing him out, Fender said, 'What did you think?'

'About Monsignor Hernandes?' She smiled. 'I shouldn't relish reporting my sins to him.'

'The story of the gloves had a curious effect on him.'

'I don't think Bacton went to one of their residences.'

He nodded reluctantly. 'And yet in what Bacton told his parents about the *Vigiles*, there are echoes of Opus Dei. The business of lay members who were to be called Co-operators — ' He began to fiddle with an ashtray on the table beside him; to add to his discontent, he had forgotten to bring his pipe. When Hebden returned, he said, 'John, is it possible there could be a small group of priests, answerable to someone very senior inside the Vatican, and charged with investigating scandalous conduct? Whose existence could be kept secret from people like Hernandes and yourself?'

Hebden shrugged. 'It's conceivable.' His voice was rather short. He crossed to the window. A sparrow was perched on the sill. From a tin he took some breadcrumbs and placed them before the bird. He smiled briefly at Antonia. 'My sub-tenant.' Seating himself opposite Fender, he said, 'Forgive me, Ludo, for saying this — but do you not think you should be more open with me?'

Fender stopped playing with the ashtray. He seemed chastened, in so far as it was ever possible for him. 'I must appear to you very discourteous. I had hoped to have some evidence from our visit here which would support the story before I gave it to you.' He paused. 'But could I press just two questions more before I explain?'

Hebden looked resigned. 'Go on.'

'Am I right that a priest, an American, who worked in the *Curia*, died in a swimming accident earlier this year?'

'Yes.'

'And that there was some scandal surrounding him?'

'I can only repeat rumour I heard afterwards — that he was involved in smuggling drugs.'

'As a result of his death, the risk that the scandal will become public is eliminated — or at least reduced — presumably.'

'I expect so.'

'My second question is this. Can you think of anyone else — apart from this American and Barralozzi — who has died

127

rather suddenly in recent times and was also about to cause a public scandal by his conduct?'

'In the Vatican?'

'Yes.'

Hebden reflected. 'One case perhaps: a Cardinal — there were a great many stories about the woman who accompanied him everywhere. But his death was not particularly sudden. He was an elderly man with a heart condition who died of a stroke. If half the stories were true one could hardly be surprised. It was certainly fortunate for the Church it happened when it did.'

Fender sat forward. 'If I told you there is a drug which if taken by an elderly person with a weak heart is almost certain to produce a fatal stroke and that traces of that drug were found in Barralozzi's body — would it give you pause in thinking of the Cardinal's death?'

'I would now like to hear your story,' Hebden said.

Through the window, wafer-edged clouds had streaked the sun. The sparrow had long departed. Hebden gazed down at the street below.

'What are your thoughts?' asked Fender.

'That you have conjured up a nightmare.'

'I'm sorry. I should like as much as you to find it's no more than that.'

'Have you considered that your pathologist might be wrong? It would not be the first time such a thing has happened. Suppose that, because of the decomposition of the body before he examined it, he made a mistake about the substance he found in Barralozzi — that it was not in reality a killer drug for a person with a heart condition after all. Without his evidence, would you be left with anything more than could be explained as the hallucinations of a sick mind?'

'You are not saying you're sure the story is untrue.'

'How could anyone?' Hebden threw open his arms. 'The conduct of some people in the Church has deeply troubled many priests in recent years. There will always be one or two, like this Spaniard, who become so obsessed with the evil they believe they see that it overbalances them. They may then

128

plunge into more evil in their effort to root it out. And if they are strong personalities, they will persuade others to join them.'

'The story goes deeper than that.'

'Yes.'

'Do you say the other part is impossible?'

'I cannot believe it. I would like to tell you it is impossible. But since I have lived here, there is a saying I have learned to respect.'

'What saying is that?'

' "In the Vatican, everything is forbidden — and everything is possible." No doubt your American journalist will be quoting that to you — if he has not done so already.' His voice was bitter.

He noticed Antonia smiling and shrugged. 'You must forgive my little paranoias. They are an occupational hazard here. Some of my colleagues blame the Russians for all our ills — that has always been fashionable. Others, like me, see journalists as Satan's principal agents. Their cynicism is much more corrosive than anything the Russians can do to us.' He sighed. 'Sooner or later, Ludo, you have to tell this story to someone more senior than I am.'

'I suppose so.'

'I could arrange an appointment with the Secretary of State.'

'We must certainly think about that.'

They had spoken the sentences without the eyes quite meeting. The words were not exactly empty; but they lacked conviction. Behind them there hung the thought that had tormented the Earl of Wadebury, brooding in his study at West Gurney with the bowl of decaying apple cores at his feet. Bad enough if the *Vigiles* were found to exist, of course. But the question that followed was far worse. To whom did they answer?

The room had darkened. Fender pulled himself wearily to his feet. 'Forgive us for having stayed so late. You can see how the *Vigiles* may hold the one key to the truth about the Ropners. I hope you will still discover a way to help us.' He carried his empty glass to the tray and paused with it in his hand. 'There is an oddity in the story I've just told you which you

129

haven't challenged — something that doesn't quite fit. It irks me.'

'What is that?'

'It concerns Rossano, the head of Laportex. I told you I believed the immediate cause of Bacton's suicide was reading of his death — because he recognized it as another of the *Vigiles'* cases, like Barralozzi and the American priest. But those two and the Cardinal you have just told me about differ from Rossano. They served in the Vatican — two of them in Holy Orders. They fit exactly with what Bacton said about the task of the *Vigiles*. But not Rossano, he was a businessman whose only connection with the Vatican seems to have been through building the hostel for pilgrims. So why was Rossano one of their interests?' Fender turned. 'Do you see what I mean? I know you said yesterday that Rossano was a crook. But there must be something more, a special reason for the *Vigiles* to pursue him, if my theory's right.'

Antonia saw Hebden's eyes slide away from Fender's face. When he replied, he was busying himself, collecting the other glasses. 'There *is* one thing I should add. Today I turned out some newspapers. One of them had an obituary of Rossano. Apparently he was well known for activities in support of the Church in Turin. But Hernandes could no doubt tell you more.'

'Why Hernandes?'

Hebden shrugged, a little too casually. 'Rossano seems to have been a member of Opus Dei.'

15

They had one more day before the rot set in.

'Sunday,' Fender said. 'How shall we spend our Sunday?' He put his head back to admire the sapphire sky through a tracery of vines. Before Antonia could say anything, he went on, 'I would like to take you to the gardens of the Villa d'Este.'

They were seated on the roof terrace having breakfast. Fender had been to Mass while Antonia was still in bed. Duly sanitized, he was ready for the role of the knowledgeable tourist. 'That sounds perfect,' she said. She went to change into flat-heeled shoes, telling herself it was best when he had his head.

From Trastevere's awakening odours, a taxi transported them at vast expense to a pavement café in Tivoli where Fender planned the itinerary with his guidebook. She had supposed that a gentle promenade through the gardens, punctuated by seated contemplation of watery vistas, would prove the limit of the expedition. Instead, she found herself relentlessly marched to every pond and waterfall, every spring and fountain, while Fender discoursed on the numbers of sprays and jets and the volume of water drawn to feed them from the obliging River Aniene.

Returning to the *pensione* through the dregs of the afternoon, spent but triumphant he said, 'Tomorrow your American will probably make touch. Then we shall see.' They dined in style on the strength of it.

But no one made touch. As Monday expired, a pall of doubt began to settle on them both. Not until late on the Tuesday afternoon was there a faint stirring: Harriet Ackerley's secretary telephoned to announce that the promised elucidation of the telephone numbers and addresses taken from Francis Bacton's diary was ready and could be collected.

Over their drinks before dinner, they combed the details provided; but the prospect that any clue to the missing months in Francis's life would emerge from these humdrum facts, suddenly seemed remote. They decided to show them to Hebden; still, there was a chance he would see something in the addresses that was hidden to their eyes, might even point meaningly to one of the twenty-three streets listed as possible answers to the riddle of 'V.d.L.'. But when Fender telephoned his office, he was greeted with the news that curial business had taken Hebden to Vienna until the end of the week. This time they drank brandy into the night to console themselves.

A call to Opus Dei's Rome office, for further information about Rossano's work in the organization had met with a bland refusal to comment. Worst of all, Stolz's telephone remained unanswered whenever Antonia tried the number. Desperation began to grip. There was no choice but to start on such of the addresses from the diary entries as warranted looking at on the ground.

As they were setting out on the Wednesday, Fender paused. 'I wonder if it is altogether sensible to assume there is nothing to be learnt at the English College? Someone might have bumped into Francis after he left.' He decided to go to see the Rector instead of accompanying Antonia. It seemed sensible enough; but she couldn't resist the reflection that he had the softer option.

When they met at dinner in the evening, she had had fruitless encounters with a clerical tailor, the matron of a refuge for the relatives of British priests who had lived and died in Rome and a spinster aunt of Francis Bacton's who shared an apartment on the Janiculum with three Siamese cats. Still uncrossed off were two addresses near the Termini railway station, someone named Zuccari in the Via Barilli, and a home for orphans in the Alban Hills.

Fender's own day seemed to have been less exhausting. He had been invited to stay for lunch at the English College. The Rector had been interesting on the subject of the life and practices of Heinrich Suso, about whom a new book had apparently been published; they had gone on well into the afternoon.

'Did you learn anything useful?' she asked, not even trying to keep the tartness out of her voice.

He shook his head gloomily. 'Only that he gave it all up in the end — the mortification.'

He had apparently missed seeing someone who had known Bacton well and was going back for another visit in the morning.

The following day she plodded doggedly to the two addresses near the station, only to discover they were both *pensioni*. When there was no reply to a telephone call to Signor

Zuccari in the Via Barilli, she decided that, for a few hours at least, she would withdraw her labour and discover if window-shopping felt more rewarding. She tried first the boutiques of the Via Condotti and Via Frattina, then moved to a reconnaissance of the Via del Babuino's art galleries. It was as she turned sharply on her heel to look again at the detail of a painting in a window that her first suspicion arose of being under surveillance.

A man, inconspicuous in appearance but with a face she found vaguely familiar, was walking towards her. As they passed, his eyes showed no flicker of interest. Something in that deliberate, almost ostentatious, indifference seemed wrong. She paused by the painting, wheeling slightly so that she could watch the man's progress. Twenty metres on, he also paused and looked into a shop window.

She walked on past him, took a left turn into the Via Vittoria and checked again. He was once more on the move. Ahead was a religious bookshop and she went in. Through the window she saw him pass without the smallest sideways glance. Amongst the books on the table by which she had stopped, she found herself confronted by a name she was beginning to know too well: Heinrich Suso, the purple dust-jacket announced. It was presumably the book of which Fender had been told at the English College. A black-suited shop assistant was hovering near her as she turned the pages, blocking her view as she tried to check the street for a possible reappearance of the man. The assistant was impressing on her the fascination of the subject, the grace of the prose, the distinction of the author: the hard sell had penetrated even religious bookshops in Rome, it seemed. She decided to surrender and buy the book. It would be interesting to discover whether her ability to read Italian had survived; amusing too, to blind Fender with the dazzle of her Suso knowledge.

Outside the shop again, she gazed carefully up and down. There was no sign of the man. She told herself that, craving something to end the nullity of recent days, her imagination had created a phantom. As a final check, she took a bus to the Villa Borghese to visit the Galleria. If she was being watched, she would surely pick the signs up there.

When she returned to the *pensione*, she had become convinced there had been no one behind her at any time. Fender was sitting in his room with the door open, waiting to pounce. 'Your American. Apparently he telephoned shortly before I returned. He left a message for you to ring him back as soon as possible.'

They went together to the telephone.

Stolz's voice sounded welcoming. Her hopes rose. 'I thought you'd gone away,' she said. 'I've been getting no reply from your number.' He apologized but gave no explanation. 'Have you any good news for me?'

'There's a piece of paper in my pocket that you ought to find interesting.'

'For me to keep?'

'If you'll have dinner with me.'

She smiled at Fender sitting opposite her, sombre brown eyes searching her face. 'Give me half an hour for a shower and change and I'll be on my way.'

She was almost out of the door of the *pensione* when she was called again to the telephone. It was Harriet Ackerley this time, not best pleased at having been summoned to the Embassy to take delivery of an Immediate cipher telegram that had turned out to be for Antonia.

'I take it you don't want me to read the text over the telephone since it's graded Secret,' she said.

'I'll come round now.'

'Perhaps you wouldn't mind hurrying — I'm due at a dinner party.'

She was behind her desk, reading the *Corriere della Sera*, when the security officer on duty at reception ushered Antonia into her room. This time she was wearing white silk polka dot pyjama trousers with a simple little top and a simple rope or two of pearls. She nodded silently, pointing to the telegram on the side of the desk.

It began 'For Strachan from Baxter'. Reading it, Antonia could see Baxter's smirk as the sentences rolled off his tongue into the tape recorder.

1. Director is concerned at absence of progress report. Meeting with PM scheduled for Friday evening. Please telegraph full account of results achieved to arrive no later than 1200 hours that day.

2. Reference suspected *Vigiles* agent: Barralozzi's lunch companion firmly identified as Stefan Weber, 28, Swiss, unemployed chemistry graduate at present lodging at 312a, Hauptstrasse, Murten, Switzerland. This is for information only — Director will decide whether action desirable *vis-à-vis* Weber in the light of your report and other developments here.

She glanced at the battery of telephones on a side table. 'May I make a call?'

Harriet Ackerley turned a page casually. 'Trouble with Golden Boy?'

'He's restive for news.'

'You'll have to watch out. He gets *very* physical when aroused. But perhaps you've discovered already.' She lifted her eyes from the newspaper. They were a flinty grey, rather fine.

There was an interminable delay before Fender came on the line. Apparently he had been in the bath. She read him a discreet précis of the message and listened to a grunting, mirthless laugh. 'Do you want me to come back with it now? I can ring Stolz to say I'll be late.'

'No, that's unnecessary. But tell me where Murten is.'

She was stumped. 'Hold on.' She tried the question on Harriet Ackerley.

'I think you'll find it's on the edge of the Murtensee about twenty-five kilometres west of Bern.'

Impressed, she relayed the information to Fender. He ruminated. 'I suppose it must be on a railway — these Swiss towns always are.'

'You're not thinking of going?'

'Possibly.'

'But if Stolz has come up with evidence that establishes the case against our man, there would be nothing to be gained.'

'You mean murder doesn't matter — ' He was deliberately avoiding her point.

Grimly she said, 'No, I was simply bearing in mind the extent of our brief and the fact that the telegram says — '

'Yes,' he said. 'Well, we'll have to see. You'd better be off to Stolz.'

She ground her teeth and rang off. Moving towards the door with the telegram in her bag she noticed a gazetteer still open on the top of a filing cabinet. Harriet Ackerley had seen her glance. 'Places I always remember, distances I like to check.' She didn't explain why she'd bothered to look.

The door of Stolz's apartment was opened by a balding Italian in a white jacket. He had a casual manner for which she decided she didn't much care. On the way through to the main reception room, they passed Stolz talking on the telephone about the deadline for some article he was writing. She accepted a Martini from the Italian and sat down beside a coffee table. In the centre of the table a flower holder had been placed. It contained a single Madame Hardy bloom.

When Stolz appeared, he said, 'Antonia Strachen — how very nice.' He still seemed taken with the sounds the name made. He was dressed more formally then the last time, in a dark blue lightweight suit with a tie to match. Holding his glass out to the Italian for a refill, he said, 'This is Franco who was away when you came last week. He puts me together in the morning and winds me up.' The Italian smiled, examining her legs as he poured Martini from the pitcher.

Sitting down beside her, Stolz asked, 'Progress?'

'Not much.'

He shook his head sympathetically. 'You had a tough assignment. Those guys in the Vatican never let anything out if they can avoid it. Ask the correspondents whose job it is to cover the place. And so far as Barralozzi's activities are concerned, you're faced with an even deader silence than usual.' He put his head back and studied the frescoed ceiling above them. 'What puzzles me is why your government didn't send you to talk to me at the beginning.'

'I can't answer that.'

'Didn't Rollo Pawson report at the time what I told him? Or is it your people just didn't want to know then?'

She gazed at him in silence, smiling.

'You're not going to tell me?'

'No.'

He sighed. 'Well, maybe I'll know one day. Meanwhile — ' he felt in the inside pocket of his jacket — 'strictly for your sake and not the British Government's, here is a little gift. Just don't ask how I got it.' He took out two folded photocopies, stapled together, and handed them to her.

The top copy showed the front and reverse of an envelope postmarked in London and addressed in a neat hand to Barralozzi at what was presumably his private address in Rome. The other was of a single sheet of notepaper headed 11, Downing Street and dated, like the envelope, about eighteen months earlier. The letter was written in the same neat hand.

My dear Aldo,

Alida passed me your kind message when she returned from Rome last night. Thank you for your congratulations which I gladly accept, although it has been one of those occasions when a Chancellor can only point the way; the backing of colleagues and officials is really what matters. But — yes, it was a very successful operation with which to end some dreadful days. I am happy at the thought that the institutions and individuals who were going short of sterling so enthusiastically have had a bloody nose. They will not forget it in a hurry.

As for our little concurrent venture, we feel agreeably *fortified* by the outcome! None of it would have been possible of course without your help. I hope you found the occasion equally profitable.

Come and see us soon and we will drink to it all in your favourite champagne. Or perhaps in this instance it should be Coca-Cola!

> With best wishes,
> Yours ever,
> Charles

She took a drink from her glass, trying not to look disappointed.

Stolz said, 'There's a detail you need to know. Some of the stock that Barralozzi made available on loan to Alida Ropner was in the Coca-Cola Bottling Company.'

'There's no chance, I suppose, of your getting another photocopy which will establish *that*?'

'None, there wouldn't be a record. He wouldn't have been such a fool.'

She grimaced and was conscious of Stolz looking at her in a half-amused, half-resigned way. 'I'm sorry,' she said, 'I'm being greedy.'

He grinned. 'Just a little. But unnecessarily, I suggest. Would you care to be in Ropner's shoes and find yourself being asked to explain that last paragraph?'

'We can use the letter in whatever way we choose except as legal evidence?'

'Provided you don't reveal that I obtained it for you — yes. But I'm relying on you keeping my identity secret.' He put his hand on hers.

She was conscious that she had been churlish in her reception of the letter. 'Forgive me, I must have appeared ungrateful. Of course, you have my promise.'

She placed the letter in her handbag beside Baxter's telegram. Through the open doors to the terrace came the pealing of bells across the city as they chimed the hour, a disorderly tumbling of sound. Gently, Stolz took her hand and led her outside. 'Come and listen.'

It was a universe of golden light and sounding bronze. On a flat rooftop far below them, a man in a practice suit working on ballet steps stopped suddenly. A woman wearing a bright yellow headband had joined him. They were drinking from a bottle of wine.

Stolz pointed to the nearest campanile. 'An owl lives in that tower. I've never seen him. But late at night, when the traffic noise has gone, I hear him call. Sometimes I reply.'

'Perhaps you're his only friend.'

He turned towards her. 'Are you married?'

'Not now, he was killed in an accident. Are you?'

138

'Sort of —'

'Sort of?'

'We can't meet often — Because of circumstances. It's rather complicated. I shall see her again at the end of August.' As though to pre-empt more questions, he went on, 'Do you not want to re-marry?'

'At times, yes.'

'What about your Ludovic Fender — would *he* do?'

She smiled. 'A little on the mature side. Also too maddening. I should certainly put ground glass in his coffee one morning.'

'What will he be doing at this precise moment? Eating a lonely dinner and wondering about you?'

She reflected. 'I have an awful fear that he is planning to take a train somewhere tomorrow morning.'

'I thought you were supposed to be working in harness.'

'Yes. But there is a mystery which happens to fascinate him. He can't let things go — he has to discover *everything*.' She spread her hands resignedly and laughed.

'If you try to discover everything, you end up knowing nothing,' he said. 'You ought to persuade him of that.'

'I wouldn't even begin to try.'

Franco appeared on the terrace. Stolz glanced inquiringly at him, then turned back to Antonia. 'Franco is hinting we ought to go. Otherwise we run the risk our table will be taken by a couple of cardinals out for a night's plotting.'

As they went down in the lift she said, 'I didn't understand that — why cardinals particularly?'

'We're going to a French restaurant called L'Eau Vive. Most of those who eat there have some connection with the Vatican — it's run by a missionary order with some quite cute girls as waitresses. I like to go occasionally to see who's conspiring with whom. We must be careful not to stay too late or we may have to sing a hymn. But I'm quite sure you'll like the food.'

Their table was in the opposite corner to a statue of the Virgin. Antonia gazed round the room: they seemed to be surrounded not by clerics but *glitterati*. 'Show me a cardinal,' she said.

139

Stolz stood up the better to survey the patrons and sat down again, shaking his head. 'It must be "Dallas" night.' He had adopted a mock-serious manner which she had come to recognize as one of his tricks.

As their wine was being poured, she said, 'I thought financial and economic affairs were your speciality.'

'That's right.'

'You seem more interested in the Vatican.'

'It's hard to resist when you've been in Rome a while. All those old men jostling for power! When they come here, I wonder if it ever occurs to them that the price of their bottle of wine would feed a family for a week in some countries?' He gestured towards the other tables. 'Is this really where they think they ought to be?'

'It's not as simple as that.'

He ignored her remark. 'Se Cristo vedesse — if only Christ could see.' When she looked puzzled, he went on, 'Vatican car plates have the initials SCV for Stato Città Vaticano. But that's not what they're really saying.'

His eyes were very dark. For the moment he had lost the laid-back manner, the air of disengagement she had thought of as his strongest characteristic. She watched him for a while. 'I can see they're not going to like your book at all.'

He sat forward. 'I have a story coming together now which makes everything else about that place seem trivial. You can forget about cardinals' women and crooked finance and all the other stuff the hacks on the mass circulations keep peddling. What I have is going to waste them all. Right up to the Pope.'

'You can't whet my appetite like that without telling me more.'

He grinned. 'Sorry. You'll just have to wait until the book comes out.'

As they were leaving, she spotted a Cardinal's red cap Stolz had somehow missed; or perhaps it had arrived since his inspection of the patrons. Beneath the cap was a face of parchment pallor, delicate and very old. A young priest was seated opposite, talking earnestly. As Antonia and Stolz passed the table, the Cardinal smiled at something the other had said and

140

patted his arm gently. His manner conveyed a kindliness that was totally unaffected.

Outside she said to Stolz, 'Who was that?'

'I forget his name — one of the curial cardinals.'

'And you're going to waste *him*?'

'Probably.'

'He's a *good* man — you can see that. Is that so unimportant in the balance?'

He took her hand. 'You're spoiling the book.'

Refusing a taxi, they walked the streets back to the Corso and rose in the wheezing lift. Franco was no longer visible but a coffee pot was on a low burner beside the terrace doors. A faint perfume came from the flowers. Seated among the darkened bushes, they drank the coffee.

'Will you go back to the States when your book is finished?' she asked.

He shrugged. 'I'm not sure. Probably not. London maybe — the political and economic scene there is interesting. Where shall I look for an apartment if I come?'

'St James's would suit you. Hideously expensive of course. But if you can afford this apartment, that ought to be no problem.'

He looked back through the terrace doors. 'Don't judge by what you see. I have to make a show.' He was, for some reason, embarrassed.

She looked at her wrist-watch but before she could speak, he said, 'Stay — you haven't heard my friend, the owl.'

She stood up and gazed across to the campanile. Stolz moved to her side and she felt him kiss her neck. 'He has a message.'

'For me?'

'I was to deliver it if he wasn't around.'

She raised her eyebrows.

'He would like you to sleep with me.'

'Did he suggest that as the price for the letter?'

'No, I told him you couldn't be bought.'

She laughed.

'Will you?' he asked.

'I might start to think of your wife.'

'We have an understanding. She sleeps with someone else.'

She shook her head. 'I'm sorry. Making love on the wing somehow doesn't work for me. Owls should understand that.' She kissed his cheek.

He sighed. 'So I must come to London.'

'That would be nice.' She reached for her bag. 'Could you get me a taxi?'

As he opened the door of the cab for her he said, 'You won't leave Rome without saying goodbye — '

'I promise.' She reached through the window and kissed him, briefly, not wishing to discover reasons for changing her mind. But as she rode back to Trastevere, she was remembering his mouth and hands, and regretted them.

16

Picking up Ropner's letter to Barralozzi, Fender went to the window to push the shutters wider apart. The sky was covered with cloud, for the first time since their arrival in Rome. In an apartment opposite, he could see a woman drawing up, from someone in the street below, a basket of groceries attached to a rope. He needed time to think but Antonia's presence in the room somehow made that difficult. Her arrival at this early hour, before he had completed those rituals, from teeth brushing to examination of eye-whites, which formed a necessary overture to his days, had caught him off balance. Moreover he had expected to have more time in which to decide how to tell her of the decision he had reached.

'What do you think?' she asked.

He read it through again. 'So nearly enough. A few words more and there would be no room for doubt.'

'You believe it might still have some other meaning?'

'No.' He repeated the word more strongly as his own conviction grew. 'No, I don't. But he might still claim it did and get away with it, in circumstances where this was the only evidence.'

'The Prime Minister may have to find a way of dropping him without a confrontation — one that doesn't leave the door open for Ropner to stage a come-back later.'

'Easier said than done.'

The smell of coffee, mingled with exhaust fumes, reached his nostrils from outside. He moved to the telephone. 'I'll ask them to bring breakfast here so that we can talk about what to say to London.'

When he had placed the order, he asked, 'Did Stolz give any hint how he'd laid his hands on this?'

'No. I rather assumed it was his American Embassy contact.'

'Who must have a source in the Vatican Bank — probably Barralozzi's private secretary — '

'Probably.'

'Whoever it was must have heard things as well as seen them. Difficult to believe he or she couldn't tell us more.'

'But if it *is* from the Embassy contact we stand no chance.'

Fender nodded, sighing. 'I suppose we should consider ourselves fortunate to get even this much. Stolz must have pulled out the stops.'

'I think he did.'

'And he asked for nothing in return?'

'Only that his identity as the person who'd provided it should be protected.'

'Unusual generosity for a journalist. *And* American at that.' He raised his eyes to study her face. 'You must have cast quite a spell.'

He didn't look away when their eyes met. He saw a faint flush appear in her cheeks. He wondered if she had slept with Stolz. If she had, she wasn't going to let him know. No reason why she should, it wasn't his business. He was conscious of his nails biting into the palms of his hands. He hated the idea, wanted it not to be true.

'What's your view of Stolz now?' he asked.

'I like him. He's also very well informed.'

'Perhaps I ought to meet him.'

'Why not?' she said.

The waiter knocked on the door with the breakfast tray and she went to open it. 'His views on the Vatican would interest you. They're pretty hostile. He claims to be researching a story that is more sensational than anything that has been published yet and which reaches right up to the Pope.'

He raised his eyebrows. 'The *Vigiles*?'

'I wondered that. But there seemed no way of discovering without admitting something of what we know.'

He poured out coffee and offered her the basket of *cornetti*. 'Tempting to probe him — '

She smiled. 'I'll leave that to you. I've done my bit.'

She hadn't slept with Stolz, he told himself. He was conscious of a foolish relief. He reached for the dish of jam. 'I suppose we'd better address our minds to drafting a telegram to London.'

She took two sheets of paper from her bag. 'I roughed something out when I woke up.' She placed them beside his plate. 'London's telegram to us is pinned underneath.'

Reluctantly he fumbled in his pocket for reading glasses; her efficiency threatened to become intimidating.

For Baxter. Your telegram arrived while result of approach to source of original Bank of England information was awaited. Any earlier report to you would have been pointless.

1. Source has given us photocopy of private letter sent to Barralozzi by male subject of inquiry and written on official notepaper 18 months ago. It contains phraseology which while not directly referring to successful currency speculation acknowledges Barralozzi's help in unspecified transaction that was evidently very profitable. Photocopy is being despatched by bag today together with source's account of how Barralozzi enabled subjects of inquiry to finance their speculation and his explanation of phrase in letter which appears particularly damning.

2. Source is clearly well informed on Barralozzi's activities and also appears to have excellent access, direct and indirect, to Vatican generally. He is now engaged on writing book

which he says will expose a number of high-level scandals, including mishandling by Barralozzi of securities deposited in bank for safe-keeping. In supplying us with copy letter and other information he has made condition to which we have agreed that his identity should not be disclosed at any time. We have also agreed that letter will only be used as basis for confrontation.

3. We are continuing to follow up one or two separate lines of inquiry based on Bacton's diary entries in hope they will yield further corroborative evidence.

Fender nodded. 'I think that will do splendidly — splendidly — with perhaps just one small addition.' He reached out and took the pen she held in her hand and wrote at the bottom of her draft.

4. Your reference to details of Barralozzi's lunch companion being for information only is noted. Unfortunately inquiries already on foot are now likely to make early meeting with Weber unavoidable. We shall handle this with great care. Need to ensure there is no prejudice to Director's future freedom of action will of course be borne in mind.

He watched Antonia's face tighten as she read it. She looked up finally. 'Is that — quite accurate?'

'Near enough.'

'I mean about a meeting with Weber being unavoidable.'

'In a sense.'

'So you've decided to go to Murten.'

He smiled cheerfully. 'Yes. I've made a reservation on a train for Bern today. I shall be able to get a connection on to Murten tomorrow morning.'

He could see her struggling with her feelings. Eventually she said, 'I'm sorry, but I don't see how it can be justified. Or how any interview can be carried out with Weber which doesn't risk putting him to flight — assuming it *was* Weber who administered the drug to Barralozzi.'

'I think I can manage that problem.' He poured her more coffee. 'Remember, we don't have watertight evidence against the Ropners yet. Weber could provide the clue that leads us to that.'

That was true enough. But it wasn't the whole truth. He knew he was taking a gross advantage of her loyalty. 'You feel very strongly it's wrong to do this?'

Instead of answering she asked, 'When will you be back?'

'Not later than Sunday I hope. I'll telephone you from Bern or Murten.' When she avoided his eyes, he went on, 'Put "From Fender" in front of that paragraph. Then it will be clear it has nothing to do with you.'

She nodded briefly. 'I'd better leave you to get ready. I'm still in the middle of drafting a note of what Stolz said the first time we met. It can go in the bag with the letter if I hurry. I'll show it to you if you haven't gone by then.'

'What will you do while I'm away?'

'I'll finish checking out the addresses in the diary.' She gathered up the papers she had brought. Her second cup of coffee was untouched. 'If there's another telegram from London in the meantime, I suppose you leave any action to my judgement.' Their relations were at lowest ebb.

He called to her when she was at the door so that she had to turn. 'I understand why you disagree with what I'm doing. I hope you'll forgive me. Quite apart from the Ropners, getting to the bottom of the rest of the Bacton story has become very important to me. Please try to understand my feelings — as a Catholic.'

She nodded. There was the merest trace of a return of the warmth he had come to depend on. 'I wish you luck.'

The booking-office clerk at Murten station stepped outside his office to point Fender in the direction of the town. '*Sehen Sie da, Philosophenweg.*'

He could hardly believe he'd heard the word correctly until he saw it confirmed by the street sign: there it was, boldly displayed. 'Philosophenweg.' In crisp morning sunlight he walked up the hill, smiling. Fellow-philosophers were working in their gardens as he passed; one swept the pavement in front of his house with a small brush and pan.

Music greeted him as he entered the Hauptstrasse. From the direction of a clock-tower which straddled the street at its far end, a band was marching, men and women in shirts and

146

sashes and silk-braided hats, their eyes fixed solemnly on the way ahead. There were no banners, no evident signs of festival. From the arcaded pavements on both sides of the street, passers-by clapped discreet encouragement.

He watched until the procession was out of sight, glancing now and then at those beside him. Amongst these sober citizens of Murten, perhaps Herr Weber himself was also standing, proud *Ultor* in a braided hat, applauding the local band.

No. 312a was between a grocer and a pharmacy. On a heavy wooden door, a name plate baldly announced 'Kohl'. Fender summoned up rusting German and rang the bell.

Several bolts and locks were manipulated before a middle-aged woman in apron and slippers appeared. He took off his hat. 'Am I right, madam, that Herr Weber lives here?'

'No.'

'No?'

She shook her head, unsmiling. The features must once have been handsome but had become set in sternness. She bore, like an emblem, a permanent look of disapproval. 'He left in the evening yesterday.'

'Can you tell me where I can find him?'

'He did not give the address where he was going. I cannot help you.'

It was a major blow. But if he allowed himself to dwell on the fact now, she would have the door closed on him. He summoned up what he hoped was a winning smile. 'Frau Kohl — it is Frau Kohl?'

She nodded, unimpressed.

'I am a lawyer from London. My firm has been trying to trace Herr Weber because he is a very substantial beneficiary under a will. I had learned this was where he was living and hoped to give him the news of his good fortune today. It seems we are faced with the problem of tracing him again. I should be most grateful if I could take your advice as someone who saw him so recently.'

He watched her expression relax slightly. Once more an ancient maxim was proving its truth: mention of the acquisition of wealth, even by a third party, was never uninteresting.

She led him upstairs to a room with a beamed ceiling and

147

cream plaster walls and a handsome floor of pine set in an oak surround. They were now at the back of the house; through the windows he could see the ramparts of Murten town wall. Frau Kohl sat opposite him across a round table, on which was a bowl of plastic fruit. He began, 'Perhaps you can tell me the circumstances in which Herr Weber left you.'

'It was very sudden. He had planned to be here until at least the end of the month.'

'He was your tenant?'

'Yes.'

'What caused him to change his mind about staying?'

She reached to smooth a wrinkle in a lace mat under the bowl of fruit. He sensed that she was, reluctantly, beginning to thaw. 'There was a telephone call, something important. He told me he had to go immediately to join a friend.'

'Do you know where the call was from?'

'From Italy. It came through in the afternoon while Herr Weber was out. The person who spoke asked that when he came back he should call a number urgently. I was to tell him it was his friend Felipe.'

His hopes soared. 'You took down the number — '

She nodded. 'I gave it to Herr Weber when he came back. He went to the post office to telephone so that the charge would not be on my account. When he returned he told me he must leave at once.'

'Can you remember what the number was?'

She shrugged. 'I paid no attention.'

'Could he have left your note of the number in his room perhaps?'

'No, I have already cleaned it. The note was not there.'

She was at her happiest offering negatives, a Molotov of a woman. He ground his teeth but managed a sigh. 'Without the number, the chances of Herr Weber hearing about his legacy seem very small. I'm sure he would be most grateful to you, if you could remember it.'

Frau Kohl frowned. 'It is possible that I wrote it on another piece of paper first, a newspaper.' She was fighting a rearguard action against sounding hopeful. 'But it will have been placed with the rubbish.'

148

'I would naturally not wish to give you the trouble of searching through rubbish yourself, but if you will show me —'

She rose abruptly; it was clear that the idea of him in her rubbish made her shudder. 'Please wait.' She went out, closing the door behind her.

He found it difficult to remain still. If Frau Kohl returned empty-handed, his journey would have proved useless. He tried concentrating on the photographs of her forebears in their carved wooden frames on a sideboard. As he would have forecast, none was smiling. Above their heads hung a tapestry into which a religious text was woven. There was another text on the opposite wall. Herr Weber had chosen a God-fearing household in which to rest between labours.

She returned in a mood that for her was almost mellow. He saw, with renewed hope, that she was warmed by success in her search. Between her fingers was a crumpled piece of newspaper on the margin of which was written a telephone number. Placing it in his notecase he thanked her ornately. 'Herr Weber will be much in your debt.'

As she was conducting him down the stairs to the street door, he asked how Weber had come to her.

'He was sent by the Tourist Office. He explained he had been living in Sion and was having a holiday before taking up an appointment in Geneva.'

'Did he ever speak of a visit to London earlier in the year?'

'No, he was very quiet and spoke little. He spent much of his time walking and reading the Bible. A very devout man.'

He nodded. 'A zealot, perhaps?'

She was impressed by his use of the word. '*Ja, vielleicht.*' She opened the door and stood back for him to squeeze past her apron. '*Ja, ein wirklicher Zelot.*'

He made his way slowly back along the Hauptstrasse. It had been a near thing to almost total failure. True, the visit had provided the first direct evidence of a link between Weber and the Spanish priest, Felipe. But without the recovery of the telephone number from the rubbish, his return to Rome and Antonia's questioning gaze would have been humiliating.

Seeing a post office, he went in to check the locality of the telephone number. The code turned out to be for Todi which he vaguely remembered as being well north of Rome. Presumably that was where Felipe had re-established his *Vigiles*. It seemed an inconvenient choice if he was really hoping to keep abreast of goings-on in the Holy City. But perhaps Francis Bacton's defection had persuaded him of the need to lie low for a while.

What needed to be considered before anything else, however, were the implications of Weber's disappearance only hours before his own arrival in Murten. Coincidence could surely be ruled out. Someone interested in protecting the *Vigiles* must have known about his journey. Felipe had been warned in time to put a telephone call through to Weber when he himself was actually on the train to Bern. But how could that be, when the only person who had known he was making the trip, and why, was Antonia?

He had come to the end of the Hauptstrasse and found himself opposite a small public garden. Through a screen of shrubs could be glimpsed a giant's chess set arrayed for combat. Entering the garden, Fender found that, within a gravelled portion, a chess-board had been created, with benches for spectators to watch the game. At either end, the chess pieces stood in their neat rows, waiting for the philosophers to arrive in search of relaxation. No one was there now, except for a woman seated on one of the benches, with a small boy of four or five beside her.

Fender took a bench on the other side and brooded. The Ackerley woman had been with Antonia when she telephoned him from the Embassy. She would have known the contents of the telegram from London and might — just might — have deduced from the interest he was showing in the location of Murten that he was thinking of going there. But why should that be anything to her? Whatever chicanery she might be pursuing in her twilight world, it could surely not stretch to acting as guardian angel to the *Vigiles*?

There seemed only one possibility left: Antonia's call had been monitored by someone who had also heard his later calls when he checked on train times to Bern and on to Murten. That meant a tap on the telephone at the *pensione*. The obvious candidates were the Italian police or the intelligence people. But he had given them no cause to be tapping his calls and they were as unlikely as the Ackerley woman to wish to protect Weber and the *Vigiles*. The Vatican perhaps? If the *Vigiles* really did enjoy favour at the highest level there and his reasons for being in Rome had become known — perhaps through Hernandes talking to someone in the *Curia* about their meeting — it might have been decided that an eye must be kept on what he was doing. But even in these days of terrorism and assassination attempts against the Pope, it was difficult to imagine telephone interception had become part of the Holy Father's armoury; certainly not outside the Vatican itself. That left only the *Vigiles* themselves. Yet whatever aspirations the Spanish priest might have for his mini-Inquisition in the future, surveillance of that sort somehow didn't fit into the picture Francis Bacton had painted.

Whoever it had been, there was no more to be discovered in Murten. Fender took out the train timetable he had collected in Bern. It was too late for him to hope to catch the afternoon express back to Rome. That left the night sleeper. While it would arrive at an unattractively early hour tomorrow, at least, emanating from this country of still immaculate and civilized trains, it offered the prospect of a good dinner and a fair night's rest.

He had almost settled on it when the thought of the Todi telephone number returned. He examined the map in the back of the timetable. From Orvieto, on the main line to Rome, there seemed to be some sort of branch connection with Todi. It seemed a pity not to stop off and see what more he could discover. It would probably not add more than a day to his trip. On the other hand, perhaps it was unreasonable to leave Antonia alone in Rome, coping with whatever diktats Antrim might be cabling in his absence.

Unable to make up his mind, he decided to leave the choice open for a while. He rose from his bench and walked across to the waiting chess pieces. An urge to discover how heavy they were had gripped him. His audience was now three; a man in shoes of bright orange suede had seated himself at the end of the bench occupied by the woman and the small boy. Fender advanced a couple of pawns, then took one from the rear with its own bishop; the pieces seemed to be made of plastic with metal weights inserted into their bases. The three spectators watched him with stolid interest.

As he left the garden he saw from the corner of his eye that the woman had despatched the small boy to restore the situation. The man in the orange shoes had risen as though to supervise. With great care the boy replaced the pieces in their former positions so that no one should know a vandal had been there.

Seated in his sleeping compartment, Fender sniffed cautiously at the neck of the bottle of wine he had purchased in the buffet at Milan station. Too late for remedial action, he had discovered that the dining-car no longer existed. Hurrying to the buffet he had reviewed with distaste the snacks offered and settled for the wine, a packet of biscuits and the consolations of self-pity; this was yet another sign of the receding tide of civilization, like the felt-tip scrawls in the lavatory and the radio pulsing from the compartment next door.

He hung up his jacket and filled the wine glass, which the conductor had produced from the recesses of his cabin. By now Antrim would have read Antonia's telegram but could not have seen the Ropner letter; presumably that would reach him on Monday, the day after tomorrow. It would be a notable trophy to dangle before the Prime Minister. But the latter was unlikely to be satisfied. Whatever suspicions that final paragraph might seem to strengthen, he would see at once it was not, by itself, the weapon for chopping off Ropner's head. More evidence would be demanded.

So Antrim was almost certain to telegraph that further efforts must be made. That might incidentally help to repair his own relations with Antonia. If Stolz was not going to come up with anything more, she would have to acknowledge that their only chance lay in running the *Vigiles* to earth and discovering the information they had collected.

He had begun to unpack his pyjamas when a knock came at the door. He opened it, expecting to see the conductor, but was confronted instead by a woman in jeans and T-shirt. She was perhaps thirty, with earnest eyes and short-cut hair that needed washing. In a rush she said, in German, 'Excuse me, but the conductor believes you are English. Is that so?'

He nodded.

'We have in the next coach an English lady who is sick.'

'I'm afraid I'm not a doctor.'

She shook her head. 'It is only that she is trying to ask for something and we cannot understand. Could you please come?'

He turned and reached for his jacket on the hanger. Only when he heard the door click again, did he realize there was something wrong about the visitation. Swinging round, he found the woman had disappeared. She had been replaced by two men as tall as himself but a good deal more athletic. He had no time to see more before the first man grabbed him and kneed him savagely in the stomach. As he stumbled, gasping for breath, they were on him, thrusting him back on to the bed. The neck of a bottle was forced between his lips and cognac flooded his throat until he gagged and felt it spurting down his cheek and neck. He was hit again, this time across the jaw, hard enough to daze him. Raising his head briefly he glimpsed through a haze the orange suede shoes of the larger man and knew it was not the first time that day their paths had crossed. Then a rug, or something similar, was wrapped tightly round his head and he was being dragged off the bed and through the door into the corridor.

He could guess what was in store but was powerless to resist or even to shout through the rug; he could only brace himself for the drop. Even with the material muffling his ears, the noise when the door was opened seemed deafening. There was a pause: the two men seemed to be waiting for some particular section of the track. Then the rug was removed. For a few seconds, stacked on his knees as though in prayer, he confronted a rushing, shouting darkness. Outside was eternity's black hole and no heaven or hell to break his fall. The push, when it came, was gentle compared with their earlier attentions. He shouted once. Then he was gone, over and over into the void.

17

On this visit to the Embassy, it seemed she was to be spared the laser scrutiny of the Ackerley Woman as Fender called her. The Ambassador's morning prayers were over-running and immediately afterwards another conference would require her presence; Heather, her secretary, bringing this news to Antonia at the Embassy reception desk, offered the welcome prospect of effecting despatch of letter and telegram to London unmonitored.

Large-boned and cheerful, blue velvet ribbon coyly binding Alice in Wonderland hair, she led Antonia to her own room and found a chair beside the coffee machine for her to sit on. Alongside the typewriter on her desk was a snapshot of a tortoise, slotted unevenly into a silver frame: a riposte perhaps to the studio portrait of the cat in the Ackerley sanctum. 'Edgar,' Heather said. 'My favourite man.' She began to type out the telegram, fingers devoid of any symbol of further commitment.

Antonia drank coffee, while waiting to read over the telegram. Through the window, the sky was changing: the early cloud had broken up, its scattered wisps evaporating fast into an all-conquering blue. Heather paused, unscrewing her Tipp-Ex bottle. 'It's going to be super but terribly hot.'

'Do you think so? I was on my way to try to find a Signor Zuccari who has a house in the Via Barilli where nobody ever answers the telephone. Or there's a place in the Alban Hills I ought to visit. Perhaps I should go there this morning.'

'Oh, definitely the Hills!' Heather sat back, the better to enthuse. 'Super place! If you've got walking shoes here you could climb Monte Cavo. You can see for seventy miles from the top. And there are the two lakes — I can tell you of a terribly good trattoria on Lake Albano for lunch — oodles of delicious fish.'

Impossible to respond to that with polite evasive noises; in any case, the prospect was seductive. 'Right,' she said, 'To the Hills!' and took advice on where to hire a car.

Setting out with map and walking shoes on the seat beside her, she glanced at her watch and thought, with only faint rancour now, of Fender, entrained and heading north for a different set of hills. If this orphanage, with a telephone number Bacton had found reason to note in his diary beneath that of his aunt with the Siamese cats, this grandly named Istituto S. Giovanni dei Colli Albani, proved against the odds to be the lair of the *Vigiles*, confronting Fender on his return would yield an agreeable triumph. But it hardly seemed a likely scenario.

Negotiating the noon traffic in the centre of Rome took more time than she had expected. When finally clear of the city, she abandoned her plan to go direct to the orphanage and drove instead to Heather's trattoria for lunch. At the side of the building, a small garden overlooked the lake. She chose a table beneath an umbrella, beside the trattoria wall. The breeze off the water gently lifted her hair and her mood. Rome might be baking now, but here it was a perfect balance of sun and whispering shadow. In this moment she was glad to be alone, ready even to be sanguine about all the moments in the future when she might still be alone. Her confidence, mauled by the disastrous day of the visit to West Gurney and by Antrim's decision to bring in Fender to run the investigation, had without her noticing it, recovered. After all, the progress that had been made since their arrival in Rome, was due to her alone. No longer valuing Antrim's approbation, even despising him now, she still wished he could know that. She conjured the spectacle of him, confronted by her in his office and forced to acknowledge it; having to admit through his teeth he had been wrong not to leave the inquiries in her hands; even perhaps begging her to take over as head of one of the investigation sections. Then would be the opportunity to tell him that such an offer was the last thing she would consider, that she was in fact resigning — resigning because the Bureau, now that he was Director, had become a place where expediency was the watchword and trimming the only style.

But after that intoxicating encounter would come the moment of truth. There would be nowhere to go. Certainly not to the police: someone from the Bureau, and a woman at that, would scarcely get a welcome there. The Civil Service too were hardly likely to want her, at least at any salary she could live on. The intelligence and security people might take her in; but she had to reckon with Antrim's past association with that world. He would surely block her chances of being accepted for all except the most junior jobs.

She gazed down at the roses beside her table. There was blackfly on them. Down in Shropshire the blackfly would still be feasting too, no doubt. For the first time since she had gone to Ottawa with Fender on the Stradbrook investigation, she had escaped from the web of family for a whole week, been spared those plucked emotions as the telephone minutes ticked by. It would be waiting for her when she got back: there was no resigning from that. Antrim could be told to go to hell, but not the web.

The waiter came with the wine she had chosen; he was flat-footed and old and courtly. 'Not sad, signora, best Frascati wine, you drink.' He waited, smiling, while she lifted a glass to her lips. She drank. When he at once refilled the glass and waited again, she laughed, and he said truly, 'No more sad.'

After lunch, gazing through a wine haze at Cavo's peak, she decided without hesitation that the walking shoes had been simply a token of goodwill; the view from the summit for seventy miles could wait for another day, even for ever. Putting her head back against the wall beside her, she let the garden's warmth embrace her and dozed.

Perched on the southern slopes of Monte Cavo, with a view that took in Lake Albano, the Istituto S. Giovanni dei Colli Albani proved easy to find, its orange walls visible for several kilometres along the road from Grottaferrata. It was difficult to imagine what the architect had had in his mind; or perhaps the money had run short in the middle of building. For roughly half the façade, it was an imitation castle with towers

156

and battlements. The remainder, together with the sides, was totally plain and had a barracks-like air. To the front was a weed-infested lawn with evergreen shrubs and a single antique cannon standing on a marble base. The area immediately inside the iron gates which gave access from the road, had been asphalted and children of varying ages were playing there in sex-assorted groups. A narrow path continued the entrance drive beyond the orphanage building and up the hillside to end at another smaller building. This had no martial trimmings, was self-confidently domestic, a large villa with a terrace along its sides.

A middle-aged woman detached herself from one of the groups of children and came towards Antonia as she opened the entrance gate. '*Si? Desidera Signora?*'

Antonia launched into the laborious Italian of her, by now, standard opening. 'Forgive me, have you a group of holy fathers living in the Institute?'

The woman laughed a little bitterly. 'In the Institute? No, that would be quite impossible! Some of the children have to sleep in the corridors, we have so little room.' She was appraising Antonia as she spoke. 'You are English?'

'Is it so easy to tell?'

The woman shrugged. Even standing in full sun, she had a shawl drawn tightly about her shoulders. She changed to speaking in an English that had hardly a trace of accent. 'I am used to recognizing these things. Before I came to the Institute I was a teacher in a language school. And, after all, you look English.' She laughed again, a pleasant, graceful woman, still beautiful, even though the features had given up the struggle to hold fatigue at bay. 'Was it Father Rodrigues you were hoping to see?'

'I'm sorry — I understood — '

'Not in the Institute. Up there in the villa,' she pointed to the house higher on the hillside. 'That is their place.'

Her spirits leapt. 'So the villa is not part of the Institute?'

The woman made a grimace which was both weary and philosophical. 'It's a complicated story. Years ago, before we came here, this house and the villa were built by the father of Signor Maderno who now owns all the property. The father

157

was interested in the care of orphans — he had been one himself. When he was old, Cardinal Lanciani, who was then the parish priest of the village down there, persuaded him to allow the Institute to use the house. He went to live in the villa himself and when he died we were allowed to take that over as well. Some of the staff lived in it. Last year Signor Maderno came to tell me we could no longer have the villa. He said he had decided to allow it to be used by some priests as a retreat. Since we are dependent on him for almost everything, we had no choice but to move out.'

Antonia nodded in sympathy. 'I'm sorry. Perhaps you will get it back one day.'

'Perhaps.'

'Did you meet an English priest among them earlier this year? His name was Father Bacton.'

The woman shook her head. 'No. Apart from Father Ligorio, who brought us vegetables once or twice, only Father Rodrigues, who was the director, called at the Institute. He was a Spaniard. He often used our telephone because there is no line to the villa and would stay to talk to the children. The others never came. We saw them when they went walking of course. But they would never stop. Even Father Rodrigues talked very little to us. The only person who went there was the old woman who cleaned for them.'

A chill had begun to rise from the words as Antonia listened; the prize, proffered only moments before, was being withdrawn.

'Are they no longer there?'

'They went away nearly two months ago. One day they were here, the next — gone.'

'And you have no idea where they went?'

'None. Probably back to Rome — Father Rodrigues said to me once that they were living there until Signor Maderno made the villa available. He told the old woman who cleaned that he would send her a message through the Institute when she was to get the villa ready again.'

It all fitted — the air of secrecy, Rodrigues' nationality, even the fact of their leaving suddenly at about the time Francis Bacton had made his break with them; fearing Bacton might talk, Rodrigues would probably have reasoned it would be prudent to leave the villa for a while. And the fact that the Institute had the only telephone would have been the reason Bacton had recorded the number in his diary.

'Could you give me Signor Maderno's address? Perhaps he would be able to tell me where they have gone.'

The woman was calling out to the children to finish their game. 'His house is in Castelgandolfo. But you will not find him there — he is visiting his estates in the Argentine and nobody knows when he will return. I would like to see him myself. Unless we can have the villa back, we must have an extension built here. We need his permission and help over the cost. I spoke to Cardinal Lanciani the last time he came to visit the children and he has promised to try to get us some funds from the Church. Signora Brizzi, the opera singer, is our other hope — she is Signor Maderno's sister. She talked about arranging a concert to raise money. But she is singing in New York now. Everybody is somewhere else, you see. So we are helpless.' Clearly the problem was weighing heavily. She smiled wryly. 'You are not a millionaire?'

'I'm afraid not.'

Most of the children had disappeared through a side door of the Institute. One girl stood with a beach ball, waiting to hand it over. There seemed nothing more to be gleaned today. On the point of returning to the car, Antonia remembered a final question. 'Has the villa a separate name from the Institute?'

'Yes. It is called the Villa dei Laghi, because from its terrace one can see Lake Nemi as well as Lake Albano. Your friend should have given that as his address.'

Antonia gazed down at Lake Albano. Shadow was creeping like an indigo tide from one end. Somewhere, invisible, was the trattoria garden. The flat-footed waiter would have removed the tablecloths and umbrellas now. It seemed a long time since she had rested her head against the wall and dreamed she was floating on the lake under a cloudless, timeless sky. She turned back to the woman, thinking of that neat script in Francis Bacton's diary: 'V.d.L.'. 'He almost did.'

As she walked into the sudden gloom of the *pensione*, a familiar

159

face topped with short sandy hair rose from an armchair. 'Mrs Strachan,' Hebden said. He looked relieved. 'I was in two minds whether it would be sensible to wait. But they told me that you had been out all day and I felt you would surely return in time for dinner.'

He was having to look up at her. In his apartment she had failed to notice quite how short he was. 'I hope you have enjoyed this lovely day. Where did you go?'

'The Alban Hills.'

'Ah, how splendid — the most wonderful view of Rome from Cavo.' He was trying to peer round her shoulder. 'Ludo is following — ?'

'No, he's away — until Sunday probably.'

His face fell.

'Is there something —?'

'The Secretary of State called me when I returned to the Vatican from Vienna this morning. He wished me to arrange for Ludo to meet Signor Panzani, who is on his personal staff, today if possible.'

She frowned. 'How did the Secretary of State know we were in Rome?'

'Monsignor Hernandes spoke to the President-General of Opus Dei after his conversation with yourself and Ludo. The President-General then called on the Secretary of State.'

'Do you know why?'

'There is apparently concern in Opus Dei that its good name might in some way suffer as a result of the inquiries you are making. The Secretary of State didn't tell me exactly what had passed between him and the President-General. But that is what I understand.' Hebden was looking embarrassed and a little short in temper.

Antonia had become aware that a man was seated in an armchair at right angles to the one from which Hebden had risen. His head was turned in their direction. He was obviously trying to listen to the conversation.

'Is that Signor Panzani there?'

'Yes.'

'What is his function in the Secretary of State's office?'

'I am not sure. He is seconded from the Italian intelligence people or the police — one of the two. I have not met him before.'

The man saw that he had attracted Antonia's attention; he sprang to his feet and bowed. He was in his middle thirties and powerfully-built, with a litheness about his movements that suggested an athlete. The silk suit he was wearing showed a great deal of shirt cuff.

'*Signora* Strachan.' The words were accompanied by a gesture in which apology for intrusion, desire to be of service and high-minded interest in the configuration beneath her clothing, were simultaneously conveyed.

She nodded.

'I am very happy to meet you, Signora.' He spoke English easily but with a marked American accent.

'Mr Fender's away. What is it you wanted exactly?'

He was clearly torn between a wish to flatter her and an inclination to suppose she was not to be taken too seriously. 'I could perhaps explain that to Signor Fender when he is available.'

He had quite an attractive way of speaking, his voice soft and deliberate. But she was hot and tired and in no mood for put-downs. 'If we're to make progress, you'll have to explain to me.'

Hebden said grimly, 'I think it would be helpful if you did that, Panzani.'

'Of course.' He spoke on a rising note as though that had been his intention all along. 'I understand you are making some inquiries on behalf of your government about a British priest and are interested in those with whom he was associated. If I could be informed of the reasons, it is possible I can save you some trouble. I should also be very interested to learn of the progress of your inquiries.' He paused fractionally. 'For example, on your visit to the Alban Hills today.'

'Have you been having me followed?'

He looked taken aback. 'I heard you mention to Father Hebden a few minutes ago — '

'All right, but what about last Thursday?'

He shook his head with vehemence. 'Have you reason to suspect someone has been doing that?'

161

She shrugged. 'I don't know.'

Hebden still had his air of embarrassment. She began to feel sorry for him. More amiably, she said to Panzani, 'I'll discuss your request with Signor Fender when he returns to Rome. I expect it to be on Sunday. If you will give me a number to ring, we will let you know our answer.'

Panzani took a card from his pocket and handed it to her. 'I shall be in my office all day on Monday. I look forward to hearing from you, Signora. The Secretary of State will be most grateful to hear of your co-operation. The matter is very important to him. And to His Holiness.'

If he wanted to pretend their co-operation was a foregone conclusion, that was up to him. When he bent to kiss her hand she was assailed by a heavy perfume in which violets seemed the main ingredient. He was altogether the last person she would have supposed to be on the personal staff of the Secretary of State. But, after all, she had never been inside the Vatican, to observe the fauna of the Holy See.

When Panzani had gone she turned to Hebden. 'What did you tell the Secretary of State when you spoke to him?'

It sounded graceless in the way it came out. She flushed and saw that he also had gone pink. 'I'm sorry, I thought that you had perhaps felt obliged — '

He interrupted her. 'I explained when he questioned me about our meeting with Hernandes that what I had heard separately from Ludo and yourself had been conveyed in confidence. He perfectly understood that.' His tone was irascible and she couldn't altogether blame him.

'I appreciate your position has become difficult.'

'Yes.' The authority, the intimations of a caustic wit waiting to break the surface, were quite absent on this occasion. Hebden had faced a conflict of loyalties and found it painful. She decided she would not tell him what she had learnt at the Istituto S. Giovanni dei Colli Albani; it could only add to the disagreeable burden of knowledge which he clearly felt should be passed to the Secretary of State, or at least to the odorous Signor Panzani. But, so far as Panzani was concerned, perhaps what she had learnt this afternoon would not be entirely new. He had certainly shown awareness that there had been something of interest in the Alban Hills. And he had not minded her seeing he knew that.

Hebden was gathering himself to depart. She felt obscurely guilty about him. 'Won't you stay and have dinner?'

He shook his head. 'Thank you, but there is a mountain of work on my desk which piled up while I was in Vienna. I shall be summoned to the headmaster's study if I don't get on with it.' A faint version of the smile had returned. He placed a hand on her arm. 'I hope you will persuade Ludo that he should not hold back any more. As I recall, he is inclined to hoard secrets rather as a miser hoards gold — for the joy of counting what he has. On this occasion, I should find it exceedingly uncomfortable if he decided to continue doing that. Please tell him that the fears which made him hesitate — and which I allowed myself to share for a while — are quite groundless, I'm sure.'

She smiled. 'I don't really have much influence with him, you know.'

He gave her his most sardonic look. 'That is not my impression, Mrs Strachan. Not my impression at all.'

18

Later, when it was all over, she realized that the characteristic ambiguity of Fender's telephone message from Bern had, in a sense, been a blessing. Without the hope it offered that his return was merely postponed, it would have been hard to concentrate on the events that followed the fresh telegrams from London.

Throughout Saturday morning and much of the afternoon, she had waited at the *pensione* for his call; then, deciding she would risk a ten-minute airing, she had slipped out, only to be greeted on her return with the news that he had been through. The message was brief and open-ended: he expected to be on the sleeper arriving Sunday morning but might be delayed for a few hours in Orvieto.

She set to decoding this. The possibility that the delay would be anything other than self-imposed could be virtually excluded. He was toying with the idea of pursuing some further inquiry there. It must mean that he had discovered, from his meeting with Weber, something that made a stop in Orvieto attractive. Perhaps he had already decided firmly on it when he made the call but foresaw an outright statement of intent as likely to revive the irritation she had shown earlier. She concluded that Sunday afternoon, or even Monday morning, were the most likely bets for his reappearance.

By the afternoon of Sunday other thoughts were in command. Heather had telephoned earlier from the Embassy to say she had been summoned to take delivery of two Immediate telegrams from London. She undertook to bring them round to the *pensione*.

This time, they announced themselves as being from Antrim himself. Prepared for hackles to rise and even curl, Antonia seated herself on her bed to read. The tone of the first was almost disappointingly reasonable. Satisfaction was acknowledged at the acquisition of Ropner's letter to Barralozzi. The Prime Minister, visited, it appeared, on Saturday evening at Chequers (another first for Golden Boy, Antonia could hear Harriet Ackerley murmur), had himself spoken favourably of the achievement. However, it was Not Enough. A source with access to Barralozzi's private correspondence, the PM had said, must surely be well placed to provide more information. The obtaining of evidence that was unambiguously incriminating was now of an importance, if anything, even higher than before; they would please get on with this. If payment for the evidence proved essential, this was now authorized: Harriet Ackerley was being instructed by her master to make ten million lire available from her own office funds. A report on progress with the aid of this carrot was to be sent by noon on Wednesday.

The second telegram was for Fender alone and adopted curter language. Any inquiry or contact which might lead to a meeting with Weber was to be dropped immediately. Confirmation that this was understood and was being followed was requested.

She let it fall to the bed and groaned; but there was nothing she could do. Fender would have to unscramble his own eggs when he got back. Heather watched sympathetically from her chair on the other side of the room. Today she had discarded her Alice band and drawn her hair back to achieve the effect of a shaving brush that had wilted with hard use. Her clothes indicated that she must have been playing tennis when summoned to the Embassy to take delivery of the telegrams. 'Tall order?'

'Very.'

'You can only try.' She had the calming quality characteristic of large dogs of certain breeds.

'Presumably Harriet doesn't know about these?'

'No, she's in Florence for the weekend.'

'I was wondering about the ten million lire.'

'That'll be all right, we've had a message to supply you with it. The currency ought to be available for Priscilla to hand over by, say, midday tomorrow. I'll get on to the bank first thing.'

'It sounds a lot of notes. How big a bag shall I need? Or should it be a suitcase?'

'Don't worry, we'll dig up something. If you have it in ten-thousand-lire notes, it won't be too bulky. Presumably you won't be carting the stuff about on your own.' She looked vaguely in the direction of the door. Obviously she had expected Fender to be visible.

Antonia folded the telegrams and put them away in her bag. 'I'll manage.'

She saw Heather off, back to her tournament or Edgar the tortoise, and returned to her own room to ring Stolz's number. Even contacting him wouldn't be straightforward, she feared. Stolz had been difficult enough to get hold of last week. He was obviously a man who took off frequently and once out of Rome could be difficult to track down. Half expecting failure, she listened gloomily to the ringing tone for half a minute and, when his voice finally answered, was almost too surprised to reply at once.

Their conversation began at cross-purposes, Stolz assuming

165

that she had simply called to tell him her return to London had been fixed. He sounded amazed when she explained that more evidence was needed.

Doggedly she tried to get him into a more reasonable frame of mind. 'I realize you've helped as much as we've a right to expect. But if he invented an explanation for the last paragraph that couldn't be disproved, there's nothing else to hit him with. Don't forget he's a powerful minister with a lot of support. He might decide he could brazen it out.'

He made noises that signified scorn showering in all directions. After a while she asked despairingly, 'Are you saying you won't even try to get me anything more because London doesn't deserve it?'

There was a pause. He came back more gently. 'No, I'm sorry, I didn't mean that. Because I think your Prime Minister is lily-livered is no excuse to sound off at you.'

'You'll help?'

'All right.'

'We've got authority to pay money this time.'

He grunted. 'We'd better talk anyway. I'll come round.'

He arrived looking more equable than she had expected. They sat on the *pensione* roof and shared a bottle of wine. He looked about him. 'Not that I'm complaining with only you for company — but do I get to meet the handsome Ludovic?'

'I'm afraid not.'

'Away?'

'Yes.'

'Until when?'

'I'm not sure.'

He was grinning. 'I don't think the guy exists.'

She glanced at her wrist-watch. It was already past seven-thirty. A bubble of anxiety surfaced in her mind. She hoped he hadn't made a sick joke.

'How much money can you pay?' he asked.

'Up to ten million.'

'Lire?'

'Yes.'

'That's peanuts in this town.'

'I can't help that.'

166

His expression softened and she felt hope stirring. 'Listen, there is one chance. I know — although my embassy friend doesn't realize it — the identity of his agent who reported on Barralozzi and also, incidentally, produced the letter. It's a woman. I've never tried to do business with her in case it got back to my friend. What I might do — perhaps — is put *you* in touch with her.'

'When will you know definitely if it's possible?'

'Tomorrow maybe. Telephone me around four o'clock and I'll try and have some news.' A waiter appeared and began setting tables for the evening meal. Stolz rose. 'I'd ask you to have dinner but there's something I must do tonight.' He picked up one of her hands and kissed it lightly. 'Don't worry. Nothing matters that much.'

'I'm not worrying,' she said.

He took two of the fingers of the hand and crossed them.

Midday Monday came and there was still no sign of Fender. Concern for his safety began to fret her like an aching tooth. It was out of character for him not to have telephoned again, if he had decided on extending the stop at Orvieto for more than a day. He should have reached there by Sunday morning at the latest; it was now more than twenty-four hours later. She studied the newspaper for fatal accidents involving trains, cars or fat Englishmen. Besides anxiety, a more ignoble emotion was taking shape, a vague but perceptible resentment. Once already he had nearly died on her, during that trip to Ottawa years ago. Had he done the job properly this time, in some anonymous hotel bedroom here in Italy — leaving her to find and pick up the pieces? At some moment, not far distant, she would have to tell London that he had gone missing, admit that it had happened on a private venture, for a purpose explicitly prohibited: a venture about which she had failed to inform Antrim, contrary to the instructions he had given her.

A call from Heather postponed further grim reflections. The money would be waiting for her to collect at two o'clock. She arrived at the Embassy on the hour and was shown into Harriet Ackerley's room. A large shoulder bag stood on the side table. In neat rows beside it were bundles of ten-thousand-lire notes. 'Come in, darling,' Harriet Ackerley said. 'We're going to make you *very* rich.'

Her mood was surprisingly mellow: the weekend in Florence seemed to have put her in a good humour. As Antonia signed a receipt, she said, 'You have a weapon of course — ?'

'No.'

'Nothing?'

'No.'

'This isn't Virginia Water, you know. It's really quite a violent city.'

'I'll just have to be careful.'

She shrugged and lit one of her small cigars. 'Well, I hope the lolly shakes some juicy fruit from the tree. If you find there's anything particularly tasty which you don't need, you won't forget us, will you? Our palates are very catholic.'

As she opened the door into the corridor, she said, 'You seem to do all the leg-work, darling. Are we going to see your shy partner in crime sometime?'

It seemed that everyone was suddenly interested in seeing Fender. Antonia hoisted the bag on to her shoulder and summoned up a smile. 'I hope so. But don't count on it.'

There was a call coming through for her as she entered the *pensione*. Hope surged and she ran to the booth in the reception hall to take it. But it was not Fender's voice.

'Signora Strachan?'

Her temper came close to snapping. 'Signor Panzani, I promised I would telephone you after talking to Mr Fender.'

'Of course.'

'He is not yet back.'

From the complete absence of surprise in his voice, she guessed he had already learnt that from the switchboard. 'I hope there is nothing wrong.'

'So do I.'

'Do you know where he is?'

'No.'

'Could he have run into some danger perhaps? If I knew something of his movements I would be able to make inquiries.'

168

'I'll remember that.'

She got rid of him at last and went to her room to telephone Stolz. She could deduce nothing from the tone of voice in which he answered and he tantalized her for a while by checking her reaction to something he had just typed in an article. Finally he said, with elaborate casualness, 'By the way, you're in luck.'

Her breath felt constricted. 'I am?'

'Yes. Provided you've got the money.'

'It's with me now.'

'Right. Take five million of it to a bar you'll find on the corner of the Corso Vittorio and the Piazza Sforza Cesarini. It's not far from the Tiber. Be there at six o'clock. Franco will be looking out for you.'

'Franco?'

'Yes.' He registered the surprise and lack of enthusiasm in her voice by making a clucking sound. 'You obviously don't appreciate Franco. He has many talents. It's through him that you're going to be able to meet the person you want.'

'She's agreed to talk?'

'Better than that — much better.' He sounded in triumphant mood now. 'Wait and see, you'll be the saviour of Whitehall. When you've finished, come back here for a drink and tell me how it went.'

'How do I know she won't be making something up for my benefit?'

He was amused. 'Just — wait and see.'

She had almost rung off when she remembered what he had said about the amount of money. 'I can be sure that five million will do the trick, can I?'

'That's the deal she's expecting. Don't take any more. Get yourself something with the rest.'

'Or a present for you?'

'You know what I'd really like,' he said. But his tone was light enough for her to shrug it off, if she chose.

The bar seemed full of students carrying books. Presumably there was a college nearby. In a corner one of them was reciting a rude poem about President Reagan to a grinning audience.

169

Her eyes were still searching for Franco's head when she became aware of someone behind her, a hand touching her bare arm for rather too long. Dressed for the street, he looked quite presentable except for the three-tone shoes and the chain about the wrist. He glanced at the shoulder bag. 'The money?'

'Yes.'

'Wait here, please.'

He disappeared for perhaps ten minutes. When he returned he was breathing hard but looked satisfied. Standing beside her at the counter, he ordered a *cappuccino*. 'She has come. Go to the parking area in the Piazza della Chiesa Nuova which is over there.' He pointed across the street. 'Immediately in front of the church you will find a white Fiat. The woman inside is named Flaminia.'

'Has she been told what exactly I want?'

'Yes, she has it for you.'

'What has she been told about *me*?'

'Nothing except that you will pay for the information.' He was very businesslike. It struck her forcefully that he was playing a role in which he felt more at home than when serving drinks in Stolz's apartment.

The woman sat smoking and watching through the windshield as Antonia approached. She waited until Antonia was standing beside the passenger door before leaning across to open it. From the seat behind, a small brown poodle in a jewelled collar rose to its feet, sniffed at Antonia's hair as she seated herself and settled back in a doze.

'*Chiedo scusa — Lei é la Signora Flaminia?*'

'*Si, sono io.*'

'*Credo che Lei abbia qualcosa per me.*'

The woman was plump and fortyish with black hair drawn down from a centre parting and restless, hot-tempered eyes. A mole at the corner of her mouth had been darkened with eyebrow pencil. In passable English, she said, 'Do you understand Italian well?'

'Fairly well.'

She took from her handbag a small tape recorder, with a cassette already fitted, and passed it to Antonia. 'Then you can listen.'

'What shall I be hearing?'

'A conversation between Signor Barralozzi and his sister one morning. The time and date are written on the cassette.'

'You made this tape?'

Flaminia smiled. 'I did not say that.'

'But you worked in Signor Barralozzi's office — '

'Yes.'

'Are you still employed by the Institute for Religious Works?'

'No.'

'Have you other tapes like this one?'

'Plenty. But none that would interest you.' She reached forward to the ashtray and stubbed out her cigarette. 'I suggest you listen now. I would like to look at the money while you do that.'

The reproduction was tiresomely uneven with a background hiss for much of the time. By the end of the third listening, Antonia found she had understood no more than half what was said. To be sure of what she had got there was no alternative but to settle down and make a written translation. She took a notebook and pen from her handbag and began.

By the end of half an hour, she was confident that, with Flaminia's occasionally interjected advice, she had it straight. She sat back and read the notes under her breath.

1st Female Voice Signor Barralozzi?

Male Voice Yes.

1st Female Voice Your sister wishes to speak to you from London.

Male Voice Put her through.

[Pause]

2nd Female Voice Aldo?

Male Voice Alida, yes.

2nd F. V. Charles has just left the big man — he telephoned me.

M. V. So, do we have the news?

2nd F. V. Yes. The big man has agreed the action. It is to be announced later today. They first have to tell the others —

the Committee — you understand? — they all have to be told.

M.V. When?

2nd F.V. They meet in half an hour.

M.V. And the Committee have to agree?

2nd F.V. Yes. No, it is a formality. Charles says there will be no argument now the big man has agreed. It is certain.

M.V. Good. So how much time have I got before the announcement?

2nd F.V. It cannot be made before this afternoon. So at least four hours. Charles says you should start our business immediately. His people will not start their move before this afternoon. But he wants you not to wait at all.

M.V. Leave it with me. I will telephone your house tonight.

2nd F.V. We depend on you, Aldo.

M.V. Don't worry, I will make the calls now. Did he say anything else?

2nd F.V. No.

M.V. Goodbye then.

2nd F.V. Goodbye, Aldo.

Flaminia was talking to the poodle. She had zipped the shoulder bag up again, apparently satisfied. 'It's good?'

'It seems to be what I need.'

'You know who the big man is?'

'The Prime Minister.'

'And the Committee — ?'

'There was a Cabinet meeting that morning.'

'Ah.' She was mildly interested to be given the gloss. 'So now you have all you want.'

Antonia bit her lip, fearful to accept the luck of it. 'He said he was going to make some calls. Were they not caught by the tape?'

'He used another telephone, a direct exchange line. I know who they were to, but I cannot give you the proof.'

'Who did he call?'

'A contact in Switzerland — Geneva — who dealt for him in the markets there when he had private business. Also one in Singapore I think.'

172

'You didn't hear them — '

'I went into his room while he was speaking to Geneva. It was about buying pounds. He stopped and asked me to leave. The Singapore people telephoned him back during the day using the official switchboard. He refused to take the call but said they were to be told he would ring them himself.'

'Did you hear him call his sister in the evening?'

'No, he left the bank early. He was very — ' she moved her hand from side to side to indicate excitement — 'very pleased, very active. He asked for his wife to be telephoned that he would be late home because the Bank of Rome had called a special meeting.'

'Why was there a special meeting?'

Flaminia looked in the car mirror, examining her make-up. 'You don't understand. There was no meeting.' She pursed her lips and then sat back, content. 'He went to his mistress in Parioli. That is what we called her in the office — Signora Banco di Roma.'

As the taxi turned into the Corso, it became apparent why progress for the past ten minutes had been minimal. A procession demonstrating against nuclear arms filled almost the width of the street. A few of the signs and flags being carried belonged to foreign peace groups. Somewhere in the throng, perhaps, would be the handsome Claire from Chawton Wood.

The taxi came to a complete halt. Antonia paid it off and began to make her way on foot to Stolz's apartment. She was on the wrong side of the street for it, but noticed that others did not treat the procession as an obstacle: when they wanted to cross, they inserted their bodies between the ranks with swift gliding movements, ignored by both the demonstrators and the police marching alongside them.

Stopping at the café opposite the *palazzo* where Stolz had his apartment and waiting for a cluster of banners to pass, she became aware of someone at the edge of her vision, someone not so much familiar as dimly remembered. She turned and saw, about to seat himself at a café table on the pavement, the man who had seemed to be following her in the Via del Babuino the previous Thursday. When his eyes caught hers,

173

they immediately slid away. There could be no room for doubt now: she had been under surveillance that Thursday morning — and perhaps ever since. For a moment she was gripped by the idea of challenging him. But that would be stupid. He would turn away, shrugging in that characteristically Roman way, appealing to the world against this neurotic woman who wished to imagine she was interesting enough for him to follow. The cluster of banners had passed. She ran to the narrow gap before the next batch of protestors, passing through with no more than an appreciative sampling of her left buttock by a youth dressed as a bomb.

Franco opened the door of the apartment. He was shorn of the purposeful authority of an hour or two back and had resumed his white jacket. He nodded silently, his manner still disagreeably familiar, but this time more that of a co-conspirator. She nodded back. 'It worked out as you said. Thank you.'

He led her through to Stolz in the main reception room. Stolz was listening to the radio news but switched it off as she entered and stood, expectant. 'Success?'

She held up the small tape recorder. 'I don't know how to begin thanking you.'

He handed her a drink. 'It gives all you want?'

'The reproduction's awful and the Ropner woman's voice is hard to get at times. But the meaning's clear. If this doesn't satisfy London, nothing will.'

'They'll award you a medal.'

'Did you know this tape existed when you got me the letter?'

'No, or rather, yes — ' He looked apologetic. 'I knew my friend at the Embassy had something like this. What I didn't realize until last night was that his wasn't the only copy. That shrewd cookie, Flaminia, had taken a copy of the original tape before she handed it over to him.'

'Why should she do that?'

'She must have had some idea of blackmailing Barralozzi with it one day. Now he's dead she can't do that.'

'She could still have gone to London and blackmailed the Ropners with it.' She paused, frowning. 'In fact, I suppose she

174

may have kept yet another copy with the idea of doing just that one day.'

'True. But is it anybody's worry except Ropner's, once he's out of your government?'

'I suppose not.'

She carried her drink to the terrace and stared down at the Corso. The procession had passed. 'What are you looking for?' Stolz asked from behind her shoulder.

'A man. Someone has been following me about. I don't know what his interest is but I hope it doesn't include separating me from this tape.'

'Why are you certain you're being followed?'

She told him the story. He fetched binoculars. 'Tell me if he's still at the café table.'

Through the binoculars the man was clearly visible. His gaze was on the entrance to the *palazzo*. She passed the binoculars to Stolz. 'What do you make of him?'

He studied the man and shrugged. 'Impossible to guess. Let's get Franco to find out.'

'Franco?'

'Yes.'

She frowned, shaking her head. 'What exactly will he do?'

'When the guy hands over to somebody else, as he's bound to do if you stay long enough, follow him back to wherever he came from.'

'Is Franco good at that?'

'He'll love it. I told you — he has many talents.' He grinned, relaxed as ever. 'If you came here more often, you'd get to appreciate him in the end.'

When he returned from briefing Franco, he was carrying a tray of food. He handed her a napkin and gestured towards paté, caviar, dry toast and biscuits. 'We may as well eat something now and maybe go out to dinner later when Franco comes back with news. Or we could always stay here.'

He was being totally casual this time, not by appearing indifferent, but by making it clear that he left it to her how the evening — and the night — went. She was conscious that when the time came, it might be hard to leave. But, inside her stomach, the anxiety about Fender, forgotten in the tension of the last few hours, was back. Something had happened to him, she was now convinced. And staying with Stolz was postponing the moment when she would face, as she must, the full implications of that. Still she shrank from a decision about when to go, adopting an unnatural vivacity to shut out other thoughts. Once, Stolz placed his hand briefly on hers and asked her to tell him what was wrong. But to share this problem, after allowing him virtually to solve everything else for her, would seem like abandoning all responsibility.

Two hours went by before Franco reappeared at the entrance to the terrace. He had not put on his white coat again and looked agitated. He didn't move forward but stood waiting for Stolz to join him. She saw them go to one of the inner rooms, then return to a corner of the main reception room. The sun had long set; across the terrace, a bird wheeled on some late mission, almost brushing the creeper above her head.

When eventually Stolz came back, his face had changed. He seemed to have become wholly remote. 'I'm sorry, we're going to have to break this up.' He might have been addressing a roomful of people. 'I have to go out for a while.'

'I see.'

The message was unmistakable, he could hardly wait for her to leave.

'The man who was following me — does — '

He shook his head. 'You don't have to worry, he's not after the tape. If you see him again, spit in his eye. But you probably won't.'

'Is your problem to do with him?'

He shook his head, more as a refusal to answer any more questions than in denial. He walked towards the apartment's outer door and she followed him, struggling with bewilderment mixed with hurt that she had become so abruptly redundant. On the threshold, Stolz seemed to emerge from preoccupation for a few moments. He placed his hand gently on her forearm to turn her towards him. 'Forgive me.' He kissed her with surprising tenderness.

She drew back. 'That's all right.'

'It's just that suddenly things have come up, difficult things affecting the future.' He looked into her eyes. 'I would like you to know that meeting you — ' He broke off and gave a curiously defeated laugh.

'Well,' she said. 'See you in London perhaps. Shall I give you the address?'

'I can get you through your office, can't I?' He was brushing the idea aside, she knew he had no thought of their meeting again. For some reason, she was being turned into an unperson. She smiled back through the lift gates, making the best of it. 'Thanks for your help. I hope things work out.' He had turned into the apartment before the shaft of the lift cut off her view.

It was just after ten o'clock when she got back to the *pensione*. The reception desk was deserted; she could hear the proprietor arguing with somebody in the lower regions.

There was no message in the box under her key and no light under Fender's door as she passed it. She was possessed by a sudden, heart-stopping conviction that she would never see him again.

Entering her room produced the same sensation of loneliness she associated with the flat in Little Venice, heightened here by the indifference of unfamiliar things. She went into the bathroom and looked at her image in the mirror for a while, then cursed it with slow deliberation. The image stared back, unmoved as ever.

She wanted a drink, a large drink, before she faced the night thoughts. Returning to the bedroom to open the bottle of scotch she had bought on the plane, she stopped suddenly. On the table beside her bed was a small package. Opening it, she found, inside a jeweller's box, a brooch of luminous blue enamel and gold filigree. It was shaped as a butterfly; the wings bore tiny diamonds. On a card beneath the brooch was familiar writing. 'I hope I am forgiven, L.F.'

She ran to his door. The room was in darkness but, slashed across by the corridor light that entered with her, was the familiar massive shape, wedged in the armchair, head thrown back, eyes closed, breath coming evenly. A white triangle of cloth, extending across the chest, she slowly recognized as an arm sling. Damn you, Ludo, she thought, How could you

177

have done these things to me? But she could have kissed him all the same.

Either the corridor light, or her movement as she approached him, had disturbed his doze. He gave a brief snort and smacked his lips reflectively, as though appraising the memory of a dream. His free hand dropped down the side of the chair so that the knuckles rested on the rug beneath. Finally, he opened his eyes. 'Antonia,' Fender said, without apparent surprise. 'How very nice.'

19

'Good tailoring,' said Fender, 'is never a waste of money. I remember my father telling me that.'

He inserted plump fingers into the jacket armhole, to indicate where the branch of the olive tree had thrust and been held fast. Gingerly extending himself sideways, he stretched over the arm of the chair, so that she could see how the other branch had supported his stomach, suspending him above the ravine, a portly Icarus, aloft but motionless, waiting for rosy-fingered dawn to discover his plight.

After the fall from the train, mercifully senseless, he had rolled down an embankment, cushioned by thickness of flesh from more than superficial injury *en route*. Where the embankment gave way to the vertical drop to the ravine, the tree had miraculously reached out, had brought him to agonized consciousness by snapping his left wrist, only to make amends by offering its ancient limbs as sanctuary.

The worst moments had been waiting for the truck driver, who had first caught sight of him, to come back, bringing the villagers and their ladders by which to lift him down. While the rising sun began to search his wounds, the pain from the wrist and from scraped flesh had woven a garment of twisting knives. Delirium came and went. When, while they worked to

178

free him, one of the villagers pressed a cloth soaked in water to his face, he had supposed himself to be in some terrible tableau, the principal actor in a representation of Christ on the Cross. He remembered nothing more until he awoke in a hospital bed, cleansed and bandaged and was told it was Sunday evening.

'You sent no message,' Antonia said.

He looked mildly apologetic. 'Since I had said in my message on Saturday that I might stop off in Orvieto, I thought you wouldn't begin to worry for a day or so. Then this afternoon I decided I was fit enough to make the journey.'

Apart from the plaster enclosing the wrist within the arm sling and a few scratches on his face and hands, he looked astonishingly unaffected by his experience. But she noticed that when he crossed to the bathroom to fetch a glass for her whisky, he was moving with even more than his usual deliberation; presumably there were a number of hidden bruises.

She shook her head when he came back. 'You shouldn't have been allowed up.'

'I did have some trouble convincing the doctors. But I am perfectly mobile, as you can see. I wanted to satisfy myself that you were all right. We seem to have fallen foul of some rather violent people.'

'You mean *you* have.'

He bowed his head in an unconvincing display of meekness.

'Panzani spoke as though he suspected you might be in danger.'

'Did he? That's interesting. I wonder why?'

'Who do you suppose attacked you?'

'Not the *Vigiles* anyway — these were professional thugs.'

'Why shouldn't their *Ultores* be thugs?'

'Because it wouldn't be consistent with what we know about them. We can assume that everyone who has joined the *Vigiles*, even to act as an *Ultor*, has done so out of conviction, a perverted sense of mission. According to Frau Kohl, Weber went about reading his Bible and behaving like a very respectable young man. We agreed that he was a zealot. Christian zealots, like other sorts, can occasionally become convinced that fighting the Devil means having to kill men. But those

179

who soaked me with brandy and threw me out of the train didn't belong to that category.'

'So who were they?'

He raised his eyebrows in resignation. 'For the moment that defeats me. But we obviously have to take care.'

'So you'll talk to Panzani —'

She watched him laboriously filling his pipe with the fingers of one hand, while he searched for reasons for saying he wouldn't. 'I think Father Hebden's position would be very difficult if you were to refuse.'

'Yes, I must consider John Hebden,' he said, a shade reluctantly. 'But Panzani — after all who *is* he? Some sort of policeman apparently, who happens to be working for the Secretary of State instead of in the Office of Vigilance. I'm not sure I want to deal with him — not initially anyway. I want someone in the Church with sufficient authority to give me assurances in return for my co-operation.'

'What sort of assurances?'

He extended a hand to the side, assuming what she recognized as his grand manner. 'That the *Vigiles* are acting without authority of any kind; and that the Church is determined to root them out. Those would be the minimum.'

He was back to his private obsession, the fascination that Antrim had foreseen would grip him, once he got into the world of thuribles and monstrances and men in birettas scurrying along endless marble corridors. She sighed silently. 'So what *will* you do?'

Fender looked up at the ceiling as though a thought was forming only gradually in his mind. 'I think — I shall insist on seeing — the Secretary of State himself.' He brought his eyes down to hers, simulating a tentative inquiry for her reactions to this sudden idea; it must, she guessed, have been in his mind from the moment she had told him about Panzani's visit. 'I could perhaps speak to John Hebden tomorrow and explain that. In gentle terms of course.'

'And if you're then satisfied with what the Secretary of State says?'

'I shall be very happy to tell him what we know about the *Vigiles*.'

'Together with the telephone number you got from the woman in Murten — '

He seemed inclined to wriggle but then sighed. 'In my present condition, further research of my own would perhaps be foolish.'

She breathed out thankfully. 'I think so.'

He picked up the tape recorder from where it lay on the table between them. 'I have not really congratulated you enough on your success.'

'I hope that's what it is.'

'Antrim could hardly ask for anything more effective with which to challenge the Ropners. Combined with the letter it's unanswerable.'

She sat in silence. He eyed her for a while. 'What is worrying you?'

'I'm not sure. Mostly the ease with which it dropped into my lap. Even the fact that the tape existed seems remarkable. Have I just been terribly lucky? Or is there something wrong? Have I paid out five million lire for a forgery — a piece of private enterprise on the part of this Flaminia woman in league with Franco?'

'A lightning piece of forgery if that's what it is — have you considered the time-scale? And what about Stolz — are you suggesting he would allow that to be done to you?'

'He may not have known. In any case — ' She wanted to articulate the puzzlement she had felt at Stolz's abrupt change of mood earlier. Yet it didn't seem relevant to the misgivings she had been expressing; and she couldn't believe he had wittingly played her false.

Fender switched on the tape and listened once more. 'You think these voices are not necessarily those of Barralozzi and his sister.'

'The reproduction of the woman's voice is so rough that I doubt if even someone who knew her very well could swear to it. Since the tapping was obviously done inside Barralozzi's office, why is the tape so poor?'

'It is, after all, a tape of a tape if what Stolz said about Flaminia's idea for private enterprise is correct.'

'I still find it odd.'

He smiled. 'You're in the grip of horrid doubt.'

'I feel we can't send the tape off to London without somebody confirming that the male voice is Barralozzi's. If we can be sure of that I shall stop worrying.'

He nodded. 'I agree. Why shouldn't I ask the Secretary of State to confirm it? If he can't do so from personal knowledge, there must be someone on his staff who can oblige.' He watched her as she still hesitated. 'You can't be against that?'

'I was only wondering if we owed it to anyone not to let the Vatican know about the tape.'

'Flaminia told you she'd left the bank. So her job won't be at risk. You can be sure they won't take court proceedings against her. And as for Stolz and his Embassy contact, there's nothing to prejudice them. I don't really think you need have scruples.'

Fender yawned prodigiously. She realized that he had suddenly become very tired and stood up to leave him but he raised a hand. 'Before you go, perhaps I could take a look at the London telegrams you told me about.'

She handed them both to him. He read the first with only mild interest. The second one, addressed to himself, he took more slowly. He gave a sigh of pleasure. 'A little nervousness there, would you say? I wonder how many times Antrim has regretted having Barralozzi's corpse dug up?'

'You must admit that going to Murten was a risk.'

'In the event no harm was done. And as a result I may be the only person who now knows where the *Vigiles* are.'

She decided that he might as well know also just how difficult he had made her position. 'Before we left, Antrim told me I was to inform him if you carried the investigation beyond Barralozzi's relationship with the Ropners.'

He was fascinated. 'Did he, indeed? He was mistrustful of me, was he? So did you telegraph him when I went off to Murten?'

'No.'

'Why not?'

'Perhaps I have more respect for you than for him.'

He stared at her, his face a little pink, then looked away. At the door she said, 'Thank you again for the brooch. It's

182

miraculous it stayed in your pocket when you fell.'

'Everything was miraculous.'

'I shall treasure it.'

He shook his head as though to say it was nothing. 'I caught sight of it in the jeweller's shop at the hotel in Bern where I spent Friday night. I realize it could scarcely replace the one your husband gave you. But it seemed pretty.'

He was settling himself more comfortably in his chair with the rest of the whisky, as though bed was now the last thing on his mind. 'I hope you weren't worried.'

'Of course not,' she said. 'Why should I have worried?'

The room was grander and more comfortable than the one in which Hebden had received him on his first visit to the Vatican, but it had the same impersonal, unlived-in air. He had supposed he would meet the Secretary of State in his own office. Apparently it was not to be. When the frail, smiling figure in the scarlet buttoned soutane and sash had appeared in the doorway of the waiting-room and, after the briefest of greetings, had seated himself at the other end of the sofa, Fender had felt irritated, even put down. But at once he found that, if he was not to miss anything, his attention would have to be wholly concentrated on the other's mouth. It was not that the Secretary of State's command of English was in-adequate; he spoke with an exactness and occasional pedantry that was attractive to Fender. But the voice assumed a total stillness in the environment and an utter absorption on the part of the listener. To catch it, the ear was compelled to strain, as though reaching out for the notes of some distant music carried on a capricious breeze.

He moved away from pleasantries without the smile chang-ing. 'I believe we are to talk about the *Vigiles*, Mr Fender.'

'Yes.'

'The word has become disagreeably familiar to me recently. I last encountered it in a different context. Did you have a classical education?'

'I did, but I don't seem to remember — '

'The *Vigiles* were the fire-fighters of Rome in the time of Augustus. I had not reckoned with their being revived for the

183

benefit of the Church.' He put his head on one side. 'Father Hebden has explained to me that you have certain fears which he did not feel free to specify.' He was examining Fender with the bright penetration of a bird. 'Do I conclude that having learnt of the existence of the *Vigiles*, you suspect you have stumbled upon some sort of Vaticangate? Or worse?'

For such a direct assault, delivered in a silvery, scarcely audible voice, Fender found himself unprepared. He cleared his throat. 'From Father Bacton's description of what he was told and what he saw, it did seem possible — '

' — that they are invested with some sort of authority from here?'

'From the Pope perhaps.'

'Ah.' The Secretary of State clasped his knees in an unexpectedly youthful movement. He leaned back so that the light from the chandelier above them crept into his nostrils. 'I see.' He was getting some bitter satisfaction from the moment. 'Then let me not delay in giving you immediate reassurance. They have no approval whatever from His Holiness. Indeed his knowledge of their activities is confined to the reports which I have made to him from time to time. Perhaps it will remove any hesitation you may still have if I tell you how we first learned of the *Vigiles*.

'Some time ago, the President-General of Opus Dei came to tell me a sad story. It concerned a member of Opus Dei, a priest named Father Felipe Rodrigues, living in one of their residences here in Rome. Father Rodrigues, although held in the highest regard for his devotion to God's work, had begun to show signs of mental instability. Some difficulty had arisen with him at an earlier date apparently, because of his advocacy of stricter discipline within the residences of Opus Dei. I understand he had been pressing for the adoption of practices of the fourteenth-century mystic, Heinrich Suso, whose life he seems to have studied in great detail. At the same time he had expressed strong views about the need for a number of expulsions from Opus Dei of laymen in different countries whose conduct in their commercial careers he saw as unbecoming and injurious to the reputation of Opus Dei. He had gone on to argue that a proposal should be submitted to His Holiness for

184

the establishment of a Special Commission, which would investigate reports of corruption, dishonesty, immorality and so forth throughout the Church. It would start its work here in the Vatican.

'All this, in the ordinary way, would have been a problem with which Opus Dei itself had to deal. As you may know, its founder was fond of emphasizing that the Church was contaminated with evil.' He pursed his lips delicately. 'I suppose one must not be too surprised if its members occasionally develop such thoughts to the point where they favour exceptional measures to stamp it out.'

'Cauterizing the flesh — '

The Secretary of State paused, his head on one side once more. He gazed at Fender impassively, then took a cigarette from a small silver case. 'I see you are familiar with Father Rodrigues' gift for imagery. Yes, the idea of cautery seems to have appealed to him as expressing the requirement. I understand his language often tends towards the dramatic.

'However — when the President-General called on me, the situation itself had become dramatic. Father Rodrigues had left his residence, taking with him two other priests who had been won over by his arguments, particularly as to the need for the Special Commission. There have, of course, been a number of unfortunate incidents here, especially in connection with the Church's finances, which have caused concern. These, no doubt, were preying on their minds. A third priest also considered leaving with Rodrigues but changed his mind and after some soul-searching informed the President-General of Rodrigues' plans. Rodrigues had apparently told him and the others that his views on the need for a — ' He hesitated while he reached for the word he wanted — 'a cleansing of the Church had found favour at the highest level but hostile forces in the *Curia* were considered too strong for the time being to permit any public move. He had therefore been charged with establishing in secrecy a group of priests, assisted by dedicated laymen, as the executive instrument for the proposed Commission to use in due course. One of the first tasks of this group would be the training of priests of different nationalities who would constitute investigators and listening-posts in their own countries. In the meantime the group would also be assembling information about those falling short of proper moral standards in the Vatican.

'The President-General had a concern similar to your own — to discover whether Rodrigues did indeed have some form of approval from here. I was able to reassure him on this point. But we were, of course, faced with the threat of grave embarrassment from the activities of the group if they became known. Apparently Rodrigues had said that information would be reaching him not only through Vatican sources known to him but also through an intelligence organization belonging to a foreign country to which the Pope had directly appealed for assistance.'

'Which country was this?'

With the hand holding the cigarette, the Secretary of State made a graceful gesture of regret. 'You must forgive me, Mr Fender, if I do not tell you. The Holy Father is still considering how to deal with that aspect of the matter.'

'So there is something in it — ?'

'To the extent that Rodrigues does seem to have access to the intelligence service of a foreign government — unfortunately, yes.' He shook his head grimly. 'With the Holy Father's approval I decided to have some inquiries made into the group's activities. Signor Panzani was lent to me by the Italian Government, together with a small team, to conduct investigations on my behalf without the matter being widely advertised. He was faced with the immediate problem that we did not know where Rodrigues and the others had gone. However, by patient inquiries, Signor Panzani traced them to a villa in the grounds of an orphanage in the Alban Hills. He arranged for observation to establish what the group amounted to and what its movements were.'

'And what visitors it received presumably.'

'There were no visitors.'

The Secretary of State's pectoral cross had caught in the opening of his soutane; it leaned sideways towards Fender and winked at him. He lifted his eyes. The Secretary of State's face was expressionless. 'I see. How long did the observation last?'

'From January to the middle of April.'

186

'And Rodrigues received no visitors.'

'None.' The Secretary of State raised his eyebrows. 'That surprises you?'

He could have challenged him then with what Bacton had said but he wanted time to reflect. 'It just seems rather unlikely.'

'Panzani discovered it was the practice of Rodrigues, and of the Italian priest who seems to be his principal assistant — a Father Ligorio — always to meet those who were collaborating with them away from the villa — usually in Rome, sometimes in Castelgandolfo. By following them, he was able to identify one or two junior employees of the Vatican who had been drawn into providing information. But what Panzani was unable to discover was the use Rodrigues was making of the information. Was he collecting it in the hope that a Special Commission, to which he could hand it, *would* come into existence? Or was he planning to pass it on to someone — perhaps one of the critics the Church has within its own ranks — who would then use it in some way embarrassing to His Holiness? Panzani invited me to consider ordering a young priest on my staff to contrive an apparently chance meeting with Rodrigues on one of his visits to Rome and to get drawn into the *Vigiles* so that we should be better informed. I was examining this proposal when I learnt that they had suddenly abandoned the villa and gone to an unknown address.'

'They'd presumably become aware of Panzani's investigations.'

'No, we think not. We concluded it was because of the departure of Father Bacton which was observed by Panzani's watchers. Rodrigues must have become apprehensive that Father Bacton would talk about what was going on at the villa and have decided it would be wise to move.'

'Bacton was anxious to report on his experiences but he told his parents he couldn't decide in whom he should confide. Surely you could have had him questioned?'

'He was followed to a hostel in Rome. It was evident from his appearance that he was in an extremely agitated condition. I decided that if we were to get his fullest co-operation, someone must win his confidence. A member of my staff of about

Father Bacton's age went to stay in the same hostel and sought to make friends. He believed he was reaching the point when he could persuade him to open his heart when Father Bacton without warning left for England. When we had established his whereabouts there, Panzani himself would have gone to England to question him. But the President-General of Opus Dei told me you had given Monsignor Hernandes news of his death. A sad business.' The Secretary of State sat back. 'Those are the facts as we know them. When the President-General told me you were in Rome and making inquiries that clearly showed you had some information about the *Vigiles*, I decided it was important to discover whether you could help our search.'

He reached forward to tap away cigarette ash in the ashtray on the table beside them. Beneath his skull cap at the back a new moon of scalp gleamed, pale as milk.

'What will you do when you finally locate them?' Fender asked.

'They will be brought here to be questioned.'

'By force?'

'Signor Panzani will be an effective persuader, I'm sure. We shall then accommodate them in the Holy City until we are satisfied we have the whole story, together with assurances that they will refrain from any further activity of the kind.'

'They might, of course, refuse — '

He seemed surprised at being invited to consider the contingency. 'Then they would stay until they recognized their error.'

'Under restraint?'

'We have a prison like any other state. It admittedly has had little use in recent years but the facilities are there. From the cells there is a pleasant view of St Peter's.'

Fender shook his head. 'You speak as though no problems exist outside canon law.'

'I see nothing to interest the ordinary police.'

'Do you not think "cauterizing" was an odd word for Rodrigues to use in talking about the work of the group?'

'Odd? A little.'

'And sinister perhaps?'

188

For a barely perceptible pause, the Secretary of State held the stub of his cigarette above the ashtray before he crushed it. 'I think there is something you wish to tell me, Mr Fender.'

'Within the *Vigiles*, there is an inner group — perhaps of only one or two people — whose functions Rodrigues probably keeps from most of the others. They are known as *Ultores*. They have been responsible for the death of at least one person formerly employed in the Vatican and, I believe, of others.'

From a distance came the faint sound of military orders being given: the Swiss guards were on their way somewhere. The Secretary of State said very softly.

'You say you *know* these *Ultores* exist?'

'Yes, one of them is a man named Weber. I went to interview him in Switzerland at the weekend but someone warned him to leave before I got there. I have the telephone number of the person who gave him the warning. It belongs to the area round Todi. I believe it would lead to where Rodrigues and the *Vigiles* are now.'

The Secretary of State had become very still. 'I see. That could be — very important.'

'I would be happy to give you the telephone number if —' he paused.

'If what?'

'I could feel confident these activities are not being supported from within the *Curia*.'

'Why should you suspect that?'

'It was Father Bacton's belief.'

'Then Father Bacton was mistaken.'

'I have your assurance?'

'The activities are totally without sanction.'

He looked into the Secretary of State's eyes. There was nothing at all to be read there except determination and a trace of impatience. 'Very well,' he said.

The Secretary of State walked to a telephone on a side table. 'This would be a suitable moment for Signor Panzani to join us. I would be grateful if you would tell him all you know.'

'I have a request to make in return.' Fender took the tape recorder from his pocket. 'I need confirmation that the voice of the man speaking on the tape in this recorder belongs to a particular person.'

'Someone in the Vatican?'

'He was employed in the Institute for Religious Works but he's now dead. His name was Barralozzi.'

Hand on the telephone, the Secretary of State gave a sigh. He repeated the name with weary resignation. 'Clearly, Mr Fender, you have been sent to torment me.'

When he returned to the *pensione*, Antonia was not in her room. He found her on the roof terrace, reading *Il Tempo*, a tray of tea on the table beside her. She had chosen a spot where the vines provided a dappled shade, but it was still too hot for comfort. Some unrest of mind had driven her from the shuttered cool below.

The main headline in the newspaper was about the Vatican. Seating himself opposite her, he pointed to it. 'What does *Il Tempo* have to tell us?'

'The Vatican have refused to comment on reports that the Institute for Religious Works owns a bank in the Antilles which has just failed.'

'Par for the course, I think.'

Her lips shaped a faint smile. 'You've had a long day. How does the wrist feel?'

He glanced down at the sling. It was becoming grimy. 'Inconvenient but no more. Bruises apart, I seem to be uncommonly well. Perhaps I should fall out of trains more often.'

He watched as she lit a cigarette. The anxiety in the way she played with the lighter afterwards was painfully obvious. He realized that she was dreading the news he had brought about the tape. Reaching forward, he pressed her arm.

'I have something good to report.'

She looked him squarely in the eyes for the first time.

'The Secretary of State was personally acquainted with Barralozzi and agreed to listen to the tape himself. He says it sounds like his voice.'

'Only *sounds* — no more than that?'

Gently he said, 'The tape *is* very rough. But he thought it was Barralozzi speaking. Could we have asked for more?'

She still seemed reluctant, almost afraid, to accept reassurance.

'I have another piece of information. Together with what the Secretary of State said, I think it will satisfy you. After I had talked to him, I went with Panzani to his office so that he could make a record of the information we have about the *Vigiles*. When he was still in a suitable mood of gratitude, I told him I would like to know if he could identify a woman you had met, who called herself Flaminia and claimed to have worked in the Institute for Religious Works. He went away to make some inquiries there and then. When he came back he said he could confirm that a Flaminia whose appearance corresponded to the description you gave me, including the mole on the cheek, worked in Barralozzi's office at the bank as a secretary. She was a very able woman who was thought capable of doing a much more demanding job but always refused a transfer. She was dismissed from the bank within a fortnight of Barralozzi's successor being appointed. He had found her taking copies of confidential bank papers for which he hadn't asked. She was given a chance to explain but refused to say anything. They thought she was probably being paid by a journalist to get the papers.'

'They never discovered she had been taping Barralozzi's calls — ?'

'Apparently not. But it would have been very easy for her to do so, according to Panzani.'

He could see her shoulders begin to slacken as the tension left her. 'So the tape really is all right — '

'I think so.'

'By midday I'd convinced myself you were going to come back with the news that I'd paid out five million lire for something worthless. I don't believe I could have faced going back to the Bureau after that.'

He shook his head at her, smiling. Sooner or later, she would have to be told the other information he had gleaned from Panzani; but that could wait. It didn't, after all, cast doubt on the genuineness of the tape. And he still had to work out the implications.

191

Her eyes had become alive with the intense, faintly challenging expression he remembered best about her, from the moment she had first walked into his office at the Bureau years ago. 'The thing that really threw me was Stolz's change of attitude last night. Something had happened. From being very friendly, within a few minutes he suddenly couldn't wait to get rid of me. I began to have doubts about everything then. Had he really been genuine about helping me? Suddenly everything seemed wrong.'

An obscure satisfaction crept over him. He stared down at the great wasteland of his abdomen, rising and falling in weary compliance with the heart's demands. What had been changed by her words? All they signified was that whatever relationship had existed with Stolz was over, gone. And he was pleased. So this was what he had come to, the meanest of pleasures: enjoying the denial to others of what he himself was denied.

'You haven't told me how you got on with the Secretary of State,' she said. 'Were you reassured?'

He forced his mind back to the day's events. Was he reassured? Gazing into the trellis beside his chair, he tried to identify what he really felt. 'In some ways. He did *seem* to be frank. And yet — ' He glanced at his wrist-watch. 'Perhaps you should ask me again at about this time tomorrow.'

'What happens tomorrow?'

'While I was with Panzani — who struck me as intelligent and resourceful even though he does wear a revolting scent — he spoke to the police in Todi. The telephone number I got from Frau Kohl belongs to a house a few kilometres outside Todi. It is occupied, say the police, by a group of priests who moved there in April, and is thought by the locals to be being used as some sort of retreat. So I was right — this is where Rodrigues and the group moved when they left the Villa dei Laghi. Early tomorrow morning, if the Pope approves, Panzani intends to take off from what he calls the Vatican's *helicoptorum* with four of his men and descend on the house without warning. They'll gather up the *Vigiles* and anybody else who happens to be about the place and bring them back to the Vatican. There they'll be questioned. Panzani said that if I call at his office at six o'clock tomorrow he'll tell me how it's gone.'

'He'd had no hint before that Todi was the place to look?'

'None. From the time Rodrigues abandoned the villa, he'd been out of touch.'

'They owe you a lot.'

'They owe me *everything*.' He laughed, seeing no point in modesty in the face of fact.

A waiter appeared to remove the tea tray. Antonia said suddenly, 'I'm going to take you out to dinner. After all, we both have something to celebrate. There's a restaurant called L'Eau Vive which might amuse you. With luck you'll see a cardinal or two at play. And beautiful maidens, chosen for their purity.'

His limbs ached and pain had reawakened where skin had been scraped from his hip in the fall from the train. But no doubt a bath and a stiff drink would put all that right. He heaved himself out of the chair. 'A Roman orgy, how clever of you to think of that!'

Stepping from the lift behind Antonia, an hour and a half later, bathed, clean-shirted and almost restored, he saw through the *pensione* entrance a man and woman emerging from a limousine. The male was a lanky, cadaverous figure with a naked dome to his head and parchment cheeks. All three buttons of his jacket were fastened and there was a silver clip on the edge of his tie: obviously he was American. The woman was harder to place, a wintry blonde with thin smart legs and wearing an expensive-looking black dress.

The blonde advanced on Antonia with a murmur of satisfaction, at the same time thrusting a hand at Fender. 'Harriet Ackerley. So glad to meet you at last.' She turned to her companion, her other arm extended to display him. He might have been something up for auction. 'I'd like to introduce a colleague from the American Embassy who very much wants to make the acquaintance of you both. Aaron Kinghorn.' She shot Kinghorn a sub-Arctic smile. 'Aaron's a very old friend.'

Antonia said, 'We were on our way to dinner.' Her expression was not much warmer than the blonde's. It was clear to Fender that she and the Ackerley Woman had not got on in any way.

193

'I'd be glad if you'd both have dinner with me,' Kinghorn said. He managed to convey the impression that he had no doubts of the invitation being accepted.

'I'm afraid this is urgent, darling,' Harriet Ackerley was saying to Antonia. 'Aaron has had rather a shock today. He hopes you may be able to tell him why.'

20

Kinghorn's apartment was a penthouse in one of the newest blocks on the Janiculum. The marble and glass perspectives of the entrance to the building, the bronze fountain with its attendant palm trees, the glittering cages of the lifts as they soared heavenwards, the faint perfume of leather hanging in the air — all attested to the quality of those who lived within.

In the apartment itself, no cheese-paring by the Embassy's accommodation section had been allowed to affront the visitor with anticlimax as he entered. Dutch flower paintings glimmered on walls lined with blue velvet in the reception room. The lamps were milky globes, held aloft on the manes of leaping horses. A sculpture of a woman's head and shoulders stood on an ebony column in one corner. The smell here was of sandalwood.

Kinghorn gestured towards three sofas, which formed an open square about a coffee table, and moved to a drinks cupboard. They were five, including Kinghorn himself. From the depths of the limousine in which they had come, a neat brown gnome in saucer spectacles had surfaced. 'Sy Gebler,' Kinghorn had said, by way of laconic introduction. 'One of my analysts.' For a moment, Fender had toyed with the possibility that the forthcoming discussion was to have a medical input. But Gebler, it soon became apparent, dealt in facts, not minds; he was a talking book, to be opened at need by Kinghorn, a survival from an age before computers had made memory a mere indulgence.

There had been little conversation in the car. When, in search of enlightenment, Fender had begun a question, Harriet Ackerley had nodded in the direction of the driver and smiled him into irritated silence. In the seat next to her, Kinghorn had mostly stared out of his side window, sucking on an empty pipe that bore a nicotine trap. It was evident that he regarded her as having a custodial relationship with Fender and Antonia. Handing Antonia the first of the drinks, he said only half humorously, 'I guess Harriet is keeping a close eye on you while you're loose in her town, Mrs Strachan.' By the time a tumbler of whisky, heavy with uninvited ice, had been thrust into his hand, choler had reached Fender's throat.

He began a speech designed to wither Kinghorn. 'Since we have very little time — ' but Harriet Ackerley had already turned to him with a glacial smile.

'Aaron shares one of your interests, Mr Fender.'

'What interest is that?'

'A man named Frank Stolz.'

'I have not in fact met Mr Stolz.'

'But Mrs Strachan has.'

He nodded irritably. 'She has talked to him, yes.'

Kinghorn sat down with his own drink, immediately opposite Antonia. 'I take it you were after information, Mrs Strachan.'

'I was consulting him.'

'And you saw him several times.'

Fender could see a tightening round her jaw-line. If Kinghorn was hoping this foreplay would lead to an admission that Stolz had been passing her information he'd got from the Embassy, he was going to be disappointed.

'Mrs Strachan,' Kinghorn said with an air of wanting to be reasonable in the face of trying circumstances, 'let me make something quite clear. I'm not asking what Stolz may have given you. You were at his apartment last night until around ten. What I'm after, is what he said about his plans. Did he tell you he was going on a trip?'

'No.'

'He said nothing at all about leaving Rome?'

'Nothing.'

'What sort of a mood was he in when you left? Did he seem worried? Pleased? Or what?' He pointed the stem of the pipe at her in emphasis of each question. She raised her eyebrows at the pipe and then at Kinghorn. He looked oblivious to the possibility that his manner might be counter-productive. There was an uncomfortable silence.

'Aaron, for God's sake,' Harriet Ackerley said irritably. 'They *have* to know. Tell them.'

Kinghorn took the reproof with what Fender judged to be a studied absence of emotion; it was almost as though he hadn't heard it. But he fixed his eyes on Fender this time, as being, if not exactly on his side, at least male.

'Mr Fender, for your strictly private information, not to be disseminated outside this room, Frank Stolz is a Soviet agent. More precisely, he's an illegal operating under the cover of being a US journalist. I take it you know what an illegal is?'

'I'm not sure I do exactly.'

'An illegal is an intelligence officer who does not operate from the residency in a Soviet Embassy. He's out in the world on his own, usually with a radio link to Moscow for his instructions.'

'Are you saying that you know this for certain about Stolz?'

'There's no question — that's what he is. We've had a special team studying him for twelve months. That is, until today. Today, along with a support agent who works with him, Franco Mongiardina, he flew out to Geneva with a lot of luggage. In Geneva, they caught another flight.' He drained his glass and stood up. 'For Moscow.'

Fender stared at him. Once he had digested the news, his reaction was not so much surprise as annoyance. It was as though Kinghorn had drummed up these facts simply to spoil what had been a successful operation for Antonia and himself. 'Let me get this quite clear. You are saying that Stolz, an American journalist, was recruited by the Russians — '

'Not an American, a Russian, hundred per cent kosher.' Kinghorn began to go round collecting other glasses for refills.

As he passed Gebler, he placed a hand on his shoulder. 'Tell them, Sy.'

Gebler's drink was almost untouched; he held the tumbler in his hand as though it was his crystal ball. Behind his tongue, a regiment of facts was assembling. He was inspecting them as they fell in, rank upon orderly rank, a grand parade awaiting his command to march.

'Frank Stolz's true name is Viktor Aleksevich Dolnytsin. He was born in Moscow thirty-five years ago, the son of a Soviet admiral and a Bolshoi dancer. He married ten years ago and has one son, Yuri, who lives with his mother in a Moscow apartment. We don't know anything about his education or exactly when he became an intelligence officer. The signs are that he must have been an English language specialist from very early on. Eight years ago he arrived in the States from Australia as Frank Stolz, the son of American missionaries who had died in China. The real Frank Stolz had been taken to Australia after his parents' death but died there at the age of four. Dolnytsin was equipped with Frank Stolz's birth certificate and some forged papers to support his story of having been to school and university in Australia. In fact he spent just three months in Sydney and Melbourne on his way to the States, getting together local knowledge so that he could live his legend. In New York he took a degree in journalism and did a couple of spells on newspapers. We know he could already speak Italian well so the transfer to Rome was probably planned from the beginning. Very soon after he got here he took the apartment on the Corso and started entertaining in a big way. We estimate his books and free-lance work for papers in the States and elsewhere wouldn't have covered more than a third of his outgoings in the past year. So the Russians have obviously been subsidizing him quite heavily to help him build his lines into Italian governing circles.'

'And into your Embassy presumably,' Fender said.

'We don't believe so,' said Gebler.

Kinghorn had seated himself again. He passed a hand over the dome of his head, as though checking it was still there, and lay back. It struck Fender, watching his eyes rest on the ceiling, that his earlier impression that Kinghorn was both supercilious and insensitive, had been wrong. He was a man under pressure from disagreeable thoughts; the remoteness of manner was part of a defensive mechanism that was showing signs of stress.

'Why don't you think he had lines into your Embassy? It seems an obvious thing for him to aim at.'

Kinghorn was shaking his head. 'He didn't want to attract attention in the Embassy so he left it alone. He came in just enough to ensure he wouldn't stand out from the other American journalists living here. But it wasn't one of his targets. That was fortunate because we couldn't risk briefing the Embassy staff as a whole about his true identity in case it leaked back to him.'

'He was never supplied with information from Embassy sources — '

'Never.'

Fender gazed at melting ice in his glass. He wondered how Antonia was taking it but couldn't bring himself at the moment to look at her face. 'So he was a spy against the Italian Government.'

Gebler sat forward, anxious to get his show on the road again. 'Stolz wasn't a spy — at least only to the extent that any journalist is. Espionage wasn't what he was here for. We believe he had two main briefs. First a disinformation role, with the Italian Government and other NATO governments as his targets — acting as a channel for stories that would undermine the alliance and discredit Italian and other European politicians who were considered to be particularly anti-Soviet in their attitudes. His other task was a destabilizing operation against the Vatican. This Pope constitutes a major headache for Moscow. They need to destroy his credibility with Catholics in Eastern Europe — and everywhere else if possible. In recent months this is where Stolz has been investing most of his effort.'

'We know furthermore that he believed he was on to something good,' Kinghorn said. 'Quite what it was isn't clear. There are always a few scandals floating around that place. Linking one of them all the way up through the hierarchy to the Pope himself was the trick he had to turn.'

'The name of the game was Vaticangate,' said Gebler shyly.

It was odd to hear that word again, within the space of a few hours. Perhaps, thought Fender, the Secretary of State had also listened to a story from Kinghorn's talking book. And what would have been the occasion for *that*?

Kinghorn began filling his pipe from a jar with a coat of arms on the side. 'Occasionally the Vatican operation was used as a vehicle for getting at other targets. Perhaps I could make a guess at what Stolz has been peddling to you. I'd say it's a story about your Treasury minister, Ropner, tying him into a corrupt deal with the guy in the Vatican Bank who died in London, Barralozzi.' He lifted his gaze to Fender's face. 'Right?'

There was no point in denying it. On the other hand, there was no reason, either, to accept the implication they'd been gullible. 'There was collateral from elsewhere.'

'I'll bet.'

Kinghorn struck his match. Beside him Gebler gazed demurely at his reflection in the lacquer surface of the coffee table. 'There'll have been collateral for sure. What you need to look at is, where "elsewhere" got it. The answer could prove very interesting.'

'Aaron, how did you know he was surfacing material to discredit Ropner?' Harriet Ackerley asked abruptly.

Kinghorn took a long drink. If he had had hatches to batten down, they would have been closing fast. 'Well, Harriet, it just so happened that we got some audio coverage of a meal Stolz had with a British banker — a guy named Rollo something. Unfortunately — '

'You didn't tell me.'

'Right, I didn't tell you.'

'Aaron.' She was leaning across Gebler, her eyes like flints. 'Have I joined some new release category nobody's bothered to mention? Who am I with nowadays? Cuba? North Korea?'

He held up a placatory hand. 'Harriet, Washington were calling the shots on anything to do with Stolz. They decided we had to hold back for a while. Our assessment was that your people would never buy an uncorroborated story straight off.'

He seemed to want it to sound reasonable; but the words

carried a sardonic flavour which none of them missed. Before Harriet Ackerley could erupt again, he turned quickly to Antonia. 'Now you can understand why we need to know if you heard anything — *anything* — when you were with Stolz that would explain why he took off in such a hurry.'

Fender was watching her face now. When she glanced in his direction, he smiled encouragement. At the corner of her jaw the bone was once more showing white. He wished with an intensity that surprised him that he could spare her having her triumph smashed to bits in this way.

Her voice sounded calm enough. 'The man you called his support agent, Franco, came to him with some news that obviously worried them both. They went off to another room to discuss it. When Stolz reappeared, he said a problem had cropped up that meant he had to go out. He was very preoccupied. It may have been connected with a man outside his apartment I'd told him about earlier.'

'What man?' Kinghorn asked sharply.

'It was someone who had been following me.'

Fender saw Gebler's eyes lift for a moment to study the expression on Kinghorn's face, then drop again.

'You told Stolz that you'd been followed by this man?'

'Yes.'

'What did *he* do?'

'He sent Franco out to watch the man. He was to follow him back to wherever —' she stopped and thrust a hand through her hair, staring at Kinghorn. 'But of course! He wasn't following *me* that day! He was working for you — *covering Stolz*!'

Kinghorn put his head back. He was reading his stars again on the ceiling and they were not favourable.

'When I went to Stolz's apartment for the first time you presumably wanted to find out who I was. So you had me followed back to the *pensione*. Then for some reason you decided to go on with it — at least you had this man following me round the town last Thursday.'

Kinghorn said, without looking at Antonia, 'We needed to establish your identity, and whether you were working with Stolz. We got your name and address from the *pensione*. While we were waiting for Washington to tell us what was known about you, we kept some light observation on. When we learnt that you belonged to the Central Crimes Bureau in London, we guessed you were following up the Ropner story and took the surveillance off.'

'But, Aaron,' Harriet Ackerley said softly, 'you don't have your surveillance people calling at the Embassy when they finish, do you?'

'It can happen.' Kinghorn's voice was brusque.

She nodded, keeping her face straight but only just. 'So Franco discovers you're on to them and tells Stolz who goes off to whatever little cubby-hole in Rome houses his radio and asks Moscow what they want him to do now. Afraid you may be about to tell the Italians to pull Stolz in, or are working up to making him the sort of offer he can't refuse, Moscow decide to withdraw him. Exit Frank Stolz.' Briskly she drained her glass. 'You've had him, Aaron darling.'

Kinghorn didn't move his position. Fender imagined him already drafting in his mind that tricky telegram to Washington, giving the tidings that he had lost Stolz and how, especially how. A servant appeared to announce to him that dinner was ready. He lowered his gaze and nodded. Then with a composure Fender had to admire, he rose to usher them into the dining-room. As Harriet Ackerley passed him, he reached out and touched the necklace of crystal about her throat. He fingered it as though in admiration. 'Harriet, how very pretty!' Fender knew that Kinghorn hated her more than anything else in the world at that moment — more than Washington, or Moscow or Frank Stolz alias Viktor Dolnytsin.

By the time they came to leave the apartment, Kinghorn's driver had gone off duty, so it had to be a taxi back to the *pensione*. Harriet Ackerley went with them, to be dropped off at her apartment block lower down the Janiculum hill. Kinghorn's bereavement had made her genial. 'So that wraps it for you,' she said. 'Antrim can tell the PM he doesn't have to worry after all. That should be popular. At this rate it won't be long before he gets his "K.".'

'Were you completely in the dark about Stolz?' Fender asked.

'Until today when Aaron discovered he'd flown the coop and wanted my help in finding out if you knew why.'

'Will he ever come out of Russia again?'

'He might. He's young, they won't want to waste him in Moscow, seducing the typists in foreign embassies. With a little plastic surgery, new papers, who knows? — you might get him in London one day. You can be sure that having got used to the *dolce vita, he'll* be rooting for it. It won't seem much fun back home with all that snow and the little wife dressed like the Michelin man.'

As she stepped from the cab, she said, 'If Aaron had let me in on the act, he wouldn't be in this mess. He has no imagination and no flexibility, he always asks Washington. Then he blames them if it goes wrong. Not that he can this time.' She opened her bag to take out keys. In the lamp above, her hair was like a frozen sea under moonlight, not a wave daring to move. 'But there you are, our gallant allies think they can do everything without nanny's help these days.'

The taxi moved on towards Trastevere. 'Quite formidable,' Fender said. 'Another iron lady, do you think? Perhaps stainless steel is more appropriate. I should have enjoyed seeing her and Antrim lock their egos together when he was still in that world. Am I right in remembering that you were told she's supposed to have a glittering future?'

'Yes.'

'I felt tonight that Kinghorn would enjoy extinguishing it.'

'Now that he's lost Stolz, he'll need all his energies for looking after his own.'

She sounded as though, after all, she was managing to take the news of Stolz's true identity in her stride. He decided it would probably be for the best if he told her the other half of the story now.

'About Stolz,' he said. 'It so happens I have some more news, something I learnt from Panzani this afternoon.'

She gave him a crooked smile. 'Don't tell me he worked for the Vatican as well.'

'Nothing like that. But Panzani did know him.'

'In what way?'

'While the *Vigiles* were at the Villa dei Laghi, Panzani ran quite a sophisticated operation in his efforts to discover what they were up to. He took over a small farm building opposite the gates of the orphanage and installed an automatic camera which recorded everyone who went up and down the path leading to the villa. He also had a surveillance team with a car there some of the time, although not unfortunately the night when Rodrigues decided to abandon the place. The team followed Rodrigues on various trips he made to Rome and saw him meet one or two men who work in the *Curia* — very low-level people apparently, but quite useful sources of gossip. However, the team also established he was having regular meetings, sometimes in restaurants, sometimes in a car, with a man who had nothing to do with the Vatican. They followed him back to an apartment on the Corso. It was Stolz.'

She stared at him.

'When Panzani told me all this, I remembered your saying you suspected Stolz had picked up something about the *Vigiles*. My immediate thought was that he had happened across Rodrigues one day, gained his confidence as a sympathetic journalist and was managing to wheedle information out of him to work up as material for his book. Panzani said he was satisfied there was more to it than that: Stolz was twice seen to hand papers to Rodrigues during their meetings. And, of course, we can see now there *was* more to it. Stolz was obviously one of the sources outside Church circles whom Bacton was told about — possibly the only one. He was also the reason for Rodrigues' claim that he was getting information from the intelligence service of a foreign country to which the Pope had appealed for help. The reference to the Pope was poetic licence on Rodrigues' part, of course. But the rest of what he said was correct.'

She took a few moments to assimilate it. 'You mean that Stolz persuaded Rodrigues, in the same way that he persuaded me, that he was providing information from American intelligence sources.'

'Yes.'

'Whereas he was feeding him with Russian information — disinformation, rather.'

'A mixture of both, I suppose. Some of the stories he gave

him would have been accurate — factual intelligence from the Russians' own sources in the Vatican — Flaminia would have been one of them. In that way Rodrigues' confidence in what he was receiving would have been built up. Once that was achieved, he could be persuaded to accept — and act on — fabrications.'

'You say "act on". Do you believe the Russians knew about the *Ultores*?'

'Of course. Stolz may even have planted the seed of the idea in Rodrigues' mind — persuaded him that until the Special Commission finally came into existence, everything was up to him. All that remained was to concoct convincing circumstantial evidence pointing to some link between Rodrigues and the Pope. Then the whole thing could be surfaced to the world. Perhaps the book Stolz spoke about was to be the vehicle for that.'

She gave a half sigh, half groan. 'So it's as Kinghorn said — the collateral evidence on the Ropners, which we believed the *Vigiles* had, was not collateral at all. Everything came from the same source.'

'The Russians obviously had total coverage of Barralozzi. They must at some point have asked themselves how, bearing in mind Ropner's strong anti-Russian attitude, they could exploit Barralozzi's link to Ropner through the sister in such a way that Ropner's political career would be finished. The answer was to surface suitable material through Stolz. Of course, the Government's failure to follow up the opening chapter of the story when it was planted on the Bank of England man would have been a disappointment. Presumably they were busy thinking up another ploy when we appeared on the scene, having taken the bait in a way they can't have foreseen — through the defection of Bacton from the *Vigiles*.'

'I wonder if they really thought the forged letter on its own would be sufficient.'

'They must have hoped it would be. The tape was obviously kept in reserve as a last resort — rather a risky one, bearing in mind modern techniques of voice analysis. They presumably had tapes of genuine conversations between Barralozzi and his sister to work from. But even making the reproduction fuzzy couldn't remove the danger entirely.'

She relapsed into silence. Only when the taxi had been halted by some traffic lights was he able to glimpse her face again.

'What are you thinking?' he asked.

'That I now see how you almost came to be murdered on that train.'

He shook his head, frowning. 'Tell me.'

'The evening I collected the London telegram giving Weber's address in Murten I went on to Stolz's apartment. The telegram was in my bag. There was a moment which I suppose must have been planned beforehand when Stolz took me out on to the terrace. I left the bag on a coffee table in the room where we'd been sitting. The man who acted as his servant, Franco, was somewhere about. He would have had time to photograph anything I had in the bag before we went inside again. Later in the evening, Stolz casually asked about you, what were you doing. I remember saying that at that moment you were planning a trip. I also made a joke about your determination always to get to the bottom of things. Together with the contents of the telegram, that could only mean you were off in pursuit of Weber and there was a risk that you would expose the *Vigiles* before it suited the Russians.'

'So Stolz was in a position to warn Rodrigues that Weber's address was known and he'd better get him out of the way.'

'Yes. Rodrigues had presumably given him the Todi telephone number.'

'But once he'd warned Rodrigues, there was no need to have me killed. And in any case, why not do it before I got to Murten? Why risk my picking up some information there — as in fact I did — and perhaps telephoning it to you?'

'Killing you was the only certain guarantee against trouble in the future. But the time factor didn't allow for doing it on the day you travelled to Murten. I don't imagine Stolz would have had the authority to take a decision of that sort — he'd have needed to refer to Moscow. Once they'd decided to kill you, they had to get an assassination team briefed from amongst their people in Italy or Switzerland. The obvious thing then was to have the team look out for you in Murten and choose its moment to strike. When you joined the sleeper back to Rome, to arrange an accidental fall from the train was the obvious answer. If it hadn't been for the olive tree, they would have succeeded. And it would have been my fault.'

For a moment or two he was back there, with the brandy running from his nose and mouth, the roar of the train wheels and the blackness waiting for him.

'There is nothing you can reasonably be blamed for,' he said. 'Absolutely nothing.'

There were lights about them now but her face was turned away so that he couldn't see the expression. He thought of putting an arm round her shoulder to comfort her but feared her wanting to shrink away. 'Well,' he said, with an attempt at lightness, 'at least Antrim will be pleased. He'll be able to announce to the PM that he has exposed a foul plot to deny the ablest man in the Cabinet the chance to take over from him. The Ackerley woman's right of course — his name will be made with No. 10. And he'll owe it all to you.'

At least he had got a response from her. 'To *me*?'

'If you hadn't spotted Kinghorn's surveillance and blown it to Stolz, we would never have discovered the truth.'

She gave a grim laugh.

'You can't deny it.'

'All I know is that I failed utterly to see through Stolz. You wouldn't have made that mistake. You would have realized early on that everything was being made too easy for you.'

She reached out a hand and placed it on his. 'But thank you for what you said.'

Her fingers were cool against his skin. He made no move, only wanting her to leave them there. But the taxi was stopping outside the *pensione* and she took the hand away to open the door.

Entering the lift behind her, he felt her hair brush against his mouth. He closed his eyes and was aware of a sensation not very different from that when he knelt helpless on the floor of the train and faced the rushing darkness.

At his door, he said, 'It's still quite early. Would you consider joining me? For a drink?'

She looked him full in the eyes. He was suddenly appalled at the possibility that she had read his mind, had seen the absurdity of the desire that possessed him. He said hurriedly, 'But I expect you're tired.'

She was smiling. She had somehow succeeded in pushing away the events of the evening. 'No,' she said. 'I'd like to come.'

When she didn't drop her gaze, he knew that in some inconceivable way she had accepted the knowledge of his desire. And, more, that it was not absurd at all.

21

She had bathed and was lying on her bed, listening to the voices of the waiters as they set out tables for the evening meal at the restaurant across the street, when she heard Fender's slow footsteps in the corridor. His door opened and closed. She got up and dressed, certain that in a few minutes he would arrive, wanting to talk over his visit to Panzani.

After a quarter of an hour, there was still no sign. She went to listen at his door for sounds of him moving about. All was silent. Back in her room, she smoked a cigarette and then decided she must discover what was wrong.

He sat motionless in the armchair, his head thrown back, the white triangle of his arm sling luminous in the darkened room. The sound of his breathing told her he was not asleep. 'Hullo,' she said.

He reached sideways and switched on a table lamp. The brandy they had been drinking the previous evening was beside the lamp but he had not bothered to pour himself a drink.

'All right?'

He gave a slight nod and a smile. He was sweating a little but he didn't look unwell.

'I sent the telegram to London letting the Ropners off the hook. I said that we proposed to fly back the day after tomorrow unless we received word to the contrary.'

He nodded again.

'How did Panzani get on?'

He made a gesture with his free hand; it seemed he could hardly bring himself to speak. 'The operation took place. Some of the *Vigiles* were picked up. The ones who really mattered had disappeared.'

'Rodrigues?'

'He and the Italian, Ligorio, with two others, had all gone. Forty-five minutes after the Pope finally gave his approval for the raid last night, Rodrigues apparently took a telephone call from Rome. The four left the house an hour later.'

'And no sign of Weber?'

'None.'

She shook her head. 'So they were warned.'

Fender pulled himself to his feet and went to switch on the room's overhead light. 'As you say, they were warned.'

He looked at her bitterly before sitting down again. 'Yesterday the Secretary of State was bemoaning the fact that the founder of Opus Dei, Escriva, was fond of talking about the Church being contaminated with evil. "Authentic rottenness" was apparently one of his expressions. I'm coming to the conclusion that Escriva had it about right.'

She watched him for a while without speaking, then said gently, 'I still have my bottle of scotch. Why don't you join me for a drink in ten minutes?'

By the time he appeared in her room, washed and slightly spruced, he was struggling to be more sociable. He launched into the story as soon as she had pressed the whisky into his hand. There had been signs that all had not gone well in the embarrassment with which Panzani had received him. He and his men had landed by helicopter in the grounds of the house near Todi shortly before eight o'clock that morning. By previous arrangement, two police cars from Orvieto were stationed out of sight a few hundred metres away, on call if Panzani needed them. As the helicopter came in to land, a battered Volkswagen passenger truck could be seen, just inside the gates to the house. Two priests were tinkering with the engine, trying to get it started while others stood about. There were six priests there in all. They had planned to leave in the truck some hours before, but it had broken down. Bewildered at first by the arrival of the helicopter, when Panzani explained who he was, they began to look pleased; it took him some time to convince them that he hadn't been sent by the Holy Father to make sure they got safely away from the house. They told him that, at about nine-fifteen the previous evening, Rodrigues had announced he had had an urgent telephone message from the Vatican. The Holy Father had become aware that elements hostile to the work with which they had been charged were planning to visit the house in order to disrupt their studies and perhaps to destroy evidence from the investigations Rodrigues had been conducting. He wished them to avoid this by moving to another address without delay. Rodrigues and Ligorio had loaded their files into a small Fiat Rodrigues used for his trips to Rome and, with two other priests, had left to make arrangements for their new accommodation. The remaining six were to meet up with Rodrigues not later than seven-thirty that morning in the Piazza della Republica in Orvieto. But their truck had broken down. If it had not, Panzani would have found the house deserted when he arrived. He had sent two of his men in a police car to Orvieto in the hope they would find Rodrigues still waiting. But there had been no sign of him.

Fender's gaze moved bleakly round the walls of the room. He looked more resigned than bitter now.

'Of course I asked Panzani who else knew the raid was going to take place. It seems about half a dozen senior people in the *Curia* were told — I couldn't get him to tell me the names — all, of course, above suspicion, according to Panzani. He thought some Private Secretaries would also have got to know. He says he will ask for an inquiry. But he's an outsider and he may not get his way. Even if it's agreed to, I think we can be sure the inquiry will run into the sand. Panzani himself appears to believe that Rodrigues is a Russian agent working to embarrass the Vatican, with an accomplice somewhere amongst the Private Secretaries.'

She poured him a second drink. 'At worst he's only half wrong. And it could be true. Why should we assume that Rodrigues was unconscious of what Stolz really was? He may have been his agent.'

He paused with the glass halfway to his lips and frowned; then he shook his head. 'I don't think so. Rodrigues is simply a fanatic who began to go off his head before he left Opus Dei and has become steadily madder ever since. He sees his mission in life as rescuing the Mystical Body of Christ from the total decomposition which will result if people like Barralozzi don't have their heads chopped off.'

'You can't be absolutely certain.'

He smiled grudgingly. 'If he'd really been working for the Russians, I doubt if the *Vigiles* would have been having to make do with a clapped-out truck.'

'What did Panzani say about the six priests he did manage to catch?'

'They all seem to be young and earnest and very gullible. They speak of Rodrigues in reverent terms — he must be an exceptionally powerful personality. Four of them are the same as were in the Villa dei Laghi when Panzani had it under observation. There are two newcomers, a Canadian and a Brazilian, replacing two who are said by the rest to have returned to their own countries and now send regular reports to Rodrigues as *Quaestores*. They all saw becoming a *Quaestor* as a tremendous thing — a mark of the Pope's confidence in them as individual priests. It took Panzani a long time to break through their conviction that they had the Pope's blessing for their work. Only when they got into their cells in the Vatican did dawn really begin to break. The story they told corresponded exactly with what Francis Bacton told his parents. The cases of Barralozzi and the American priest in the *Curia* who smuggled drugs had been described to them as successful investigations carried out by Rodrigues and Ligorio personally. They don't seem to have viewed their deaths as anything more than the hand of God. Rodrigues told them that he reported personally to the Holy Father on the progress of investigations and the Pope then decided what, if any, action might be taken. In recent weeks, Rodrigues has been concentrating on someone in Vatican Radio who he believed was having an affair with a leading member of the Communist Party of Italy.'

'Had they seen Weber?'

'One of them described a man who arrived a few days ago to stay the night. He was referred to by Rodrigues as a co-operator from Switzerland. "Co-operator" — obviously an echo from Opus Dei — Rodrigues plainly borrowed a few ideas from his old firm. That must have been Weber. But he left the following day.'

'They hadn't heard of the *Ultores*?'

'No, Rodrigues seems to have been careful to keep that side to himself.'

She shook her head. 'I wouldn't have thought there was much justification for keeping them in prison. I realize the Vatican's a sovereign state and can do as it likes. But they've committed no criminal offences. Have they even done anything serious against canon law?'

'I don't know.' Fender levered himself out of his chair and went to stare from the window at the street below. 'Probably not. Once they've promised to say nothing about Panzani's raid and what they were doing with Rodrigues, I expect they'll be released. And that will be the end of that. Hardly a wrinkle in the carpet to show what has been swept under it.'

'They surely can't leave things as they are?'

'I'd like to believe not. But I begin to despair. Living at a safe distance in England, one can maintain a sort of exasperated loyalty. For the sake of the Church, one puts up with things like the mess they make of sex, and the apparent belief that remarriage is rather worse than murder, and a bank that sometimes seems to be run by chimpanzees. It surely won't get worse, you think. Then one comes here and finds they can't even control something like this!'

He turned back from the window with a sigh and paused at her bedside table to glance down at the book about Suso she had bought in the Via Vittoria. 'I find it difficult to believe you're enjoying that.'

'I'm stuck on page fourteen. My confidence that I could still read Italian fairly well was misplaced.'

He grunted. 'Panzani discovered that Suso standards of mortification were still the order of the day for the *Vigiles*. One of the six requires medical treatment.' He sat down again and closed his eyes.

'I wonder why Rodrigues was so obsessed with Suso?'

'God knows.'

Reaching feebly for something that would stir him out of this mood, she said, 'At least Panzani seems to want to get to the bottom of it all.'

'I'm not even convinced of that. Everything that has come out so far points to Bacton having been a reliable witness. Now Bacton spoke of Rodrigues being visited more than once *by somebody very senior in the Curia*. At the time Bacton was with the *Vigiles*, they were living at the Villa dei Laghi. Panzani admits he had an automatic camera recording all movements into and out of the villa. But he swears there were no visitors of any kind. The Secretary of State said the same.'

'Bacton could have been simply repeating something Rodrigues had said.'

'Yesterday I was prepared to allow for that possibility. In view of what happened over the raid, I'm not any more.'

There was a silence while he gazed at her, challenging her to disagree with him. Then he drained his glass. 'Let them rot! I suggest we go and eat.'

She was aware that her mind was refusing to follow his words, instead had tracked back to an incident a few moments before. Something about the Suso book was demanding her attention. She went to the bedside table and opened it. Fender raised his eyebrows. 'Dinner-table reading? That man must have a strange fascination.'

'G. Lanciani,' she said. 'The author is G. Lanciani. Very distinguished, the man in the bookshop said. I paid no attention at the time. But so he is. A cardinal in the Vatican, no less.'

'Where does that lead?'

'The woman at the orphanage mentioned a Cardinal Lanciani who had been interested in the Institute's work from the beginning and came to see the children regularly. On his last visit he apparently promised to see what could be done about raising funds from the Church to pay for an extension to the building.'

'Go on.'

'Rodrigues also made a point of visiting the orphanage. What better place to meet someone like Lanciani and discuss the work of the *Vigiles*? The contact couldn't be observed and there would have been no risk of news of it getting back to the Vatican.'

She had stirred him at last. He sat forward, frowning. 'Francis Bacton wrote to his mother before he joined the *Vigiles* that Rodrigues had been engaged on some research for the Vatican into Catholic history. If one substitutes Lanciani for the Vatican, that fits.'

He rose and took the book from her to read the text on the dust cover. He seemed to have become larger, as though air had been pumped into him. 'I suppose I have to accept the possibility that Panzani's camera was covering no more than the path leading up to the villa — it would have seemed pointless to record people going to the orphanage as well. In which case Lanciani would never have appeared on the film.'

'So that leaves only one question,' she said. 'Was Lanciani on the list of those who were told there was going to be a raid on the house at Todi?'

She watched Fender walking up and down between her bed and the window, tapping his empty glass against his stomach in punctuation of his thoughts. 'What will you do now?'

'I shall telephone Panzani first thing tomorrow and demand a straight answer as to whether Lanciani was on the list. If he was, I shall speak to the Secretary of State and say I want an audience because I have something very grave to discuss. When he asks me what about, I shall add that it is connected with Cardinal Lanciani and the raid to pick up the *Vigiles*. I shall refuse to say more at that stage — which he may not like. But he has to weigh the risk — the virtual certainty — that I have some very damaging allegation to make. He won't want a leakage of whatever it is. The only hope of controlling the situation is to get me on their side.'

He began to hum beneath his breath. They were back to

Elgar, she noticed. 'He's not exactly going to welcome you with open arms when you arrive.'

He shrugged. '*If* he's present.'

'But you said — '

They stared at each other. Then Fender laughed. 'You misunderstand.' He made a gesture to indicate she was thinking unacceptably small, that events had moved on to a grander plane.

'I'm not asking for an audience with the Secretary of State. Why should I accept *his* assurance that everything will be taken care of?' He paused once more by the window, triumphant this time. 'No mere underlings now!'

22

Watching from her vantage point where the vines gave the deepest shade, she could see, as Fender approached from the lift, that his appearance was smarter than it had been since their arrival in Rome. He had abandoned the lightweight suit, scarred by its encounter with railway embankment and olive tree, in favour of a blue flannel one. The tie too was different, a striped affair, insignia of some club or college.

'When do you leave?' she asked.

'The audience is an hour from now. They're supposed to be sending a car.'

'They want to flatter you.'

'More likely a trap,' he said comfortably. 'Having lulled me into a false sense of security with a limousine, they plan to clap me into one of those cells they recently cleaned out.'

'Ms Ackerley and I will organize a plot to free you.'

He was dabbing his brow already. She wondered if he had brought the suit to Rome in the secret hope or expectation of this occasion; but it was hardly meant for a Roman summer. 'Do you expect anyone else to be with the Pope?'

'The Secretary of State. And, if the Vatican is anything like

Whitehall, there'll be a Private Secretary taking notes, as well.'

'I hope you have your bones ready.'

He frowned. 'Bones — ?'

'You told me on the way to Tunbridge Wells that you had bones to pick with the Pope.'

He inclined his head. 'If he can spare the time, I have a little collection.'

She moved her chair so that he could join her in the shade. 'You are looking very smart.'

'You are looking very beautiful.'

She saw him colour after he had spoken. The words had slipped past his guard because he was kindled by the thought of the interview that lay ahead; since the night when she had gone to him, she was aware of moments when he seemed changed, to be living in the skin of an earlier self, not yet bloated, still uncaged by shame.

She lit a cigarette. 'How do you think it will go?'

'Nothing will be admitted. On the other hand, nothing will be explicitly denied. He will have been given an assessment of what I am going to say which will be fairly accurate. He will have begun already to think how Lanciani can be dealt with if the evidence against him leaves no room for doubt.'

A breeze had sprung up, lifting the scalloped sides of the umbrellas which hung over the tables away from the vine pergola. 'Any solution that presents itself will call for breathing space, time in which to put it into effect without causing too many ripples in the *Curia* or too much wonder in the world outside. So he will want to be assured that I will do nothing to deny him that time. That will involve deciding how much it would be wise to tell me about their own investigations.'

'You still believe that the Secretary of State and Panzani held things back?'

'Consider. By their account, all they were dealing with was a foolish gaggle of priests led by a man who had persuaded himself that he must collect information about scandalous conduct in the Vatican and the Church elsewhere so that the Pope could take the necessary steps: nothing more. A potential source of embarrassment of course; but did it justify borrowing from the Italian Government a man like Panzani with a special team of men? Did it warrant Panzani establishing an observation post outside the Villa dei Laghi and installing an automatic camera to record every coming and going at the villa? Do you think all that would have happened if there hadn't been at least a suspicion that Rodrigues had an influential patron somewhere in the Vatican and was up to something worse than simply collecting scandal?'

'So they misled you — '

He shrugged. 'If all they had was suspicion, I suppose I can't criticize them too much. In their place, I would probably have done the same.' Now that he had the edge on them, he was prepared to be magnanimous.

'Even after Lanciani is dealt with, that still leaves Rodrigues on the loose somewhere. And the *Ultores*.'

'I believe the Pope has no choice now but to ask the Italian Government to look for them. I shall tell him so, if necessary.' He lifted his eyes to the shimmering green-gold web above them; she could see he was relishing the prospect. 'Monsignor Hernandes and his colleagues at Opus Dei headquarters will be hoping more than most for quick action.'

'Why?'

'Because Rodrigues obviously retains a burning interest in his old organization. Bacton's reaction to Rossano's mysterious accident can only be explained if one accepts that, in addition to delinquents in Holy Orders, Rodrigues couldn't resist cleaning up lay elements in Opus Dei. He's probably lined up quite a few more candidates.'

'Since you found Rodrigues for them this time, perhaps you'll be asked to help in the search.'

He shook his head firmly. 'I have no wish to compete with the Italian police. In any event, I have pressing business in Chipping Campden.'

At first baffled, as he began to smile she suddenly recalled his parting words to Antrim. 'Butterflies!' she said. 'So the Large Blues *are* there — '

'The man I had lunch with is convinced of it. I want to see for myself.'

Abruptly he frowned and sat forward to take a letter from his side pocket. 'Forgive me — I collected this for you at the reception desk when I went to warn them a car would be coming. I quite forgot to give it to you.'

She braced herself for news from Shropshire; rather more than blackfly this time perhaps. But the writing on the envelope was unfamiliar and the postmark Geneva. Opening it, she suddenly guessed, with a jolt of the heart, that the writer was Stolz.

The note inside was hastily scribbled and began without ceremony.

Antonia — by now, if my guess is right, you will know.

Useless to ask you to forgive. But the decisions were not mine to make, any of them. I wished many times it could have been otherwise.

At least you were not played false with the evidence, all of which was true — only with its wrapping. Perhaps, after all, they will give you a medal when they discover it!

Do you know that you never used my name? By the time you receive this, I shall no longer own it anyway. But do not think of this as being a letter from an unperson. It comes from someone who will remember you always.

She was conscious that her cheeks were burning. She folded the letter and placed it in her handbag; lifting her head, she caught Fender's eye. 'A friend?' He was polite but preoccupied with once more mopping his brow.

She found herself wanting to laugh. 'In a way.' It was impossible to tell him at this moment, she would not know how to begin — when he returned from the Vatican perhaps. Her feelings were too mixed for her to be sure what they amounted to. But the sour taste of failure had vanished, to be replaced by a conviction that, after all, there was nothing in this whole affair about which she need have regrets. Whether she could believe what Stolz had said about the evidence was almost immaterial. The whole letter might be a fraud. It would still have a mysterious value.

Fender had taken out his notebook, to study it in advance of his meeting. Into her thoughts came a vision of Antrim, returning to his office from No. 10, triumphant after giving the Prime Minister his reassurance that Ropner and his wife

217

were in the clear, of an ashen-faced Baxter following him into the room, in his hand another telegram from Rome that would say the evidence was probably a true bill after all. But how could a telegram be based on those few words from Stolz of all people? Who would believe it? Who would *want* to believe it?

The breeze was lifting her hair, twitching the hem of her dress. 'Do you think this means a change in the weather?' she asked.

He didn't look up from the notebook. 'Perhaps, for a while. I remember from the last time I was here — they have a name for it.'

She persisted. 'For the breeze?'

He put the notebook away. 'Yes, when the heat seems intolerable, so that you feel transfixed by it, there's a curious whispering along the streets. It's a westerly from the sea, called the *ponentino*. Suddenly life is bearable after all.'

Going to the edge of the terrace, she turned towards the breeze, feeling the coolness envelop her. In the street below, a car was drawing up beside the wall of the restaurant opposite. The driver got out and walked towards the *pensione* entrance. She could just make out the Vatican registration plate. 'Your car's arrived.'

Fender struggled to his feet, smoothing recalcitrant hair at the point of his parting. He looked uncharacteristically tense, his hands fumbling at the sides of his jacket to straighten the pocket flaps. She had a mild urge to adjust his tie and ask him if he had a clean handkerchief.

As he entered the lift, she said, 'Remember me to the Bishop of Rome.'

'He may not deserve it.'

'I leave it to your judgement then.'

He had his finger on the button to hold the lift. He faced her through the gate. 'There is something I've wanted to say but have found difficult. It's very simple.' For some reason he needed to have the grille between them.

'I wanted to say — thank you.'

She smiled.

His finger was still against the Hold button. 'Before that night, I'd forgotten about —' he searched for a word — 'about discovering and being discovered. You made it live again.'

She shook her head. 'Not true — you'd never forget.'

'Why do you think that?'

'For so many reasons — there'll always be Large Blues.'

His face was shadowed by the roof of the lift, so that she couldn't see whether he was accepting her words. But as the lift began to move, he said, 'I like your saying that — "always".'